D1823019

Year of the Hare

Year of the Hare
The Bowen Chronicles
Volume 1

Mark Finn

Year of The Hare

Copyright © 2001 Mark Finn

A Clockwork Storybook Publication
www.clockworkstorybook.com

All of the characters in this book are ficticious, and any resemblance to actual persons, living or dead, is purely coincidental.

No part of this book may be reproduced or transmitted in any form or by any means, graphic, electronic, or mechanical, including photocopying, recording, taping, or by any information storage or retrieval system, without the permission in writing from the publisher.

Clockwork Storybook, Inc.
P.O. Box 200126
Austin, TX 78720
comments@clockworkstorybook.com

ISBN: 0-9704841-5-1

Printed in the United States of America

For Cathy,
who fell in love with Sam before she fell in love with me.

Acknowledgements

The number of people who influenced and helped shape these stories is far too great for me to list here. However, a few deserve special notice. Thanks to Sharon Nash for advice on Shamanism, as well as a couple of cool book recommendations, Bill Willingham for suggesting the Bowen-Stonehill feud, and to Robert Van Gulik and Robert E. Howard for inspiration.

Thanks also to John Lucas, Doug Potter, Jay Tabares, and Harold Covey for art assistance that went far beyond the call of duty.

And thanks to Liza Poggemeyer for her able assistance in proofreading and revising this manuscript.

Contents

Welcome to San Cibola

The University of Northern California was immense, larger than Berkeley or UCLA. The grounds were well tended and liberally covered with the Douglas fir trees that were the trademarks of the Pacific Northwest. Large gray and cream-colored buildings jutted through the groves of trees or sat benignly on the hills that rose up throughout the campus.

Universities are all different, in that they are all the same. Only students can navigate them with any surety. However, this was probably the hundredth campus I'd stepped on in the past decade, so I had an advantage over the average visitor. I found the registrar's office and snagged one of the cheapo maps that colleges always print up. From there, it was easy to see where I was going.

The Department of History was the only building with Roman columns in front of it. I went inside and smelled the ubiquitous aroma of pine cleaner, patchouli and cigarettes as a wave of displaced nostalgia washed over me. Certainly, I'd never been here before, but it still took me back to when I was a student.

I walked into the dean's office and gave the secretary my name. She asked me if I had an appointment and I told her no. Then she asked me my name, and I gave it. Finally, she told me to take a seat and I took it. She and I were batting a thousand.

After I spent about twenty minutes of looking at my fingernails, the door behind the secretary opened, and an anxious student wandered out, followed by the man I was there to see.

Alex Crowe hadn't changed too much since I last saw him. A bit more gray in the hair, maybe. He was beardless now and also dressed in a nicer cut of suit. It didn't look right on him. I was used to sweaters with holes in the sleeves and threadbare twill jackets.

The secretary started to say something about me in a whisper, but Alex waved her off and walked over to me, smiling. "My goodness, they'll let anyone on this campus, won't they?"

I stood up. "Hello, Alex," I said, and then I was surprised by his embrace. He backed up and pumped my hand earnestly.

"Mister Bowen, as I live and breathe. The years have matured you, Sam. I daresay, you look as old as I feel now."

"Alex, I never know if you're giving me a compliment or telling me off," I said.

"Then you must always assume I am paying you due respect." He clapped me on the shoulder. "When did you get into town?"

"Last night at about one in the morning. You're not listed in the phone book, by the way."

"Precisely for that very reason," he said. "Where were you coming from?"

"San Francisco, by way of Arizona. Long story. Want to hear all about it? Over lunch, your treat, since I'm so new in town?"

"You, sir, have me at a disadvantage. I am in the middle of finals, and it's chaos and madness around here right now."

"Well, you are the dean. Geez, that sounds weird to me."

"Oh, you'll get used to it soon enough," he said. "I certainly did. Listen, I really can't split off right now, but can you come to the house tonight? Sophie would love to see you. I'll make her cook."

"Okay, sure," I said.

He walked over to the secretary's desk and wrote his address down on a piece of paper. "Here you go," he said. "Six o'clock, sharp, or I'll start without you."

"You got it," I said. "I'll be there."

He smiled again. "Just like old times."

I met Dr. Alex Crowe when he was a senior professor at Transylvania University, in Lexington, Kentucky. We hit it off famously, and by that I mean to say he took a real shine to me. Alex was the kind of guy that either liked you or didn't. He bent over backwards for the people he liked, which was not very many.

I told him I was researching my family history and why, and he immediately rose to the challenge. Crowe had a checkered past with regard to the supernatural and was fascinated with my mission and my former experiences. Next to me, he knows more about the Bowen family than anyone.

We spent many a late evening in his small study, poring over reference books and using his university access to surf the Internet on his computer, the place steeped in pipe smoke. His wife, Sophie, kept us stocked on sandwiches and coffee. She washed my clothes and I did the dishes. They were my second home for the better part of a year. In between making maps and genealogy charts, we discussed witchcraft and folklore and anything else that came to mind.

Crowe's name and his reputation opened a lot of doors for me, and he was happy to write letters to antiquarian societies and private libraries on my behalf, provided I share my findings with him. It was too easy with Crowe at my back.

That's when the University of Northern California made him an offer he couldn't refuse: a tenured position in their history department. The dean was an old friend of his and had a great interest in setting Alex up for life. And he did, when he died of a heart attack two years after Alex came to work for him. Alex had been the dean of the department for the past three years. We kept in touch through infrequent letters, so he always knew more or less where I was, and I always knew what was going on in San Cibola.

When Alex left Transylvania University, I left for the Eastern seaboard, looking for a group called the Armitage Foundation. I had received training in witchcraft, but I was eager to learn more if I was to protect myself from the family curse. That was eight years ago. Now I was standing on the West Coast. I had a lot more arcane knowledge under my belt, and a bag full of facts, research, and magical gewgaws, but I was no closer to finding Jacob Bowen, the man who started it all.

I wasn't here by chance, but by a process of elimination. Using the family records, I was able to chart a course for my far-roaming ancestor that spread from New York to California, with a detour into Mexico by way of Texas. Most of this was gleaned from family journals and letters. San Cibola was Jacob's last known address. If I couldn't find out what happened to him here, I would have to give up.

With my stomach growling, I navigated myself to the edge of campus and found what had to be the "strip" or the "drag" or whatever the kids called it here. Columbus Street started on the southern end of campus and ran for several blocks before splitting into different streets. Along the way, I found a plethora of pizza by the slice stands, taquerias, sandwich shops, and diners. Columbus Street also had a couple of record shops, bookstores, headshops, and other collegiate necessities. With less than a hundred bucks in my pocket and three weeks to go before my next check would be cut, I ate a couple of mediocre pieces of pizza and washed them down with some flat soda. Obviously, I was alone in my assessment of the place because it was packed.

I killed a couple of hours in the overstuffed used bookstore before tracing my steps back to the San Cibola Area Transit station (the locals called it the SCAT, but I couldn't bring myself to do that just yet) and checked the big map. The two terminals on this line that let off near the campus were equidistant to where Alex's house is. What the hell, I thought, buying another ride ticket. I've got the time. Dinner isn't for three hours, and as a bibliophile, I was honor bound to check out any neighborhood called the Rue Livre.

The district was actually named for that street, and it was lined with old houses that had been converted into bookstores. Each house was a specialty unto itself. For example, there was a large, two story house near the SCAT station that sold only law books. Right next to it was a creepy little cottage, surrounded by a wrought iron fence. They sold mysteries, naturally.

Going from house to house (and in some cases, translating the signs from my sketchy knowledge of French) killed the rest of my time. I looked up the street at the houses I didn't get to and shook my head. If I couldn't find a book here, it didn't exist.

I walked the neighborhood to get to Crowe's house. He lived in the nice, older, settled (and therefore extremely expensive) residential section of Collegetown. No doubt, much of the real estate was owned by the University and doled out to deans and professors as a perk for their services.

I was a little early, but no one minded. Alex's wife, Sophie, greeted me at the door with a huge hug and ushered me into their home. She hadn't changed a bit; the model college-professor wife. She was charming but not too much so, a great cook, and possessed the patience of Job. She kept herself well and kept to herself when Alex would lecture at parties, leaning against the fireplace mantle to gesture emphatically with his pipe. It was strange to see furniture and things I associated with one home now rearranged into a larger, more attractive two-story house. Being the Dean of History agreed with Alex, I could see, as he showed me around his house and pointed out new bits and pieces he'd picked up since the last time we'd seen each other. At one point, I passed a family portrait of Alex, Sophie, and their daughter, Jennifer. "Hey, how's Jennifer?" I asked.

Alex sighed. "Same as always." I dropped the subject. Jennifer was only two years younger than me, but in some ways, she was even more messed up than I was, if that were possible. She and I were friendly, but that was it. Looking after Jennifer fell mostly to Sophie.

As I got the nickel tour, the smell of Sophie's cooking followed us through each room until we couldn't stand it any longer and practically ran for the dining room.

After dinner, and after Alex and I cleaned the dishes, Sophie excused herself to go watch television upstairs and left us with instructions to clean up any late night food raids we might make on the kitchen. We retired to Alex's study, where he poured himself a glass of wine. The house might have been different, but Alex's study was still the same, piled high with books and steeped in fragrant pipe smoke.

"Now then," he said, settling into his favorite chair. "I want to know what you've been up to all this time."

So I told him everything. My travels in the Deep South, zombie hunting in Mexico, meeting famous, reclusive wizards, fighting harpies, the whole sordid thing. Crowe listened attentively and only interrupted to get me to clarify points of my narrative. He was keenly interested in hearing about my apprenticeship to the Navajo shaman. I told him how about the educated guesses I'd made as to where Jacob Bowen ended up, and how that led me up the California coast, hopping from Chinatown to Chinatown, looking for information that might not even exist anymore. I could tell by the look in his eyes that he knew I was at the end of my rope.

"How's the Armitage Foundation doing?" he asked.

"Same as always, I guess. They're still paying me as a field agent, and I'm still accumulating information about the stuff I run into. We've settled into a nice little hands-off arrangement. That reminds me, I put your address down for my next check, until I can get a place of my own."

Alex smiled. "Well, then, I'll want you out of here as soon as possible. You're your own weirdness magnet."

I smiled, and we studied our drinks for a minute.

"Sam," he said, thoughtfully clicking his unlit pipe between his teeth, "have you ever thought about just giving up? Letting all of it go? Living a normal life?"

"I've thought about it, Alex, really I have, but what good would it do if the curse still affected anyone I married?" I shook my head. "No, if I want peace, I have to tend to this. Besides, I've got a couple of younger relatives to think about. My niece is a teen-ager already. What happens if she falls in love with someone? No, it's too chancy."

Alex waved off my explanation. "It was just a thought. I just wonder if you're not chasing a ghost. Something you can't catch."

"Entirely possible," I conceded. "But I have to try. I have to keep looking until I know one way or the other."

I spent the night in the guest bedroom at Alex's insistence. The next morning, I went back to the bus station and pulled my meager belongings out of two lockers. It wasn't much. My duffel bag, which had been with me since Mexico, and an overstuffed suitcase I picked up in Phoenix, full of T-shirts, jeans, and toiletries. The sum total of my worldly possessions. I schlepped them back over to the Crowe house, then met Alex on campus for lunch.

"I hope you can still digest cafeteria food," he said as we strode quickly down the hall of the history building. "I did some checking around, and I think I've found a place for you to live. Someplace you'll really like."

"I appreciate the effort," I said, "but I'm not exactly flush, if you know what I mean. The Armitage Foundation is still paying me, but it's not a lot, and I've got a month to wait until the check gets here."

"You worry too much, young Mister Bowen. I've also arranged for you to meet the director of student services. She needs people to tutor the students in the summer semesters and possibly beyond. It's a few hours a day, but it's good money."

We were headed across campus to the student center. People were everywhere, so he lowered his voice and leaned in. "Besides, only college staff and faculty get access to the restricted stacks at the library, if you know what I mean."

I smiled. "As usual, I don't know how to thank you."

"Twenty percent of your first book will do fine for a start," Alex said, holding open the door to the cafeteria for me. "And whatever you do, for God's sake, don't eat the tuna fish."

After a ham and cheese lunch and half a can of Coke, Alex took me to meet the woman in charge of student services, a dumpy yet pleasant woman named Colleen, who was charmed by the sudden reappearance of my Southern accent. While I filled out the necessary paperwork, Alex dazzled her with stories of my academic career, and I dutifully copied it all down in the blank labeled "Work related experience." By the time we left, Colleen had me on a twenty-hour schedule, starting next week.

"And now, Mister Bowen," said Alex as he loosened his tie, "let me show you your new digs."

"Geez, Alex, what about your schedule?"

"To hell with it. I'm the dean."

We drove through the crowded streets of San Cibola, and Alex showed me the different neighborhoods: we drove through the chateaus of the Rue Livre, the old world charm of the Canal District, down into Arcadia and its old funky buildings repainted in garish, bohemian colors, and further down into the dilapidation of Spanishtown before turning east into Chinatown.

It was a lot to take in. The streets were crowded, and Alex didn't seem to know where he was going. Eventually, he spied a cul-de-sac off one of the main streets and we drove into it and parked.

"Pagoda House?" I said, my eyebrows shooting up. I expected something fancy. This was a dump. It was, I could see, part of the real old neighborhood. Pagoda House was a four-story brownstone of a building with faded bricks, yellowed glass, and discolored wood trim. It looked like a cartoon. "Are you kidding?" I asked him.

"Don't worry," said Alex, as he got out of the car. "All will be clear soon enough. Step lively, Mister Bowen." He dashed up the cracked cement steps and threw open the warped wooden door with a bang. He was practically giddy. I followed him, still not sure what the hell was going on.

I walked in to find Alex slapping the bell in the dingy lobby. "Hello? I'm from the college," he said in an overly-loud voice.

"Look, Alex, really, this isn't necessary..." I began, but stopped when the little Chinese man floated down through the ceiling to land behind the counter.

"Okay, okay, already," he groused. "Whole building can hear you banging on bell."

Alex opened his mouth and took a step back. I could see in his eyes all the stories I'd told him about ghosts springing back to life in his mind, in full color, and all of them starring this diminutive, well-dressed Chinese man in a green and black vest.

I stepped forward. "I'm interested in a room. To live in."

The ghost looked at me curiously. "You from the college?"

I looked at Alex. He nodded mutely. "Yes, I'm from UNC."

The ghost beamed. "Okey dokey, then, I show you what I got. Come on," he said, indicating the steps to the left of the counter. "Third floor. 301." He floated back up through the ceiling and vanished.

As we walked up the rickety wooden steps, I put a hand on Alex's shoulder. "First ghost?"

He shrugged. "Sort of. I belong to this gentlemen's club. Very exclusive place. They've got ghosts there, but they don't really behave like ghosts." He looked squarely at me. "It was the entrance that got me."

I smiled and nodded. "How did you find out about this place?"

"Through the same club," he said, his composure now back in place. "This guy, this ghost, Benny, likes to rent only to old people and students. However, because he's a ghost, it sort of limits his clientele. So, he only rents to Neighbors or people on the edge of being Neighbors."

I'd heard the term "Neighbor" before. It meant anyone who was connected with the supernatural community, which was referred to as a "Neighborhood." I'd had some experience with the Neighborhood in Philadelphia, but not much. San Cibola is supposedly the largest Neighborhood in the country, but I couldn't prove that yet. I was surprised to hear the term coming from Alex. I guess he knew more than I had given him credit for.

Finally, we reached the top step to find the ghost shaking his head. "I don't know if you can handle going up and down these stairs every day. Maybe I have to get an elevator." He laughed loudly.

"I'll be fine," I said thinly.

The ghost opened the door. "Okay, look around, test the water and stuff. I be back." He melted into the floor. Unsettling. I walked in and looked around.

It was small, but furnished. Facing the door was a good-sized bed with an old fashioned metal headboard. Next to it was a mismatched nightstand with a gooseneck lamp. A threadbare throw rug covered the hardwood floor. Next to the nightstand was an old recliner, tilted for viewing the small television on the opposite wall. Past the bedroom/living room was a small wooden table and two chairs, situated to take advantage of the meager light coming from the window. The fire escape was visible, as was a sterling view of the cul-de-sac. Beyond the table and chairs was a small but complete kitchen. Off to the right of the kitchen, I found the bathroom. It had a shower, but the tub was old enough to have feet. That was cool. Back in the living/dining area, I found a closet. Underneath the window was an old radiator that I just knew would work for shit when it got cold. Everything was old, but it was cozy and homey. And, most importantly, it was in Chinatown.

"How much is this place?" I asked Alex.

The ghost answered me, walking through the wall, which made us jump. "Eight hundred a month," he said, "plus one month rent deposit."

I looked at Alex. It was a steal, no doubt about it. But I didn't have it. Alex knew it, too.

"I suppose, Mister Bowen, that this will be another one of our famous lending arrangements?" Before I could answer, he turned to the ghost. "Cash okay with you?"

The ghost beamed. "What's your name?" he asked me.

"Sam Bowen."

"Benny Wan. Call me Benny." He bowed.

I tried to shake his hand and lost the feeling in my right arm.

That night, with my arm still numb, I managed to completely move into my new digs and was ready for food. It was strange, to be surrounded by familiar friends one night and then twenty-four hours later, be in a completely alien environment. Still, I couldn't really blame Alex for wanting me at a distance. I would be coming and going at all hours, and he no longer needed my distractions to keep him busy.

Outside my window, I could hear the cars and noise that filtered in through the cul-de-sac. It was time to explore my new home. I grabbed my duffel bag, threw on my overcoat to brace me against the cool evening air, and strolled leisurely down the stairs of my new home.

Chinatown at night was scary. There were lots of people on the streets, mostly tourists, but I still stood out. I also noticed several of the more unusual members of the community that other folks seemingly missed, including a Japanese ogre, one impossibly old Chinese man with a baby dragon in his arms, and three guys perched on one of the overhanging rooftops like gargoyles who seemed to be equal parts black-bird and man. The tourists were oblivious, of course, seeing only what they wanted to see. I walked past a demon with a food cart giving directions to two Asian tourists and made my way north on the street.

I popped into the first restaurant I could find, a little dive tucked in between a laundry service and a drug store. The menu was in Chinese, but I was too embarrassed to leave, so I ordered by pointing. I still couldn't tell you what they brought me, but it was great. I've tried to figure it out since then and I can't. Probably something they bring all the white people who wander in.

By the time I finished, night had fallen in earnest and cast the streets of Chinatown in a multicolored glow of red and green neon, and Chinese lanterns with yellow electric bulbs threw pools of color on the people below. I navigated my way through the people, using the shapes and colors of the crowd to guide me. I walked without seeing, as I was taught, and let my mind's eye take in what I was supposed to see. That's how I ended up deep in the neighborhood, three blocks off the beaten path, staring at a blinking sign that said:

Ping Ping's Bar

No Minors

I hadn't had a drink since Arizona. I picked up my bad habit in Texas, and it became a good friend in Mexico. My time with the Navajo medicine man had sweated the sick-ness, as he called it, out of me. What the hell, I thought, as I walked through the door, if I was going to get to know the natives, this was as good a place as any to start.

I got no further than two feet inside the door before a wall of man intercepted me and grunted something at me in Chi-nese. I used the international symbol for drink on him and he grudgingly let me past, but not before he clapped me on the shoulder, pointed to his eye, then thumped me on the chest. "I'll be watching you." I got the message, but the encounter left me feeling a little slighted. As if I would make trouble in a place like this.

And what a place it was. The bar had a smell to it, something that cut through the funk of humanity, mixed with animal and beer. Even empty, the bar would smell off, like milk that's just gone, or Indian food left too long under the heat lamps. The crowd was a weird mix of cultures, all of them Asian. I was the only white guy in the place. Great.

I sat down at the bar next to an ox-headed man with strange metal weapons hanging off his body. He paid me no mind. I caught eye of the old man tending bar and said, "Bourbon, please."

He stared at me, and several heads at the bar followed suit. "Bourbon," he repeated in a thin, reedy voice.

"If you have it," I added, noticing that everyone else was drinking beer or some colored thing in small glasses.

He looked me up and down before saying, "Wait here, I check." Where the hell would I go, I thought.

"Hey, Round-Eyes," said the monkey on left hand side of the bar, "don't order bourbon, this is Ping's place."

"Oh really," I said, secretly thrilled with myself that I was acting as if I had grown up around talking monkeys. "What would you suggest?"

"Beer."

"Thanks for the tip," I said, as the old man came back carrying a half-full bottle full of brown liquid.

"Here," the old man said, thumping the bottle on the table, "this is four dollars a shot."

"I'll take a shot," I answered, laying a five-dollar bill down. Out of the corner of my eye, I could see the monkey shaking his head.

"Fine," said the old man, taking my money and not returning any change. He poured three fingers into a small glass.

I brought the drink to my lips, took a deep breath, and tossed it back. During the deep breath, I caught a whiff of the drink and, in the split-second before I swallowed it, realized that whatever it was, it sure wasn't bourbon.

I gagged, choked, and tried to spit it back up, but it was no use. It was down the hatch. If I was lucky, it wouldn't stay there long. "Jesus Christ," I gasped. "What the hell was that?"

"Oh, that wasn't bourbon?" said the old man, cackling madly. The bar joined in, laughing raucously.

"No, it fucking well wasn't."

"Settle down, Joe," he said, drawing me a beer. "Lesson learned, no harm done."

"Says you," I replied, wiping my mouth. "When's the last time you were poisoned?"

I drained my beer in three single gulps, but it didn't help. I ordered another one. The taste was completely gone by my third beer.

After that, things got a little cozier. I ended up in an involved conversation with the ox-headed guy, whose name was Zi Yu. I showed him my scars from the knife fight I lost in New Mexico, and he gave me a set of brass knuckles that fit my hand perfectly. I also spent a lot of time talking to Monkey, whose other name was Great Sage, Equal of Heaven, but I was damned if I was going to call him that. The old man pulling beers turned out to be Ping Ping himself. Between the three of them, I got quite an education regarding exactly how dangerous Chinatown really was.

"You lucky it's busy today," said Ping. "Ylongo there not let you in otherwise."

"Why for?" I asked.

"Because you ain't a Neighbor or an Oriental," said Monkey.

"Asian," corrected Zi Yu.

"Ah, I'll call it what I like," Monkey snarled. "I'm due."

"You're going to piss someone off someday, Monkey," Zi Yu admonished.

"So?" said Monkey, pulling a golden toothpick from behind his ear. "Anyone who screws with me without knowing the score deserves what they get."

"What, you'll throw poop on 'em?" I said.

Monkey ignored the comment. "The point is, Bowen, you don't make the cut here. This is a pity party, having you at the bar."

"Hey, I can hold my own," I protested. "How do you know I'm not a Neighbor?"

"How long you here?" asked Ping. "One day?" He laughed. "Come back in a month, then we see."

"Ah, nuts. I have to go," said Zi Yu. He emptied his mug, letting his ox tongue fill the glass like a huge blue slug. "See you around, maybe, Bowen. Nice to have met you."

"Yeah, thanks for these," I said, holding up the brass knuckles. I watched him lumber through the crowd, who parted deferentially for him.

"Nice guy," I said to Monkey.

Monkey looked at Ping, grinned, and shook his head. "I give him two weeks."

"You're on," said Ping.

"Aw, you guys suck," I said. I started to order another drink, but something crashed into me from behind and knocked me off the barstool. My foot caught in the strap of my duffel bag and sprung me back into the hardwood bar. By the time I had freed my foot, I had a close-up look at the source of the disturbance.

One of the patrons was grappling with a man in the process of turning into a snake. I watched as his neck elongated and his face tapered like a melting candle, green and brown scales bubbling to the surface of his liquid flesh. The man with no shapeshifting abilities let go and popped the cuffs of his sleeves. Twin knives, the size of machetes, slid into his hands, and he screamed in Chinese and struck a defensive stance. The snake-man was now mostly reptile and easily twenty feet long with no signs of stopping. Everyone was staying well away from the flashing knives and writhing tail. The giant serpent reared back, mouth open, and spit a glob of venom at the knife holder. It caught him right in the chest, and the man screamed as it burned through his shirt. He ran out the door, wailing like the dead.

The sudden loss of an active adversary in no way stopped the giant snake, who turned immediately to the closest patron and buried its fangs in the poor man's right shoulder and lifting him off the ground. Now the bar was moving, people crowding the door and pressing against the back wall.

I took off running, like an idiot, straight for the snake. It let go of the screaming man and faced me, its eyes glittering in the half-light. I grabbed up one of the wooden chairs and caught the snake's strike with it. The snake's fangs clattered on the legs of the chair before sliding off. I followed the movement of the head with the chair, trying to keep it between the snake's head and me. I got close enough to make a grab for the body, which was as big around as a mesquite tree, but the snake flexed and tore out of my grasp. I leapt over the coils of its body and almost got bit for my troubles.

Now I was in for it. I had maneuvered myself into a corner, literally. The snake loomed over me, a smile on its triangular face. I had brass knuckles and a chair. It was going to come in high, aiming for my head or my shoulder. I waited. Behind the snake, I got a sense of people screaming and moving, but I was locked in on those eyes. It was a test of the desert, all over again. Suddenly, the head was coming for me, fast and quick. I dodged to the left, moving the chair to the right, and caught the snake just under the head with the legs of the chair. With a desperate heave, I slammed the chair and the snake against the wall, pinning its head under the legs. I stepped over the writhing body and sang the song of friendship to the snake, telling it my Navajo name and offering it protection from the vengeful sky and the swift-flying feathered hunters. Gradually, the snake stopped thrashing, but I kept its head pinned to the wall, just to be sure.

The tail receded until it split and became two legs. I lifted the chair away from the half-human face. He looked at me sullenly, his eyes accusing. After that, a bunch of men rushed in on us and carried him out into the night. I never saw that guy again.

I walked back up to the bar with the patrons patting me on the back. At least my duffel bag was still there. Someone bought me a drink. Then another, and another.

Ping looked at Monkey and said, "The kid can stay."

I woke up on the floor of the bar, which is never, ever a good place to wake up. A broken bottle was staring me in the eye, two inches away. I got up, quickly, and leaned against the barstool when the room started moving. Everything hurt, and not just from the fight with the snake-man. Ping was behind the bar, rinsing out glasses. I got the distinct impression he never left the bar.

"Oh, look who's up."

Monkey rose to a sitting position and regarded me. Apparently, he never left the bar, either.

"You look like shit," he said.

"Funny, I thought I was looking in a mirror."

Ping smiled. "Good tough guy line."

"Christ, I hurt all over," I said.

"No kidding," said Ping. "You drink so much, I thought you died."

"When I fall off a wagon, by God, I fall off a fucking wagon."

Ping frowned. "That not a good tough guy line."

"It wasn't meant to be." My back hurt because I fell asleep on my duffel bag. I picked it up and said, "Anyone know how to get back to the Pagoda House?"

"Benny's Place?" Monkey raised an eyebrow. He glanced at Ping. "I still give him two weeks."

"Double or nothing," said Ping, refilling Monkey's gourd with plum wine.

A fellow drunkard tapped me on the shoulder. "You go Benny. I take you."

I looked at Monkey, who said, "That's the brother of the guy who got savaged last night. You'll be fine."

"Okay, let's go," I said.

"Okay, he said.

"Lead the way," I said.

"Okay," he said.

I pulled out a ten-dollar bill. "We go now."

"Right," he said, snatching the money and walking out the door. I hurried to follow him.

"Welcome to San Cibola," Ping called out after me.

The Kindness of Strangers

I didn't know anything was going down until I saw the three men by the door flip open their jackets to reveal bare chests with arcane symbols cut into them. They formed a complicated symbol with their hands, and I saw arcs of blue flame lick their fingers. I vaulted out of my seat and ran for Chu Sheng Kai's table. I don't know if I yelled, "Get down!" over and over, or if I just thought it. The point was moot, though. I barreled into the old man and his two aides, knocking the table over on top of all of us as a hailstorm of blue fireballs pelted the restaurant, catching the decorations on fire and setting off the sprinklers.

The water from the ceiling kept the pools of fire at bay. Amid the shrieks of the patrons, I felt something hot and wet on the back of my neck and panicked for a second, until I realized it was only shark fin soup. Chu's men groaned and stirred, but Chu was silent beneath me. "Are you okay?" I asked. I looked down. His eyes were closed, and he was colorless. I could see he was still breathing, which answered my main question. "Mr. Chu?"

Chu's eyes opened. He yelled into my face in flawless English, "Get off of me!"

I rolled over onto broken dishes and a pile of rice noodles. "Sorry," I said automatically, even though I was a little miffed. I did just save his life; you'd think he could be nicer. I watched the two aides pick him up, dust him off, and hustle him to the front door. They paused for a second, one goon leaning out the door looking this way and that, and the other whispering earnestly to the crying woman at the front counter. He handed her a roll of bills, and she stopped crying and started nodding. The goon joined his occupational twin in the doorway, and they hurriedly spirited Chu out of the restaurant without so much as a look back.

Great, I thought, just great. First time in three months I get close enough to the man to finally talk to him, and someone tries to whack him before I can even say hello. I picked myself up, and my left knee reminded me that it was not real happy with the stunt I'd just pulled. My jacket was covered in duck sauce and God only knew what else. I walked back through the carnage, noting that no one else seemed to be injured. I guess I had yelled, after all.

My duffel bag was sitting in the opposite chair from my ruined meal. I grabbed it and headed up to the counter where the woman was counting her money, paid for my meal, and left with the wail of sirens growing louder and louder.

Goddamn it all anyway, I thought as I moved through Chinatown, falling instinctively into the rhythm of the streets. My luck runs in cycles, and this looked like the beginning of a new batch of the bad stuff. That's all right, I thought, I was overdue anyway. The pendulum always swings the other way. I had such good luck when I first arrived in San Cibola, I knew it was just a matter of time. I just wish it could have waited another day or so.

San Cibola was that kind of town. The days are twice as bright and the nights are twice as dark. That makes Chinatown about four times at enigmatic. Chinatown actually encompassed the Japanese as well as Chinese cultures and even had a couple of streets the locals called Little India. With all the usual mundane racial prejudices suspended, the community worked under an uneasy truce, largely enforced by the triads, who in turn ran the tongs. Since what I knew about Chinese culture wouldn't fill a teacup, in spite of my nine-month stint in California and a brief visit to Philly's Chinatown, I kept my eyes open and my mouth shut. It's too easy to lose your head here to flying birdmen or avatars of Shiva. If I could do it all over, I wouldn't have lived in this neighborhood. On the plus side, in the past three months I had generated roughly fifty pages of notes for my folklore book, so it wasn't all bad.

I turned off of Pacific Avenue, glad to see Benny's Pagoda House in the distance. I walked up the narrow stoop and into the cramped lobby. Benny Wan was behind the front desk, waving paper at me.

"Sam! Sam! You get letter! No one but you get letter! You very important, huh?" He handed me an envelope. He leaned half-in and half-out of the counter in his excitement.

"Hey Benny." I took the letter from him, careful not to let any part of myself pass through him, and looked at the return address. It was from my nephews.

"This is family stuff." I told him. Actually, it was pretty important, but not in the way he meant.

Benny snickered. "Why you got food all over you?"

"Oh, I was eating at that big Chinese place over on Orchid Street, you know, Shi-Shi House? Well, I was in there with Chu Sheng Kai, and someone tried to kill him. I intervened and saved his life."

Benny frowned. "That's very bad. You get reward?"

"Nope. Not even a thank you."

Benny scowled. "Ungrateful man."

"I thought so, too. Goodnight, Benny."

"Okay, bye bye." I had tried several times to get Benny to talk about how be became a ghost, but he wouldn't go on record. Considering what I had already seen in this town, I doubt he had the most interesting story to tell. I just could never figure out why he still needed the money and insisted on running this place, particularly since it wasn't his building.

Ordinarily, I could take the steps two at a time, but the evening's entertainment took a lot out of me. I paced myself, feeling the weight of my duffel bag on my shoulder with every step. Once inside my compact apartment, I shot the deadbolt, dropped my belongings on the floor, and collapsed onto the rickety bed.

When I first arrived in San Cibola, I had nothing but a few vague assurances from a couple of Asian studies professors at Berkeley. Thanks to Doctor Alex Crowe, and the job he helped me get, I had full access to the college's resources, including a pass to the restricted stacks at Addison Memorial Library. I spent my first few weeks in town going through everything I could find there. After that, I went into the microfiche, zig-zagging through every issue of the *San Cibola Courier* and the *San Cibola Examiner*, making tons of notes and racking up a killer headache. What I did get out of it was a name: Chu Sheng Kai, a mysterious philanthropist with strong political pull in Chinatown. According to the papers and a few discreet interviews, Chu's main passion was local history. Plus, Chu had a personal library filled with esoteric books and one-of-a-kind manuscripts. The problem was, Chu had a lot of enemies and was seldom seen in public. According to one source, Chu used to be in a triad but left to start his own, legitimate organization and declared war on the other triads and tongs. The counter-rumor held that Chu was still running a triad, and all of his parks, museums, and community services were a nice front. No one really knew; it all depended on which paper you read.

Anyway, Chu was completely unavailable and made infrequent public appearances. I spread some precious bucks around and got a scrap of info from a friend of a friend. He told me that Chu occasionally ate at what is now the Shi-Shi House indoor barbecue and that I might find him there. So I had been eating there nightly for the past ten days, just working my way down the menu numerically, to the chagrin of my wallet and the misery of my stomach. Finally, he shows up and the place turns into a gas grill.

I opened my letter from Mitchell and Marcus.

> *Dear Uncle Sam,*
> *Hello, I am fine and so is Marcus. How are you? I had a birthday now I am 7. Marcus is 4 he says. I hope you can come home for Christmas I asked Paul and Stephanie and they said you could stay with us so please come home if you can. Please bring presents to but if you can not come then can you mail them to us like you did last time? Marcus wants a Spiderman web shooter and I want Hardy Boys books or a BB gun. Thank you.*
> *Love, your nephews.*
> *Mitchell Marcus*

Below the letter was a crudely drawn picture of Spider-Man labeled "Marcus" and a boy in a cowboy hat labeled "Mitchell." Mitchell was holding a rifle. Stuck to the back was a yellow sticky note from Stephanie, their foster mother:

> *Sam,*
> *I know you are busy, but you have a place to stay if you can make it in for Christmas. The kids never stop talking about you.*
> *Stephanie*

Nice. I read it with all the bitchiness I am sure she intended. I stared at their drawing until it became a blur, then a black tunnel, then nothing.

I woke up in the same clothes I'd had on the night before, which made the whole apartment stink. Looking at my cheap, drugstore alarm clock, I noticed I was about to be late for tutoring. I filled the kitchen sink up with water and detergent and let my ruined clothes soak while I showered. The feelings of yesterday fell away with the soap and water, and a full night's sleep did me a world of good. I even caught the number 13 bus that took me straight to the campus.

Thursday was my light schedule. Two morning sessions, then I was free for the day. I decided to hit the Rue Livre District and wade through all the specialty bookshops in the hope of stumbling across something useful for my research.

The labs were hopping that day for some reason, and the kids actually made me earn my keep. It was after 12:30 when the last of the angst-ridden students left. As I gathered my things together, a Chinese kid in his early twenties stuck his head through the door.

"I'm looking for Sam Bowen?" he said with a trace of an accent.

"I'm Sam, but you just missed my labs. The next guy can probably help you, though." I made a production of slinging my duffel bag over my shoulder.

The kid smiled. "I don't go to school. I am here because my employer wants a meeting with you."

I frowned. "Okay...who do you work for?"

He stepped into the room now, and I could see he was dressed in a simple chauffeur's outfit, minus the hat. He bowed deeply. "My employer is Chu Sheng Kai."

My heart sped up. "Uh, when does he want to see me?"

"Now, please." The kid was all smiles. He gestured with his hand. "Can I carry your bag?"

"No. I got it." This was all wrong. UNC was my second home. I didn't bring any of my real work to school, which made campus a safe haven for me. This kid felt like an intrusion into my world. Furthermore, after spending the better part of a year in California fruitlessly searching, this lackey showing up out of the blue to suddenly escort me to the Holy Grail was a bit unnerving.

The chauffeur noticed my apprehension. He said, "I am told you are to be his guest at lunch today and that he wishes to express his gratitude for your intervention." The kid was just mouthing the words; he obviously didn't know what the deal was. In my experience, gift horses don't come around too often, and it's best not to stare when they do. Go now, sort it out later, I thought. "Okay, sure."

The chauffeur took me back to Chinatown, through the tourist traps, past the residential neighborhoods, and into the more expensive real estate. Chu Sheng Kai's house sat on the backside of Nod Hill, so close to the Buddhist temple that I thought the two were part of the same property. His house was palatial and very traditional, with gardens in the front and back, paper screens, the whole nine yards. Telltale signs of modern living showed, like the electronic eye at the iron gate, and a security camera that quietly followed the car as we made our way up the driveway. Otherwise, it was like stepping back into a 1970's kung fu movie.

The chauffeur parked in front and opened my door for me. Two toughs appeared in the front door, but as I approached, they bowed and gave way. I nodded uneasily to them. I was escorted through several halls and rooms, each filled with artwork, scrolls, statues, vases and urns, and other items of extreme antiquity. I kept my eyes peeled for books but didn't see any. Finally, my chauffer opened up a set of double doors, and I was on a deck with Chu. He was sitting at a wooden table, half in the shade and half out, wearing red and yellow silk robes. He was pale and gaunt and did not at all look well. His short, distinguished gray and white hair was unkempt, and there was a noticeable tremble in his frame. No one knew his age, but from what I saw, I guessed he was around seventy years old. When I walked out, he was staring into his back garden, a sprawling affair with manicured rocks, flowerbeds, wooden bridges over tiny streams, and diminutive trees. Framed against the picturesque side of Nod Hill, it suddenly didn't feel like I was standing in Northern California at all.

Chu stood up, turned to face me. Our eyes met. Before I could speak, he bowed deeply and kept his head lowered.

"Welcome to my home. I asked you here to thank you for your assistance last night and to beg your forgiveness. You gave of yourself, and my fear and weakness are no excuse for rudeness. I am in your debt."

Well, shit.

Now what was I supposed to do? He remained bowed. "Um, it's all right." I said. "You're welcome. No harm, no foul. I would've done the same for anybody."

Chu raised his head. "I do not believe that. Still, you are an extraordinary man, Mr. Bowen, to risk your life for a total stranger."

"That reminds me, how do you know who I am, anyway?"

Chu smiled thinly. "I have lived in Chinatown for fifty years. I know everyone here, and they know me. You have been in my neighborhood for three months, asking a lot of questions about me. So, when these questions reached my ears, I asked some questions of my own."

"I assure you, Mr. Chu, I would have come to you directly if there was any way to actually get ahold of you."

He nodded. "I value my privacy, for my family's sake and to my enemies' frustration. It is fortunate, then, that you just...happened to run into me at the restaurant last night." He laughed, and I got the impression that he knew so much more than he was letting on. I laughed, too, still not sure of where I stood with him.

"I would be honored if you would join me for lunch," he said.

"Thank you. I've learned never to refuse a free meal." I smiled, setting my duffel bag down beside me and taking a seat opposite him. This was my chance. He just said he owed me, so I figured access to his library ought to square us right up. All I had to do now was bring it up without pissing him off. Seemed a bit silly, considering he just kowtowed to me, but something told me to use the kid gloves.

Chu poured us tea from the pot on the table. I raised the round cup and said, "To your health."

"And to yours," he echoed. We drank. I could taste jasmine and something sweet. It was excellent.

"You like my tea?" Chu asked. "I make it myself. It's an old family recipe. I have found it is best not to stray too far from the things you love, for they are often the source of our strength."

I thought of my nephews and my niece. "I agree."

A woman in traditional garb brought out a tray of appetizers. I recognized pot stickers, won tons, and egg rolls and stuck with those. Chu ate quickly and deftly with chopsticks. I followed at a slower, clumsier pace.

"You have a beautiful home, Mr. Chu." I said more to fill the space between us than anything else.

He inclined his head. "I thank you. But I suspect you do

not want to ask me about my home. Let's talk about exactly why you would risk your life to get close to me."

I swallowed my dumpling, surprised at his frankness. "Well, okay, then. I should start at the beginning." I opened up my duffel bag and pulled out the binder containing my credentials and put it in my lap for later. "I am doing some extensive research on my ancestors. You see, I am the only living adult in my family, a family that has been in this country for over two hundred and fifty years. The only other relatives I know of are two nephews and a niece that live with foster parents."

The girl reappeared with a tray full of food. We helped ourselves. "When I was a boy, my family in Kentucky numbered maybe three to four dozen people, nuclear and extended. Well, one by one, they all began to die at an alarming rate. Some of them were involved in work-related accidents, some fell by their own stupidity or stubbornness, but every so often, there was one that was just unusual." I looked at Chu for acknowledgement and got none. I pressed on.

"The first one I can remember was my Uncle Hank. Hank was killed when he was hit by lightning. He was plowing his field one day, nothing amiss, when the doctors figure he was struck by lightning. The thing is this, though...that day, the skies were clear. He was found, dead, all the classic signs of electrocution, out in his field. The plow and the mule were fine, not a mark on them. Only Hank. They called it lightning because there wasn't anything else to call it.

"The one that clenched it, though, was my older brother. Saul was killed by a wild animal that they couldn't identify. They simply don't know what did it. The forensic evidence doesn't match anything in the area, in the state, or in the country. He was taking the trash out and died in his backyard, without a sound. His wife and child were in the house and never heard his violent death. They called it a wild dog attack."

Chu cleared his throat. "I am sorry for your loss. I don't see, though, how I can help."

I paused for a minute, to get the lump out of my throat. Telling this story always depressed me. "Okay, let me get to the point. There are only four members of the Bowen family bloodline left. Myself, and three children. When I was a boy, I used to hear my family talk about some sort of curse. My mother would shush him and tell me to put it out of my mind. But after all the weird things started to happen, I began to think maybe there was something to it. So, I did some research through my family, read some diaries and conducted some interviews, and it seems that one branch of my family tree, my father's branch, believed they were under a curse. To further lend credence to the idea, I am the seventh born into my family, Mr. Chu. You know, the seventh son of a seventh son? I have crisscrossed this country in the last eight years, trying to track down every one of my relatives from the time they set foot in this country. As you can see from these, it's has been my life's work."

I handed him the binder and kept talking. It was full of letters of accommodation from a dozen or more small towns for helping them fix some haunted house or chase down the Goat Boy of Fill-in-the-Blank Woods, academic citations from a handful of private universities, my degrees, and my letters of commission from the Armitage Foundation. That was usually what got the antiquarian's attention. Chu thumbed quickly through it and handed it back to me. "I know about all of this already. Please go on."

I kept talking, hoping my surprise didn't show on my face. "Well, I am tracking down my last great great great grandfather, Jacob. Old Jake was a bit of a wild man, and he is responsible for a lot of the illegitimate Bowens that ran through my family. He started on the East Coast, traveled down through the south, into Texas, then dipped into Mexico, back into Texas, and finally traveled throughout California. I know he spent some time here, and I am looking for corroborative evidence that can back that up. I also suspect that the curse came from an ethnic community that Jake didn't take seriously. That means either the Native Americans, the Blacks, the Mexicans, or the Chinese. Please forgive my frankness. I don't share my family's viewpoint. I have ruled out all of the above but the Chinese. Which brings me to you."

Chu looked up from his food, nonplussed. " I still do not know what you want me to do."

"I'm sorry. What I need is access to your personal library. I am classified as an expert with the handling of rare documents and would not damage your books at all. What I want to do is go back through your family's journals and the diaries you have collected through the years and look for evidence of my ancestor. I would imagine that cursing a man would make it into someone's personal recollection. Let me go through them and look for something that can help me. I can also get a feel for the local legends and folklore. It would really help me out, and you can supervise my work if you..."

"No."

It took a second for the word to register, even though it was the loudest and strongest syllable he'd uttered so far.

"I'm sorry?"

"No, I am sorry, but the answer is no." He pushed his plate away for emphasis.

I took a sip of tea to disguise my anger. "May I ask why?" I said evenly.

"What you are asking me to do is unthinkable. The

amount of things I don't want you or any other outsider to know cannot be calculated! You are not Chinese, you do not understand our customs and traditions!" He paused and collected himself. "If you like, I can go through my library myself and look for a reference to your Jacob Bowen."

I bit my lip. "I certainly appreciate your offer, but that won't do. What I mean is, I often don't know what I am looking for until I sort of stumble across it."

Chu nodded. "I understand. And I am sorry, but I hope you understand my position on the matter. I can not open my family's private history to someone who is not of my family."

Just then, the door flew open and banged sharply against the terrace. A flock of birds I hadn't even noticed in the garden suddenly took flight.

A Chinese man in his mid-thirties strode through the doors. He wore an expensive suit and was carrying a bloody chicken. It was definitely not something you see every day, even in San Cibola.

"Father! It has happened again! To me this time! You must call the..."

"Sst!" Chu hissed, and the man stopped short as if he'd been slapped. "You impudent oaf! Where are your manners?"

The man finally noticed me and gave a curt bow. He turned back to his father. "Now, what are you going to..."

"Sst!" He stopped again. "Introduce yourself to Mr. Bowen." It was a command.

The man extended his left hand, as the right one had a bloody chicken in it. "Hello, I am Michael Chu."

I noticed Chu wince and look away. I took his hand in mine. "Sam C. Bowen. Glad to know ya." I looked at the chicken and noticed the blood was not even dry.

"Likewise. Now, please excuse me as I must address my father." He turned to Chu.

Chu shot me a look that seemed to say, "Do you see what I have to put up with?" "Michael is the curator of the Chinatown Cultural Exchange Center, one of my non-profit organizations." Michael nodded. "I am sorry, Mr. Bowen, but I must speak with my son. Please excuse me." He got up, bowed to me, and left the veranda. Michael followed him through the door.

I gathered up my things and tossed my coat on. No point in staying, anyway, I thought. I walked down the hallway, completely stumped about where to try next. As I neared one of the doors on my left, I could make out the voices of the old man and his son. I put my ear to the door and listened.

"Father, you must call the police."

"There is no need."

Michael stamped his foot. "It is Wan Fei Ying! This was on my doorstep when I arrived this morning!"

"You still think this is some sort of an attack on me?"

"Not an attack, but an attempt to discredit! Your enemies are always trying to make you lose face!"

"You are wrong. This means nothing."

"This is the third time it's happened! Remember your office in Chinatown? And the warehouse?"

"This is pointless. I am too important to let childish pranks get to me. This is beneath my attention."

I knocked on the door. "Who is it?" Chu asked.

"It's Sam."

Pause. "Come in."

I opened the door. His office was as lavish as the rest of the house. Chu was sitting, Michael was standing. "Pardon me for interrupting, but I couldn't help but overhear your talk..." Chu shot Michael a dirty look. "And I have to ask you, Michael, is this the first chicken you've brought home?"

Michael looked confused. "Yes, I came straight here when I found it."

"Mr. Bowen, this does not concern you. Please finish your lunch, this is nothing."

"I don't think so," I told Chu.

He gave me a level gaze. "And why is that, Mr. Bowen?"

"Because this isn't a prank."

"Oh really? What is it, then?"

"It's voodoo."

The driver stopped in front of the building and jumped out to open the door for me. "Hey, you live at Benny's?" he asked.

I stepped out, pulling my duffel bag with me. "Uh huh. How do you know Benny?"

The driver shrugged. "Every kid in Chinatown has heard of Benny and his Haunted Pagoda."

"Yeah? What have they heard?"

The driver waved me off as he climbed back in the car. "You wouldn't understand. You are not Chinese."

"I'm trying to learn!" I yelled at the retreating car. Christ, what a lunch.

I'll say this for Chu, he's a sharp one. After I explained my theory to him, he realized his current ill health matched up with the appearance of the first warning sign at his office. Then when Michael scoffed at my suggestion, well, of course Chu was going to listen to me after that. Nice to know family politics are the same from culture to culture.

Chu was being hexed, and I had no idea why. Chu knew but was keeping mum about the whole thing. Without that kind of personal information, I was flying blind regarding the type of hex being used against him. I was surprised to learn that not only was Chu unaware of what to signs to look for, but he hadn't even considered the possibility that he might be the target of a supernatural attack. He just said to me, "There are things you do not understand about this situation. Someone has risked personal honor to strike at me. I am close to a victory, it would seem." Great. I could get more direct answers to my questions from a Magic Eight Ball.

I hit my room at a run and changed into my work clothes: my black turtleneck and jeans with my black boots. I pulled out my trench coat, a recent addition since moving to the West Coast, and laid it by the door so I could grab it on the way out. That done, I cracked open my duffel bag and sifted through the compartments until I found a leather bag labeled, "Louisiana." I opened it up and dumped the contents out onto the bed. I then did the same with "Mexico" and "Missouri," keeping everything separate. I stared at the little piles of junk for a long minute, then dug into my duffel bag one last time and pulled out my working journal. I opened the book, which was keyed to each state, and read my notes. It took a while. I jumped around in the book a lot. Finally, I pulled my mojo bag out of the Louisiana pile and hung it around my neck. I opened up the paper packet marked "witches' balls" from Missouri and dumped the contents out. Two balls made of horsehair and candle wax rolled across the bed. I needed to make some more, but these would do for now. I tipped them back into their paper packet and put that in the pocket of the trench coat. As an afterthought, I added a candle stub and some chalk as well. Finally, I grabbed a heavy brass amulet from the Mexico pile and consulted it. The amulet had two dials: the outer ring, engraved angelic symbols that governed each month of the year and the inner ring, the days of the week. I set the dials to match Thursday and October and put that in the pocket of my jeans. I had no idea if Solomonic magic was any match for voodoo, but it worked against Santeria, so I thought it was worth a try. I loaded my hunting knife into my boot and replaced everything in the duffel bag. Now there was nothing left to do but wait for the phone to ring, so I caught a nap. Bad idea. I should have written the kids.

I'm back in Missouri and I am nineteen again. It's me and Tallulah and we are in the graveyard. She tells me to strip and I do it, laying my clothing on the tombstone she indicates. She shimmies out of her dress and begins to kiss me. Two people appear from the shadows, only this time it's Chu Sheng Kai and his son, Michael.

"This is pointless! Useless!" he screams at me as Tallulah leads me back to the tombstone and begins chanting. The wind picks up and Michael points at us.

"They mock our ways! Ignorant barbarians! Do not trust him!"

Tallulah is all over me, her words filling my head. I can't concentrate. I am supposed to renounce Christ here, but all I can think about is the fact that I am still a virgin and this woman will be my first. "All I want is to read your books!" I shout over the noise.

"You are not family!" Chu screams back.

"I don't have any family!" I reply.

Tallulah is up and in my arms now, around my waist, asking me questions I know I am supposed to answer. Chu and Michael turn away in disgust. The wind is deafening...

And then it was just the telephone.

I fumbled around until I hit the receiver. "Hello?"

"Sam?" I didn't recognize the voice, but it was Chinese.

"Yeah, go ahead." I reached for the pad and pencil I kept

on the nightstand.

"I have an address for you. 1697-A Rue Bijou." Looked like I would get to go to the Rue Livre after all.

"You get a name? A description?"

"Black man, long hair pulled back. Nice suit."

That would have to do. "You sure about the address? Did you follow him?"

"From Master Chu's house to his."

"Okay, tell Chu I will have this taken care of tonight." The man hung up without saying good-bye.

Once I hit the street I realized how hungry I was and decided to grab some to-go food before going about my business.

Zhu's Noodle Hut was always open. Poised at the intersection of Sacramento and Crane, Zhu offered the absolute best dollar Chinese food in town. You could get a one dollar, two dollar, or four dollar carton, and Zhu would fill it with rice, noodles, or one of five daily entrees. He served a lot of tourists who never even noticed he tended to float about six inches off the ground. For a demon, he was pretty demure.

I walked up to the rolling cart. "Hey Zhu, I don't know why you have wheels on this contraption, you never go anywhere else."

Zhu regarded me with one yellow eye and one red eye. "Very funny. That joke so old I forget to laugh."

I stepped under the umbrella and into a variety of smells that made my stomach rumble earnestly. "I need a four dollar box tonight."

"More questions about that fool, Chu Sheng Kai?" he asked as he fumbled for one of the big wax-paper cartons. For some reason, Zhu hated Chu. I think it had something to do with why he could never leave this street corner and had to sell food to tourists.

"No, I have some work to do." I looked over his dishes. "Um, rice on the bottom, then noodles, and a double order of the chicken and garlic sauce."

"Must have a hot date," said Zhu, spooning food into the box. I selected some chopsticks from the round jar.

"Say, Zhu?" I tried for a casual tone. "Do you still have any, you know, powers?"

Zhu nodded, his chin wobbling. "Sure, the power to make excellent Chinese food and the power to answer any question about Chinatown." He spat on the sidewalk. "That's it."

"Oh, wow, that's too bad." I didn't try to hide my disappointment.

"Don't be sorry, Bowen. If I had but a fraction of my true abilities back, I would have killed all the white men in this town long ago and re-established San Cibola as the new Shanghai of America."

"Ah. I see. Well, then, um..." I handed him a five-dollar bill. "Keep the change, Zhu."

"Don't try to suck up to me now!" he screamed as I walked away. "You the first person I come for when I am free!" I dug into my chicken and garlic and prayed that day would never come. He was too good a cook.

By the time I made it to the SCAT station, I had finished my meal. I decided on the train rather than the bus because the Rue Livre stop was on Bijou Street. Plus, it would be a lot quicker. My train took five minutes to show up and another five to get to the Rue Livre station. Curb service.

I ascended to street level and started walking, looking for the address. The buildings on Rue Bijou were mostly chateaus, which made a lot of sense for my mystery houngan and for the district. A good number of the houses had signs out front proclaiming them to be a business of some sort. Those without signs were either private residences or businesses you had no business knowing about. 1697 was ten blocks up. This house was a veritable mansion and sported a low brick fence and wrought iron gate. A sign over the gate read, "Chez Maison Boarding House." Give me strength. Apparently my luck was still in. As I approached the house from the opposite side, I noticed a well-dressed black man in his late forties open the gate and stride out. His long, kinky hair was held with a length of gold wire. He wore wrap-around shades and looked more like a record producer than a houngan. I watched as he quickly got into a 1973 Triumph and bolted away from the house. It was almost too good to be true. I opened the wrought-iron gate and walked around to the back. There were two guesthouses, 1697-A and 1697-B. The windows were closed and the curtains drawn on 1697-A. I walked over to 1697-B and knocked.

The door opened a quarter of an inch. I could see a woman's face peering at me suspiciously through the crack. "What?"

"Hello, ma'am, I'm from Vic's Automotive. We're here to pick up your Triumph, and I just wanted to let you know."

"My what?" she asked.

"Your Triumph Spitfire, 1973, color red, right outside? We're going to tow it to our shop to do the repairs you asked for."

"That's not my sports car, that's Mr. Dominguez's next door."

I frowned and pulled out a receipt for some dry-cleaning out of my pocket and proceeded to study it intently. "Mary Dominguez?"

"No, Beau Dominguez. He's not married, either. Are you sure you've got the right house?"

I made a production of checking the house numbers against my three shirts with no starch. "Hell, I can't read this scrawl, now it doesn't look like Dominguez at all. Looks like Dunkawitz. I'm sorry to bother you, ma'am." I backed away.

"Hey, you aren't going to tow his car, are you?"

"Not a chance, ma'am," I replied and kept going.

Well, Mr. Beau Dominguez, I hope you get back from wherever you went soon. I might be able to wrap this all up by midnight. I crossed the street to the small bookstore and wandered around until I found a San Cibola restaurant guide, then sat down in the romance section in the front, facing the window, to wait.

Dominguez stayed gone more than two hours. It was dusk when he returned. He cut the engine with nary a rattle. He must be a pretty powerful mojo man to keep that car running. Dominguez wasn't alone, either. The woman in the front seat wore a riding scarf and sunglasses so I couldn't get a good look at her. Dominguez climbed out, then ran around to help her. She was stiff from the drive, I noted, and seemed older. An accomplice, maybe, I thought. Either that or he's got a thing for mature beauties. Together they pulled a grocery sack from the trunk and walked through the gates and around the back.

Looks like a date, I thought. Still, better give it a few minutes and see what goes down, just to be sure. I paid for the book, stuck it in my pocket, and walked across the street.

I artfully dodged between the two bungalows lest the woman in 1697-B see me. I couldn't hear anything untoward, and all the windows were shut and the curtains drawn. I walked around to the back door and tried to listen all the same. Nothing. It was going to be one of those nights, it seemed. I scrunched down in the bushes, between the back door and the kitchen window, and waited.

Maybe an hour went by. I had forgotten what my legs

felt like. Then I heard the front door slam. What are the odds, I asked myself again. I stood up, letting the blood surge gratefully into my ankles, and shook myself off. I tried the knob, and to my surprise, the door opened. So, like an idiot, I went inside.

The stink of swamps and graves and something flowery hit me the second I entered. To my left was a small dining area and to my right, the kitchen. I was facing an opening that led into a living room of some kind, and beyond that, I could see the front door. The room glowed from the pale light given off by a slew of candles in the room before me.

There was no furniture in the room, only candles and a very familiar pattern on the walls and wooden floor. I could also just make out bloodstains within the pattern. Dominguez was working some terrible mojo on Chu. Chicken feathers stirred as I walked. I could feel the mojo bag jumping under my shirt and I pulled it out. I fished in my pocket for the chalk. Then I heard a board creak behind me.

"What do you want?" said a deep voice with a Cajun lilt.

Shit. Only way out of this was a bluff now. I turned slowly around, keeping my hands where he could see them, and said, "I am looking for you, Beau Dominguez." That was risky, as I suddenly realized he could have given a fake name to his landlady and neighbors. I saw surprise flicker across his face for an instant and then it was replaced with a stern look that was supposed to frighten me. It was working.

"Well, here I am, chere. Don't stand on ceremony, come on in, make yourself at home." He smiled, displaying a row of pointed teeth. Dominguez was nude and painted from head to toe in arcane black and white patterns. He was about four inches taller than me and outweighed me by forty pounds. This was such a bad idea.

"Well?" he barked. "Speak up, what' chu want with old

Beau?"

"I come to tell you to lay off the hexing." My mojo bag was practically standing straight out from my neck. This guy had power.

"Oh yeah? An' why I wanna go and do a thing like that?"

As quickly as I could manage, I hopped backward, dragging my foot through the pattern on the floor, and pulled a witches' ball out of my pocket. I dropped it in the center and said the words. The wax melted, and the horsehairs stood up like goose bumps. Dominguez shouted, but it was too late. The circle was ruined. He surged forward. "Stop!" I shouted, putting my hand up. He did so, looking at me with hatred.

"You touch that, you die."

"Bullshit," he said.

"Okay, bullshit. Pick it up, Beau. Go on. Kill yourself, I don't give a shit. But you will stop attacking Chu Sheng Kai and leave town."

He stepped forward. "I think you bluffing."

I stepped backward to match him. "No bluff." I dangled my mojo bag in front of him. "But what I got in this here bag can beat anything you can throw at me."

"Ain't gonna spell you. I'm gonna kick your dumb white ass." He started muttering under his breath. I was walking backwards, knowing the front door was just a few feet behind me. I hoped Beau had a thing about public nudity, as I fully intended to haul ass once I got outside.

I felt the doorknob poke me in the back. Then I heard, rather than felt, the pane of glass breaking behind me. Two cold pieces of wood wrapped themselves around my throat and something hissed in my ear. I was pulled back against the door and held in place. Dominguez surged forward and shot a fist into my exposed gut. Again. And again. And again. I puked up Chinese food and tried not to choke on it.

I could smell blood in my nostrils as Dominguez worked me over. Finally, he stopped. Air and pain flooded back into my lungs.

"Now, I gonna cut your heart out and send it to the Chinaman. Hold him, chere. I go get my knife." He walked into the living room and out of my star-filled sight. I looked down at what was holding me and saw two gray arms. I smelled rot and turned earth. It was the woman, or what used to be a woman. She was leaning against the door to hold me. I reached down and turned the knob and pulled with all of my strength. The door opened and she was yanked off-balance and let go of me. I ran into the living room as she righted herself and charged after me. Her mouth worked, but only papery rattles came out. I noticed she was also naked, and I shuddered to think what they had been doing before I ruined the festivities. Dominguez appeared from a side door as the zombie launched herself at me. I met her charge with a boot. I would have gotten farther kicking a brick wall. Off-balance again, I fell on my back, and then she was on top of me, claws clicking, reaching for the meat in my throat. I screamed and threw her aside. Dominguez had a knife in his hand, waiting for a chance to stab me. The zombie skittered sideways towards me. I rolled to my feet and reached for my other witches' ball. This time, I let her come and embraced her. I said the words again and pushed the ball into her back as her teeth worried through my trench coat. She made an audible gasp, and her blackened eyes seemed to focus on me for just a second. I stepped back, out of her arms. The dead skin fell off of her in great chunks as she returned to the earth.

I reached into my pocket, feeling the talisman. Dominguez looked up from the ruins of his servant. I said, "No bluff. I have one more of these, and I can throw it at you before you can get me with that knife." His arms tightened. I quickly added, "But I don't want to do that. I'm just here to make sure you don't hex Chu Sheng Kai anymore, that's it."

Dominguez looked skeptical. "I know your name, Beau Dominguez. I know the stripe of your juju. You got no power over me. That means you got no power over Chu anymore. You hex him, I'll send that hex back to you and everyone in your family, you got me?" I looked down at the witches' ball in the conjure circle for emphasis. "And if I found you once, I can find you again."

Dominguez met my gaze now. We stared at each other for a long time. "Who the fuck are you?" he finally asked.

"Bowen."

I saw a light come on in his eyes. He dropped the knife. It stuck in the floor. "Get the hell out of here," he said to me.

I backed out of the room, out the door, and limped away as quickly as I could. I made it only a couple of blocks, then my legs decided to try going in different directions. I fell to the pavement and decided that was as good a place as any to take a nice rest. I could see blood slowly pooling and I wondered if that meant I would die.

I opened my eyes to see a Chinese woman standing over me. She was smiling. "Good!" she beamed. "You are awake!"

I tried to ask how long have I'd been out, but what came out was "H-h-how...long...?"

"All day," she answered. "Wait here, I be right back."

I looked around. I was in a wooden room, simply decorated with Chinese wall scrolls. Beside my bed was a nightstand that had to be 200 years old. The door opened, and in walked Chu Sheng Kai. He was neatly dressed and well groomed. There was color in his cheeks and a spring in his step. He smiled and sat on the edge of the bed. "Mr.

Bowen. How are you feeling?"

"Like shit."

He laughed. "Good! That means you are going to live."

I laughed too, until it hurt. I sat up in bed and looked at myself. I was bandaged at the neck and shoulders, and I had multiple cuts and bruises on my arms. My back felt tight. I tried to turn my head and couldn't.

"You were badly lacerated," he explained, "and we almost didn't get to you in time."

"You were watching me?" I asked.

"It is not that I did not trust you..." he started.

"No, that's fine, I don't mind. I just wish you would've told me, I could've used the help."

Chu smiled again. "Twice now, you have saved my life. You will stay here as my guest and let me take care of you until you are well. I do not forget the kindness of strangers very easily."

"I take it, then, that you are feeling better?" I asked.

"It is as if a great weight has been lifted off of my heart."

"Actually, it was a pin, I think."

Chu smiled again. "I do not understand."

"Nothing. Thank you for your hospitality."

Chu patted my leg. "Lie back. You need rest. Ring the bell by your side if you need anything." He stood up to leave.

"Um...there is one more thing."

He looked back at me. "What is that?"

"Our deal. My payment for services rendered."

Chu sighed. "I thought we might wait until you are well. But yes, I will honor my end of our agreement." He put his hands on his hips. "While you recuperate, consider this. If you become a member of my family, my enemies will become your enemies. That means you will be in the same danger as me. No different. My enemies do not care; if they perceive a weakness, they will use it. You will also be open to sorcerous attacks, which is something you have very little experience with. Just ask yourself how much you are willing to risk in your quest for knowledge."

I nodded. "I will think about it."

"Good. I will check on you later." He left the room. I slid back down in the bed and thought about the kindness of strangers.

So, that was that. Chu squared everything with UNC, and I actually got paid for the week I was out of commission. Whoever it was that fixed me up did a good job on my back. I only had one dueling scar from that encounter, a little notch where one of the zombie's teeth scratched my shoulder. I wrote the whole thing up in my journal, adding a couple of notes to the Louisiana chapter in the process. I found out later that Beau Dominguez did leave town, and I had an old friend in New Orleans keep tabs on him. He turned up dead two weeks later. The papers kept mum about the details, but my buddy found out he was covered in small symmetrical cuts, all the same pattern. He sent me a picture of one of the cuts, which I passed on to Chu, who said only, "Wan Fei Ying. My youngest son was right. Who would have guessed?"

Roots

"Uncle Sam! Uncle Sam!"

Mitchell and Marcus ran into me full-force like two wool-covered cannonballs and tackled me high and low. We all went down in a tangle of limbs, oblivious to the other passengers coming out of the jetway. The kids babbled at me in that stream-of-consciousness manner of happy children.

"Uncle Sam, you can sleep in our room if Mommy says you aren't too big to sleep in the bed."

"Whad'ja bring me?"

"I got a big Superman thing for my birthday!"

"We got you a present but 'cept I'm not supposed to tell you what it is."

"Shut up! Uncle Sam, don't listen!"

"Can you pick me up?"

Their foster parents, John and Stephanie, finally made it through the crowd of holiday travelers. "Boys! Get up now!" she snapped her fingers emphatically. "What did I tell you? Ooh, just you *wait* 'til we get home." John helped pull the kids off of me so I could get to my feet. We shook hands.

"John, good to see you. Thanks for the assist, there."

"Hey, don't mention it." He wrangled the kids out of the flow of traffic.

"Hi, Stephanie. You look great, as always." I gave her an awkward, formal hug.

She smiled professionally. "Sam, it's good of you to

come. The boys are so excited to see you."

"Obviously." I leaned down to inspect the kids. They looked huge. "Hey guys, give your old uncle Sam a real hug!" They clamped onto me fiercely. "Good show!" I tickled Marcus to make him let go of my neck, which had the effect of winding him and his mother up at the same time. I stood and looked around. "Where's Stacie?"

Stephanie opened her mouth to speak, but John stepped in front of her. "Uh, Rog and Shelly are going to bring her by later. They're doing something with Rog's mom right now. She's in the hospital."

I watched Stephanie send a laser beam into the back of John's neck as we started walking. John and I talked briefly about what was wrong with Roger's mother, while Stephanie fumed at some imagined transgression. I could see her working it over in her mind: how dare Roger's mother get sick when Stephanie had everything planned out for everyone?

I volunteered, "Well, that's all right, then. Family stuff like that is just as important. I think it's great that the last of my kin got such great families. We'll work it out, it's no big deal." John nodded sagely. Stephanie's expression softened, like I knew it would. I dropped back to where she walked. "And thank you so much for this last-minute imposition."

She smiled a real smile this time. "It's nothing, really. We always have extra food, and since you are the boy's only blood family, that makes you part of our family. How did you manage to pull this off?"

John dropped back to hear. Marcus and Mitchell sped ahead. We all watched them distractedly. "Oh, I have sort of a dutch uncle now."

"A what?"

"Like a patron. A sponsor. He knows of my situation and told me I needed to go home for the holidays. I didn't have the cash, so he made it a present. Really out of the blue, too."

Stephanie glanced at John worriedly. John leaned into me and asked, "You realize, of course, that what you described sounded very gay...and I don't mean happy."

"What? Aw, no, man! I mean, he's a rich guy, and he's helping me out with my research, is all. That's it! He's straight! And so am I!"

John grinned, and Stephanie shrugged. "It's just that, well, we've never heard you talk about women at all, and..." She trailed off. I shook my head at them and adjusted the straps on my bags to keep them from digging into my shoulder. Mitchell and Marcus came running back up to me. I braced myself, but they slid to a stop amid parental choruses of "slow down!"

"Uncle Sam!"

"What!" I yelled back, grateful for the interruption.

"They just called your name out over the radio!" I cocked my head and listened. Sure enough. "Sam Bowen, please come to the Avis Counter" rattled through the inferior sound system. I turned to the adults.

"Looks like I am going to be less of a bother than we thought. I guess Chu-San rented me a car."

I followed the Rowland's car through the streets of Lexington as Mitchell and Marcus made faces at me in the rear window. The town had changed only slightly in my absence. New restaurants for old ones, a convenience store where a tire store once stood. It in no way compared to the urban sprawl of L.A. or the decadent sophistication of San Francisco, but it was home to me and it felt good to be back in a city where I knew all of the potholes by name. John took us out into the nicer suburbs, far away from where I grew up, and we parked in front of a two-story gingerbread house that couldn't have been more than two years old. The kids fled the car and made for the door. I pulled my bags out of the backseat and joined the adults walking up the winding path.

"Very nice, guys." I nudged John. "You do this?"

"Yep." He said proudly. "Hand-picked my crew and everything. Took us six months, but it was worth it. For a while, I was using the place as a showpiece, 'look what we can do for you,' that kind of thing. But now that the kids are a little older..."

I nodded, not really knowing what he meant. He unlocked the door, and we walked in behind shouts of glee and thundering little feet.

Stephanie always went a little nuts at Christmas. The whole house was done up in gold angels and evergreen. Their eight-foot tree didn't even come close to touching the vaulted ceiling. Its branches sagged under the weight of gold ribbon bows, dusted red pine cones, and blinking green and white lights. The effect was almost pretty. Holly wreaths adorned every wall. I took a quick Nativity count and came up with 3 complete recreations on various tables. They even had a Yule log in the fireplace. She spent a lot of time making sure everything was picture perfect, if not tasteful. Even Stephanie's genuine sentiment came off as superficial and false. "What do you think?" she asked.

"I've never seen anything like it."

She beamed. John rolled his eyes and walked into his bedecked castle. "Want a beer?"

"Sure."

He rummaged in the refrigerator. Stephanie leaned up the stairs. "Kids! Wash up! Lunch!" She turned to me. "I hope sandwiches are okay, because I'm taking a break from cooking until tomorrow."

After lunch, we sat at the dining room table and made adult-talk while the kids played in the backyard. I told them about San Cibola and California in general. They told me about PTA meetings and bad sales calls and a lack of housing contracts in the area. They showed me school pictures of the boys. Mitchell and Marcus both favored my sister a lot. We laughed at the things the boys did. They both seemed distracted, though. Something was bugging them, but neither one would say anything. Finally, I banged my coffee cup down on the table and said, jokingly, "Okay, enough of this beating around the bush. What's the story, here?"

They glanced at each other. John drummed his fingers on the table. Then it hit me. "Sam, we would like to...um..."

Stephanie cut in. "We want to adopt the boys."

I figured that would come up eventually. I nodded slowly. Stephanie started to explain about how they call her mommy anyway and Marcus doesn't really remember because he was only three months old, and so on and so on. I raised a hand to silence her. For the first time ever, it worked.

"Guys, if you want my blessing, you've got it. Seriously. You are both good people and good parents to the kids. Even though I'm older, there's no way I can care for the boys like you do. I still want to be a part of their lives, though."

They both jumped in. "Oh, Sam, we didn't think for a minute..." "Please, you are such an important part..."

I nodded. "Okay, then. I know there's some paperwork for me to sign, so maybe we can..."

The phone rang, breaking all the tension at the table. Stephanie jumped up to answer it, visibly relieved. As she talked on the phone, John looked at me squarely.

"I guess that makes you family, too."

"Well, thanks, I..."

"No, Sam, listen. We love those boys, and they love you.

It would be nice if you could be a little more visible from time to time."

"I can't do that right now, John. I have a lot of important research in California."

"It's no different from the research in Massachusetts, or the research in Texas, or Mexico." He tilted his head. "I think you're just running away from the fact that your family had some back luck. Doesn't mean it'll happen to you, you know. You gotta trust someone eventually."

John's words angered me, but I swallowed it all. He didn't know. If I had my way, he wouldn't ever need to know. The boys were still years away from being a danger. I intended to have all of the family business wrapped up long before Mitchell developed his first crush.

Stephanie sat back down at the table.

"I knew this would happen. Stacie is trapped over there, so we'll have to go get her. This happens every year, you know! Why is it that we have to make all of the effort, all of the concessions?" John moved over to pat her shoulders in a placating manner. "Steph, I can go get her," I said. "It's no big deal, really."

"But you don't know where she lives now! They moved last year, and it's on the other side of town!"

"John, can you draw me a map, please?"

"On it." He moved to the kitchen.

I looked at Stephanie. "I'll see if the boys want to come along. Then we can have some time together, all right?"

Mitchell and Marcus sang Christmas songs off-key in the backseat. Loudly. Over and over again. I was full of newfound respect for John and Stephanie. After the tenth chorus of "Rudolph the Red-Nosed Reindeer," I shushed them and asked them to tell me what was going on. Mitchell piped right up with, "Mommy and Daddy want to change our name to Rowland."

"Yeah? How do you feel about that."

"It's okay," said Mitchell.

"Yeah," echoed Marcus, "that'll be cool. Didja bring me a Spider-Man Web Shooter?"

"Nope." I patted the packages in the front seat. "You'll see what I got you when we go get Stacie."

"Yaaay!" they shouted. "Stacie's coming over! Stacie's coming over!" they chanted. Jesus, they had their mother's lungs, that was for sure.

I found the house easy enough, nestled in one of the older, settled neighborhoods on the edge of town. Stacie's foster family, Roger and Shelly Stack, were both local artists. Roger was a sculptor and landscape artist, and Shelly did wood working and was a local celebrity at the craft fairs. They were both as laid back and down-to-earth as Stephanie and John were uptight. Hanging on their door was a Christmas wreath made entirely of 7-Up cans trimmed to resemble holly leaves and Coke Cans for the berries and bow. It was very white-trash chic, and knowing Shelly, it was put up specifically to annoy the neighborhood squares. We'd just parked the car when the front door banged open and Stacie came running out.

"Uncle Sam!" she screamed.

"Stacie!" Mitchell and Marcus chorused.

"Mitchell! Marcus!" She yelled back. We all hugged again, and I felt a wave of relief wash over me. These kids and I were all still here. They were all that was left of the Bowen family. I ushered the boys back into the car and held Stacie at arm's length. It was like a punch in the stomach. The ten-year old tomboy I remembered had grown into a fifteen-year old young woman. She had her father's hair color, the Bowen blonde that ran through our family. But her face was her mother's, and she was beautiful. I suddenly realized I didn't have nearly as much time as I thought I did, and it sent a cold wave of fear over me. Stacie noticed it.

"What's wrong?" She frowned and looked down at her sweatshirt and jeans. "Am I underdressed to go over to the Better Homes and Gardens House?"

I laughed. "Cute. No, it's nothing. Come on, we'll get the family stuff out of the way, then we'll have some fun."

I let them open their presents while we drove to our first stop. Mitchell and Marcus got the same thing: a pair of wooden, articulated Chinese Dragons that were the right size to use with their little action figures. I also threw in, as an afterthought, matching brass necklaces of the Great Sage, Equal of Heaven. "What is it?" asked Marcus.

"It's a monkey!" said Mitchell scornfully.

"Not just a monkey, but the King of All Monkeys," I told them. "I got those from the Monkey-King himself. He even put a royal blessing on them for you." I didn't tell them the price for the blessing was two beers. I thought I'd save that anecdote for their graduation day.

"Where did you meet the Monkey King?" asked Mitchell.

"He lives near me in a place called Ping Ping's."

Stacie slapped my arm playfully. "You tell them stuff like that, they're liable to believe it."

"It's true!"

"Yeah, right." She turned to her present. "I know what this is already," she said, ripping the paper off. "It's a T-shirt from the college."

"Good guess, but wrong!" I told her. It was a sweatshirt from UNC. That was my standard present to her for birthdays and Christmases: a university T-shirt from whichever

campus I happened to be kicking around on at the time. She
held it up.

"Semantics. It's cool, though. Thanks, Uncle Sam."

"Thank you, Uncle Sam," the boys sang from the back
seat.

"There's more," I said. "Look in the box." I also gave
her some rice paper stationary I'd picked up last month. It
was hand-printed with orchids and was very girlish. She
squealed. "Awesome! Thanks!" I smiled. The boys dueled
with their dragons in the backseat. We continued on to the
city cemetery.

I pulled through the gates, driving by memory. The mood
in the front seat changed dramatically. Mitchell and Marcus
leaned over the seats. "Are we going to see mommy?"

"Yeah, I thought we would, since I haven't been in a while.
Is that okay?" Everyone nodded. I drove over to the area
where the family was buried and parked the car. "We won't
stay long," I told Stacie.

"It's okay," she said.

We all got out, and I walked over to my sister Laura was
buried. She was four years older than me. Her husband,
Todd, was buried beside her. They died in a car crash. Drunk
driver. I squatted down between the boys and said, "Your
mom was really pretty. She was loud and loved to sing, like
you guys. I miss her very much, and I know she would be so
proud of you right now."

The boys looked solemn. Marcus asked, "Uncle Sam,
this was my first mommy?"

"That's right."

"And Steph'nie is my second Mommy."

"You got it."

"Is it okay if I like my second Mommy better?"

I swallowed hard. "Sure, Marcus. Stephanie loves you

very much. She and John are your parents now. You love them as much as you want. If it'll make things easier for you, just think of your first mommy as my sister if you want to."

He nodded and smiled a little.

Mitchell said, "I think I remember my first mommy. She sang to me."

"Yes, she did." I looked for Stacie. She was standing nearby, looking at another headstone. "Guys, can you stay here for a minute?" I walked over. She was sobbing quietly. I put my arm around her.

My brother, Charles, was the second oldest after Saul. He was seven years older than me and we weren't very close. I remembered being in awe of Chuck. He was on the football team at the University of Kentucky. Third string, but at the time, I thought he was running with the gods. I smiled as I thought about his wedding day and how drunk I got at the reception. I was only fourteen at the time, and Dad broke a belt on me, he busted me so hard. Chuck's wife, Michelle, was one of the prettiest women I'd ever seen. Everyone agreed either Chuck was damn lucky or she was real nearsighted. Stacie leaned into me to cry in earnest.

"Uncle Sam, please tell me how he died."

"Stacie, no. Not now."

"When?" she cried. "I'm practically an adult now, I can handle it."

"I don't think so. Not now. Ask me when you're eighteen. If you still want to know by then, I'll tell you. I promise."

She sniffed and looked up at me. "That's in addition to any money you plan on sending, right?"

I smiled at her. "Yeah. I'll write it on the envelope, okay?"

She looked back down at the marker. "God, I miss them."

"I know. I do, too. How are Shelly and Roger?"

She rolled her eyes and wiped her nose on her sleeve. "Oh, okay, I guess."

"You know, you got off really lucky."

She nodded. "I know. We all did." She grinned. "Do you remember the Laskers?"

"Yeah, I do."

"God, you were so cool! I've never seen you fight before. You really saved my ass."

"Nothing glamorous about a fight, Stacie. I was mad, was all. Not that he didn't deserve it."

She kicked the dirt. "Yeah, Shelly and Rog are okay. They're not in it for the money, they really love me. Even when I'm a shithead."

"Don't swear."

She cut her eyes at me and decided now was not the time to challenge me. "Sorry."

"Uncle Sam?" The boys.

"Yeah?"

"We're bored!"

Stacie wiped her eyes dry. "I'll go watch them. You take a few minutes."

"Thanks, Stacie."

She ran off, shouting for the boys to follow her. I watched them run through the graveyard and out to the nearby grove of trees. She was a good babysitter. I really didn't want them to go; talking about the family was a lot easier than losing myself in my own maudlin thoughts. I looked over the assembled graves, roughly seventy-five percent of my family there in one area. Saul. Chuck. Matt. Laura. John. Peter. Dennis. Leslie. Mom and Dad. I was the only one of all the siblings, of all the cousins, of everyone in the family, who was still standing. I thought about the curse on my family, thought long and hard about Jacob. My grail. My missing piece. What did you do, you philandering son of a bitch, that was so awful that it killed my family? Why me? Why the hell am I the only one still alive? Am I supposed to live, so that I can know what an asshole my ancestor was? I hope and pray that whatever cursed my family is still around when I finally track it down... I was shouting all of this by now, tears running down my face, replacing the grief with anger as I had done so many times before. Now I was glad that the kids couldn't see me. I fell to my knees in front of my brother and swore vengeance for my family to every god and higher power I could think of. That done, I cried quietly, ashamed of myself.

Someone was behind me. I turned around, thinking it would be Stacie and the boys. Instead, I saw a woman in her thirties. She wore a heavy coat, bundled tightly around her, and a thick scarf over most of her head and neck. A hint of dark red hair peeked out from under the scarf. There was a lot of living in her face, and I almost didn't recognize her. Then she spoke.

"Hello, Sam." Her voice, once a husky drawl, now sounded thin and reedy.

"Hello, Tallulah." I stood up and walked towards her, embarrassed, thinking about how much of my outburst she might have witnessed. I stopped just short of hugging her when she flinched at my close proximity. I stepped back looked her over.

"You look good." I said.

"I can read your thoughts, Sam. But thank you for trying." She fumbled for a cigarette and lit it. "How are you?"

"Oh, I'm good, I guess. Working out in San Cibola. Same old, same old. You?"

"Still here. Still conjuring. You practicing?"

"Sort of." I shrugged. "I've learned some other disciplines, different tricks, but nothing major. Mostly self-defense."

She took a big drag and talked through it. "I can see it on your aura. You're a mess, kid. You've been working some pretty heavy shit."

"Occupational hazard." We made eye contact, and a chunk of old memories bobbed to the surface.

Tallulah and me sitting in her barn, and she's teaching me how to kiss. She keeps putting her tongue in my mouth, and it's freaking me out. Finally, she says, "Wanna see my boobs?"

Tallulah and me, standing at the foot of the hill leading up to her mother's home. She's showing me what she calls a hotspot. "It's where the forces of nature all come together to remind us that we are not the masters of this planet." Soon, I can feel my skin tingle, and we watch the cheap pocket watch we stole from the drugstore come apart in my hands. I drop the hot metal, and she leans over and kisses my burned palms, blowing cool air across my skin.

We are alone in a graveyard, this graveyard, and she is telling me about "the conjuring" that runs in her family. I tell her I want to know more about it.

Our parents screaming at one another. I am being pushed into the car by my father, as Mom shouts at Tallulah's mom, calling her awful names. Tallulah's mom, Miss Pickford replies by making a strange hand gesture, and Mom hurriedly gets into the car. "They're witches!" she tells me. "You stay away from them!" she screams at me.

"She's my friend!" I yell back.

"She's four years older than you! Make a friend your own age!"

I'm nineteen, and we are laying naked in the graveyard. Tallulah is smoking and asking me how I feel. I tell her I can feel things in my head. She tells me it's the conjuring making room for itself. She tells me it'll grow if I feed it.

She broke the stare first.

"What brings you out here?" I ask her finally.

"Huh? Oh, it's Momma." She pointed absently behind her.

"Oh, wow, Tallulah, I am so sorry." I move towards her again, but she keeps the distance.

"It's okay. The only thing I feel guilty for is putting her here, in hallowed ground. She was old. She was crazy. It needed to happen. "

"Well," I tried, "at least she's resting now."

"Probably not, if I know Momma." She thumped her spent butt away. "You visiting family?"

"Yeah, my niece and nephews."

"I've seen them. They're cuties. "

"So, you married?" We were running out of things to cover pretty quickly. I didn't like this. We were best friends growing up. Now she seemed so cold and impersonal.

"Hah!" she snorted. "No, I am afraid my reputation precedes me. I stay home a lot. Do my thing, charge too much for simple spells and sewing and odd jobs and shit. They all pity me."

"Tallulah, what's wrong?" I stepped in quickly before she could adjust the space between us and touched her elbow. She jerked away.

"Goddammit, how come you keep doing that? Ain't I done enough to you already? Knock it off!"

"Done enough? Done what?"

She looked at me with contempt, then wonder. "I am so sorry." She burst into tears, big jerking sobs that pained me to listen to them. "I am so sorry for what I did to you."

"What? We had sex, you gave me some of your power. What did you do?"

I looked into her tear-filled eyes. "My powers damned your family, you idiot!" She renewed her sobs. "I never meant to hurt you. You were my best friend, my only friend. I never meant to take your family away from you."

I took her into my arms so she wouldn't see me smile. "Tallulah, you doofus, you didn't do anything. My family is under a curse. You had nothing to do with it."

"You're just saying that."

"No, I'm not. Use your sight on me. Come on." She looked at me, wiping her face. I held my arms out, eyes closed, inviting her. She nodded once, then she stepped back, and her body went limp. Her eyes rolled back in her head, and I felt something gently touching my mind. I closed my eyes and let her. Gave her everything, all at once. She gasped. I opened my eyes. She was staring at me.

"Holy shit! You've been busy!"

"Yeah. Now do you get it?"

She shook her head appreciatively. "I had no idea. These powers demand a price, and I naturally thought it was your family..." she trailed off. "Oh. It was Momma, wasn't it?" She looked ready to cry again. I took her in my arms. She sobbed like she'd needed to for a long time. I watched over her shoulder as the kids came walking back in through the gate. They stopped when they saw me with a woman. Finally, Tallulah pulled away. She was pale and sniffling. "I'm sorry. I shouldn't have..."

"Shut up, will you? You're my friend, you can cry on my shoulder anytime. Now, listen, 'Lu. It wasn't your mother, okay. What happened to my family, near as I can figure it, happened a few generations back. So, do not worry about my little quest, okay? If anything, you saved my life."

She nodded, but I could tell that what I told her hadn't stuck. She behind her. "I see your charges are back. I'd best be letting you go."

"Well, okay, I guess. Maybe I could stop by later? We can catch up on what's been going on?"

She grinned and frogged my arm like she used to do. "Bowen, I just saw the last seven years of your life in color. No thanks. But you can swing by later, and I'll tell you how much I hate it here."

I regarded her for a minute. "Listen, what are you doing for Christmas?" I asked.

"Nothing. Probably go to Denny's."

"Aw, no, screw that. You're coming over to John and Stephanie's. No, don't argue, either."

"Sam, I don't want to impose on total strangers..."

"'Lu, you're not imposing. You're all I've got left, next to these kids. You're the only one I can talk to about my family. You grew up with me. That makes you family, too. So you are going to spend Christmas with your family, and I don't want to hear another word about it."

"But what about their parents?"

"Let me worry about that." I gave her another hug. "I'll come pick you up tomorrow. Wear blue jeans, nothing slinky. Okay?"

"Okay." She walked away.

"Come on, kids, I'm freezing! Your mother's hot chocolate is calling!" I yelled. They sprinted for the car.

"Hey, Sam!" I turned around.

"Thanks." She smiled at me, and the years melted away, and pretty skinny Tallulah was standing in the graveyard, waving at me.

"You're welcome."

As we drove out of the cemetery, Mitchell asked me, "Who was that lady?"

"She's an old friend. She's coming to Christmas dinner tomorrow." I looked back in the rear-view mirror for her, but she was gone. As we passed the gates, I turned on the radio. "I'll be Home for Christmas" by Bing Crosby was on. It made me smile.

The Ghost Walk

The clock tower in the Canal district chimed eleven times. I stood up and started walking down Los Angeles Street, cinching my trench coat against the cool air. The streets downtown were quiet, with few cars and fewer people. I pulled out the directions I'd photocopied from Joseph Preston's journals a week ago and consulted them as I navigated by streetlight. I turned left on Dinero and then right on 23rd. So far, so good. Not much of a Ghost Walk, really.

This was one of the more fascinating accounts I'd stumbled across in my research. San Cibola was overcrowded with legends, personal ghosts, and folklore. According to Preston, there was a specific path that a person could walk through the old downtown streets that would unlock a restless spirit. While it didn't necessarily relate to my own personal research, it was something that I had to investigate for the Armitag Foundation. A successful report of this phenomenon would keep my stipend rolling in and keep food on my table.

I kept my eyes and ears open. In spite of the sizable number of supposedly legitimate occultists who claimed to have successfully performed the Ghost Walk, it was very probable that the whole thing was a hoax.

My path was long and winding through the streets of downtown San Cibola. As I walked, I thought about the historical significance of what I was attempting. In the sketchy accounts I'd found, this had been performed maybe ten times in the last 120 years. Even at the turn of the century, these streets were old. Sometimes during my day-to-day walks, I would see curious patterns carved in the stone or bricks laid out in an attractive but eerily familiar pattern. Now that I was walking this specific route, it was clear as day that these were signposts to the Ghost Walkers. Or, more appropriately, tumblers in a giant lock. I consulted the directions I'd culled from "Ghost Walking Joe" Preston's diaries and turned left on McIntyre. The wind picked up behind my back, hurrying me along.

As I rounded the corner of Lexington and Rutherford for the home stretch, I could see the Founder's Cemetery loom into view. This was the kind of place that made historians break into a cold sweat. It was the first graveyard back when San Cibola was just a village of peasants. In the center of the immense park was a huge overworked arrangement of tombs for the seven conquistadors who, according to legend, rose up and menaced Joseph Preston during his Ghost Walk in 1921. From the amount of mist and fog surrounding the place, it was pretty easy to see how people could mistakenly see spectral forms.

Midnight. I sprinted the rest of the way and slid to a stop in front of the gates. I pulled a handful of grave-dirt out of the baggie in my pocket and made a little mound. From the other pocket came a vial of water from the Mad River, mixed with equal parts of garlic, witch hazel, and annis wort. I shook the bottle, pulled the cork, and wet the mound liberally. Finally, I produced my trusty iron horseshoe and waved it over the miniature grave and chanted "Spirits Come. To me, you are bound. But do not leave this hallowed ground."

I said it three times and waited. I stood up, peering into the mists. Nothing. No change in the temperature, no spectral whistles, nothing. I shook my head and sat down on the wrought-iron bench just outside the gate. A goddamn Emperor's New Clothes scenario, I thought. One guy tells this story about a route you can walk through town that will enable you to see ghosts, and then someone else tries it, doesn't see anything, but for some reason doesn't blow the whistle. Thus are local legends born. I pulled out my notepad and began writing. This was one legend I had no problem with debunking.

"Daddy?"

The gates opened, and the fog and mist billowed out into the street. I was not alone. I looked over to my right. A little girl was standing not six feet from me, outside the entrance near the summoning mound I made. She was dressed in a homemade nightgown that floated in the breeze. Her hair was long and dark, her eyes blue, and she was holding a flaxen-haired doll. Of all the ghosts I had chased, broken, or walked through, I never got such a sense of pain, loss, and confusion before. The fog occasionally seemed to rise up and take shape, then fell back into a patternless swirl again. For a long moment we regarded one another. Finally, she spoke.

"Daddy?" she repeated. Her voice was raspy and not at all human.

"No, honey, I'm not your daddy. My name is Sam." I really hated talking to the dead.

"Do you know where my daddy is? He said he would come right back."

"No, I don't. What's his name?"

She stared at me for a second. "Mommy called him Teig."

"And what's your name?"

She cocked her head to one side. "I'm Caitlin Ashley McGee, that's who." Her accent was Gaelic.

I smiled at her. "Caitlin, what are you doing up? You

really should be in bed."

"I'm waiting for daddy. He had to go do a job at the canals, and then he was coming back with some medicine to make my throat not scratchy no more. Only he hasn't come back yet. Do you know where he is?"

"No, Caitlin, I don't. Can I show you back to bed now?"

"Nuh!" she stepped back from me. "I'm not going to bed, I'm waiting for my daddy!" Her shout dissolved into a hacking, raspy cough that shook the bones in my ribcage it sounded so painful. She ended the coughing with a plaintive cry, and in response, the mist and fog rose up protectively over her. The temperature dropped ten degrees and I could hear the wind keening through the iron bars around the cemetery. Sticking around was suddenly the worst idea I ever had. I stood up and backed away until the bench was between us. Caitlin walked though it to stand in front of me. "Find my daddy. Bring him home. I'm tired. I want to go sleep." She stared into my eyes. "Find my daddy." And then I was looking at a cold wrought-iron bench.

I shivered, partially from shock and partially from the marked cooler air. She had been standing in cold iron. I'd never seen a ghost that could do that, but then again, this was San Cibola. Something about this town made the supernatural much more powerful that it should be. I needed a drink or five. I kicked the mound of dirt until it was spread out, then walked into the Gaslight proper where there were lights and people and bourbon and no fog or sick children.

The next morning was a mish mash of rolling stomachs, stabbing headaches, and thin coffee. I called my boss at UNC and got someone to cover my labs, then made great efforts to get showered and dressed. I more or less succeeded. As I descended the stairs, duffel bag slapping against my legs, my landlord Benny popped through the wall and scared the bejeezus out of me.

"Sam! You didn't sleep good last night! Carrying on at four in the morning! Ms. Tipplethwaite call down to me and ask me if you were killing someone!"

"Sorry, Benny. Tell Ms. Tipplethwaite I'm sorry. It won't happen again."

Benny crossed his arms and frowned at me, keeping himself at eye level as I navigated the stairs. "You sick?"

"Yeah, Benny, something like that." Ordinarily, Benny's state of being wouldn't have given me a moment's pause. Today still felt too much like last night, however, and I was in no mood to chat up another ghost, however benevolent he may be and cultural differences notwithstanding.

He nodded. "Go eat at Mama Wang's. She fix you up." He floated up as I walked down.

"Maybe I will."

"Trust me Sam!" he called from overhead. "I been here long time. Mama Wang will fix you up."

Wang's Golden Dragon sat in the No Man's Land between accepted tourist areas and the real Chinatown. The Golden Dragon in question was a huge neon sign that towered over the establishment and was probably taller than the restaurant was deep. The place was always packed. I walked inside, past the row of ducks hanging in the window, through the tourists, to the back. Mama Wang saw me and said something in Chinese, then gave me a winning horsey smile and ushered me to a booth in the back. Once I sat down, Mama Wang leaned in close, past the noise of the restaurant, and asked me, "You sick, Mr. Bowen?"

"Close. Hung over."

She nodded sagely. "I fix you up." She bustled off, screaming at the kitchen. Within minutes, I had a huge bowl of hot and sour soup in front of me and a pot of hot tea to the side. I sipped both and felt the warmth spread through me. It settled my stomach, and soon I was feeling close to normal again. Mama Wang reappeared with a huge bowl of lo mein. "You eat all of this, your sickness will go away." I dug in while Mama screamed at her wait staff. As usual, she was right. This stuff was good.

After I finished, she came and sat down in front of me. "Better?"

"Lots, yes. Thank you."

"Welcome. You get color back in your cheeks, but you still look tired." She leaned in close. "Tell Mama Wang what the problem is."

I sighed. "I just had a rough night last night, is all."

"You know what you need?" She pulled back and beamed. "You need a good woman to take care of you!"

This is why I was always hesitant about visiting Mama Wang. She had three daughters, all waitresses at the restaurant, that she was always trying to hook me up with. "Mama Wang, thank you, but not right now."

"When?" she stood up for emphasis and gestured wildly. "My useless daughters are all grown. An Yin is twenty! An old maid!" An Yin popped her head around the corner and smiled at me. She had her mom's teeth. All of them.

"Mama, I am sure you will find someone to take them off your hands." Perhaps a nice orthodontist, I thought. I stood up to pay her.

She muttered in Chinese and waved her hand at me. "You still got credit. Go on, get out of here." I gave her a one-armed hug that she squirmed out of. "And no funny stuff, either! I'm still in mourning!" I waved good-bye and shouldered my way through the crowd, swinging my duffel bag to make room. Her husband died seven months ago, but couldn't seem to get it in his head that he was really dead. I helped her put him back in the grave for good. She insisted on paying me with free food ever since. If I was him, I would've taken my chance and stayed down the first time.

I walked through Chinatown, killing time until I had to go to Chu Sheng Kai's place. I meandered up through the weekday tourists and unassuming locals going about their business. This had been my home for several months now, but it was still very new to me. City workers were busy stringing up paper lanterns and banners for some kind of street festival. Here, everything was cause for a celebration. I checked out some herbalists and a couple of general stores, mainly looking and learning. However, I couldn't quite shake the feeling that I was being watched. I didn't know if it was just me or if I was getting the evil eye from the shop keepers, but I didn't stay in one place for long. I bought some prayer candles and incense for my apartment, then turned east and made the long hike to Chu's estate.

Two weeks ago, I had been inducted into Chu's family. This was without a doubt the weirdest thing I ever had to do in order to gain access to research materials. There was a huge, complicated ceremony with lots of chanting and bowing and praying. Everyone wore traditional clothing, including myself. I was given a new family name, "Ya Shen," and a strange ranking that roughly translated means, "Last Son in Line but No Less Favored." Whatever. After that, Chu opened up his library to me and we selected half a dozen personal diaries and journals for me to pore through. That's when problem number one reared its ugly head. I can't read Mandarin.

Two guards stood ready at the gate. These were the Jen Long Tong, and they served as security for Chu's business organization, Red Moon Enterprises. Ever since Chu's voodoo trouble, they had been fixtures. Large, merciless garden statues. They bowed when I approached. I bowed back, and they pushed open the gate for me. I smiled at them and got the blank face in return. Another first-rate exchange with the locals. I hoofed it up the driveway and was greeted at the door by Su Yun, the houseboy. He smiled at me and I returned it.

"Ya Shen," he said to me, "welcome home." He bowed.

I bowed back. "Hello, Su Yun." He let me in and disappeared up the hall.

I walked the now familiar route through the living room to the study. This room was unofficially mine, now. Two comfortable chairs flanked the long teakwood table along the south wall, in front of the windows. A few books and papers lay scattered across the table. Chu gave me a simple but powerful computer system to use, but I hardly ever touched it. That chore went to my research assistant, Mi Hei, who was already at work. She was younger than me by a couple of years. Her father was Jiang Shui, Chu's second-oldest son, who ran the Jen Long Tong security force. Mi Hei was a part of that branch of the operation until she got assigned to me. Now she translated Mandarin and typed it into the computer.

"Ah, good afternoon, Mi Hei," I called, striding confidently into the room.

"Hello, Foreigner." She said in a monotone voice without turning around. Her fingers clattered on the keys as she transcribed the page in front of her.

"Fine, thanks, and you?"

"Here." She gestured to the fresh stack of papers to her left with a nod of her head. "The latest batch of useless ramblings for your approval."

"Don't talk about my ancestors that way." I admonished

her.

"My ancestors! Not yours!" she spun around to face me, her eyes narrowed.

"Nope. Mine too. I'm part of the family, now, remember? So show a little more respect, huh?"

She looked ready to throw a punch. Instead, she took a deep breath, turned back around, and resumed typing. I settled down into the chair and picked up what she worked on yesterday. This was the journal of one Xiou Dou for the year 1887. What she had translated was mostly entries about how the soil here was completely unsuitable for growing ginseng and that extensive sorceries would have to be constructed before anything of worth could be cultivated. I sorted a few papers, then turned to her. "Okay, are you at a stopping point?" I asked.

"Just...a...second..." She banged on a few more keys, then pushed away, rubbing her eyes. "What?"

I picked up Xiou Dou's journal and flipped it open. "This entry mentions a cousin of some sort. Can you translate the next section for me?"

She plucked the book out of my hands, sat back in her chair, and stared at the page. "Um...honorable cousin arrived today...blah blah blah...gifts from the homeland...um...something about an altercation on the ship over...he got into a fight with..."

I leaned forward eagerly.

"...the captain...over the theft of something...jade, a necklace..." She went on haltingly reading while I pushed down my disappointment. I hadn't entertained any notions of just walking in here and laying my hand on the one book that would give me the answers I needed. However, stranger things have happened.

"Goddammit, are you even listening?" She slammed the

book shut.

I looked up at her. "Yes, I was. I was also thinking, which is something I do when I am conducting research."

"Look, Foreigner..."

I leaned back in my chair. "You can call me Uncle Sam."

"...I am not going to tip-toe through this old, useless crap for you if you aren't even going to listen to me. I don't know why Grandfather doesn't just give you a translation spell and let you do this yourself."

I pretended to think really hard for a minute. "Maybe you're being punished. Perhaps you're paying off a Karmic debt. Do you have any old grudges against anyone? Maybe, everyone?"

She mimicked my thinking. "No, just you." She picked the book back up and said, "You want this part?"

"Look and see if it says how long the cousin is supposed to stay?"

She scanned down. "Can't tell."

"Well, then, do me a favor and translate the sections until he leaves. Can you do that?"

She shot me a look. "Yeah, I can just think of a hundred things I'd rather do."

This really pissed me off. I wanted so badly to tell her which corner of hell to go to, but I needed her to translate quickly and accurately. She was my lifeline. And she wasn't even going to try to make it easy for me. She marked the passage and went back to her earlier transcriptions. I made some notes in my family notebook and doodled in the margins until she was finished. She threw the papers at me and stood up.

"Thanks again." I said. She picked up her purse. I tried again. "See you tomorrow."

"Right." She couldn't get away fast enough. As she

stormed out of the room, she walked through Caitlin. I dropped my pen. Caitlin came and sat in the chair Mi Hei just vacated.

"I like her. She's funny," the ghost said.

I tried for a calm demeanor. She was just a ghost, and I had dealt with more malevolent spirits than this before. "I don't think you're supposed to be here, Caitlin."

She laughed, and it became that hacking cough that made my chest hurt. "Sillyhead," she finally wheezed out, "I'm following you. You said you would find my daddy."

"I did?" I swallowed the lump in my throat.

"Uh huh. And I am going to follow you around until you do!" She clapped her hands together soundlessly.

" Caitlin, I..." I started to say, but she was gone. The room was colder now. This was definitely not right. Chu's house was supposed to be shielded from magical attacks. Apparently the house didn't see my diminishing sanity as some kind of threat. I quickly packed up my things.

Su appeared with a brown paper bag. "Ya Shen, this is for your dinner." It smelled wonderful, whatever it was.

"Thank you, Su."

He smiled at me. "You are very polite man. All the time, you say please and thank you."

"That's because my momma would beat the tar out of me every time I didn't say please and thank you."

"Strong parents make strong children," he said, escorting me through the house to the front entrance.

"Well, she had a pretty mean backhand, that's for sure. Thanks, Su. See you tomorrow."

"Okay, bye-bye. See you later." He shut the door behind me. The temperature was falling but I scarcely noticed it. I made tracks for UNC campus.

Addison Memorial Library was built in the twenties and

was completely Bauhaus. The interior was warm, not sterile, and yet completely functional. What it did have that distinguished it from the other libraries on the West coast was a first-rate folklore section. Their rare books collection was even more impressive. My connections to Doctor Crowe afforded me some nice library privileges, which included coming and going whenever I pleased. I'd spent more than one night in there and was fully prepared to do it again.

The microfiche machine and I were old friends by now. Sometimes, though, she could be really bitchy. I found no mention of a Teig McGee in the *San Cibola Courier* or the *San Cibola Examiner*, which meant he probably just took off one day and never looked back. But I did find my ghost. Caitlin McGee died in 1927 of pneumonia. She was seven years old. No mention of Teig anywhere, but her mother was listed, one Molly McGee, 26 years old. Actually, I found her first. She committed suicide two weeks after Caitlin died.

I printed the articles out and took a dinner break. Su packed two smoked chicken sandwiches with Chinese lettuce and hot mustard on fresh-baked bread. He also threw in some won ton noodles and a box of his homemade dumplings, which I absolutely loved. Two cans of Coke from the library's vending machine washed it all down. Chu's family may be cool towards me, but at least the cook liked me.

"I'm hungry."

Shit. I turned around. Caitlin was behind me, looking more bedraggled than ever. I shivered against the chill she brought with her.

"I said, I'm hungry!" she croaked.

"Caitlin, I don't have any food for you." I tried an old Ozark spirit-catching trick. "Why don't you go find your mother? Maybe she has food for you."

Caitlin shook her head. "Nuh-uh. Mum is gone. I can't

find her. I think she's lost."

Of course she was. Irish family. Mother was most likely Catholic, and they don't think too highly of suicide. Christ, Bowen, use your head. "Well, I'm trying to find your daddy for you."

"If you can't find him, then you can be my daddy!" she laughed and then was gone, except for her terrible coughing. My stomach rolled. This was too much. I understood now why Joe Preston went nuts and wandered the Gaslight for nine years. He was running from the ghosts he called up.

I spent the rest of the night in the stacks, pawing through the local history and folklore sections. When I was finished, I had filled one of those metal book carts with stuff to replace on the shelves. I had a dozen pages of notes, a cramp in my hand, and no answers at all. Time to expand my search. I called a taxi from the guard's desk and waited until he showed up. I went straight home and collapsed into my bed, clothes and all. Mercifully, Caitlin let me sleep.

It was mid-afternoon when I woke up. I showered hurriedly, praying that my ghost wouldn't stick her head up through the tub. It was really distressing to think of Caitlin as my ghost. Once dressed, I called Dr. Crowe and asked for a few references for local folklore experts. He threw me two profs, a grad student, and a rare books dealer. Ordinarily, I wouldn't trust outside sources, but time was of the essence. I was jumping at shadows.

I started with the rare book dealer first. Thaddeus La Violette owned a bookstore in the Rue Livre called "Serendipity." The shop was a testament to chaos. Books filled every conceivable crevice and cranny of the poorly designed two-story building. Anything that wasn't shelved was stacked, sometimes four to five feet high. I entered the store and spent a good ten minutes wandering around trying to make sense of his filing system. Finally, I called out, "Mr. La Violette?"

"It's La Voe-lette!" came a voice from overhead. I looked up to see Thaddeus La Voe-lette descending the stairs. "Sorry, I was in the bathroom." He fastened the strap of his blue and white coveralls for emphasis. He wore them over a white T-shirt. A red handkerchief hung from his back pocket. He was portly, in his sixties, with an unkempt mane of white hair that flowed into an unkempt bush of white beard. Black horn-rimmed spectacles sat high on his nose. It was quite a look.

"Sorry." I extended a hand. "I'm Sam Bowen. Dr. Crowe at the university said you might be able to help me with a project I am working on."

He cautiously shook my hand. His was dry and papery. "Glad to know you." He spoke with the non-accent of a native Californian. "You buying books today?"

I didn't know how to take that. "Uh, maybe, I don't know. I need family records, leases, and whatever zoning information you might have for the Gaslight district, say around the 1920s."

La Violette frowned. "That's pretty specific." He peered over his glasses at me. "Just what are you working on, Mr. Bowen?"

I paused. "It's kind of complicated." So I filled him in on what I knew about Caitlin, her mother, and her father. At the mention of Teig's name, he perked up.

"I think you've got your stories mixed up," he said. "Come on back here." He lumbered off into a back room, gesturing me to follow. He stopped short at a closed wooden door and turned on me. "You're not writing a book, are you?"

"No," I said. Well, not specifically, I thought. "My interest is in genealogy."

He looked at me, blinked, and said, "Okay, then you can see this." He unlocked the door and held it open for me. The tiny room was crammed with shelves and books and newspapers tacked up on the walls. Dominating the room was a card table with a miniature model of the city laid out atop it. The buildings were fashioned out of hobby materials and impressively detailed.

La Violette dug through a stack of manila folders and handed me one. Across the label was written, MILLIGAN, TEIG (SPRIGGAN RIOTS) "What you're looking for I think is a missing person story from 1927. The man's name was Teig Milligan, a bricklayer from Ocean View. He was reported missing by his family, but they never found him. Now this was during the Spriggan Riots in Arcadia, and it was just assumed that the Spriggans got him. Anyway, they buried him a year later in an empty coffin, and that was that. He's even listed as an official casualty on the lists."

"Why do you have all of this?"

Thaddeus smiled. "Well, the Teig Milligan disappearance is one of the town's lesser mysteries. My project here is going to dispel a lot of local myths. I intend to publish a comprehensive history of the city, no sugar coating. Tell all of the neat little stories that make it so special."

"No kidding?"

He nodded. "Oh yeah. The problem is, I have to confine my efforts to this room alone, or they'll find out what I am working on and have me killed."

Oh, boy. I made a mental note to thank Dr. Crowe for the ambush and pushed a polite smile onto my face. "Well, since you seem to be the expert here, do you have any theories on what happened to Teig?"

"Oh, I know exactly what happened to him. The di Lessa bastards killed him."

I had heard the name di Lessa before, mostly in conjunction with the Canal district, and also with organized crime. Street gossip. "What? Why did they kill him?" I scanned the articles at random. Missing persons report. The headline read, "LOCAL BRICKLAYER MISSING." Two stories about the police having no leads. Allegations of foul play in the Canal District. Protestations of innocence from the di Lessa family. A handwritten note (most likely Thaddeus') to "see also the Spriggan Riots." Finally, an obituary. Death attributed to the riots.

Thaddeus shook his head. "He was running bootlegged gin for one of the Irish gangs. My guess is that he was hijacking a shipment of booze and got pinched."

"Where'd you come up with this theory?"

"An eye witness."

I closed the file. "Well, that's some pretty amazing information. I don't think it's related, though. Your file here says Teig Milligan had two boys and lived in Ocean View. I am looking for a Teig McGee with a little girl that lived in the Gaslight."

"Hmph. Suit yourself. Look around here, just keep everything in order, is all I ask. And don't take anything out of this room, or they'll know about it for sure." He turned and exited without another word. I spent a few hours poking around the files. La Violette's filing system was a mystery to me, but I honored it. I read until my eyes hurt and turned up nothing. I gave him twenty dollars for his time, thanked him, and left. I was chasing my tail, and it pissed me off. I would not give up on the idea that my ghost's father could be found.

The first thing I saw when I left the bookshop was Caitlin. She was standing on the other side of the street, waving at me. I didn't wave back. Her presence there made me realize that maybe I'd been going about this all wrong. If I couldn't track down Teig, then maybe I could get some more information on Caitlin. I turned left and caught the SCAT to the Gaslight. She followed me onto the train and stood opposite me, making faces and laughing and coughing into her hand. No one else could see her. She began to scream, "Sam! Look at me!! Lookie lookie lookie!" She was so close to me I could feel my hair rustling from her foul breath. The man sitting next to me got up suddenly and sat in a nearby seat.

I got off and made my way to St. Mary's Hospital, charmed my way (literally) into the records room, and looked up Caitlin's birth certificate. No father was listed. She was a bastard. That was it. I left the hospital and called Thaddeus. He picked it up after a dozen rings. "Serendipity, Thad here."

"Mr. La Violette, this is Sam Bowen, I was just in your shop about an hour ago."

Silence.

"Do you remember me?" I asked.

"Mr. Bowen, I am not senile, I am still holding your money in my hand. I am waiting for you to get to the point."

I bit my tongue, since I needed the son of a bitch's help. "Is your eye witness still alive?"

Thad chuckled. "Oh yeah, he's alive all right."

"I need to get in touch with him."

He laughed heartily. I knew this would be a problem. Academics were notoriously stingy with their contacts. Professional one-upmanship was always a danger. "Listen, I know this sounds odd, but I have a hunch that our two Teigs are actually one in the same. Moreover, if I am right, I will give you my findings, no strings attached."

He stopped laughing. "Tell me your theory, Mr. Bowen." I told him. He was silent for a long minute. "Okay, if you can prove that, it's worth giving up my source."

"Great!" I fished around in my duffel bag for paper and a pen. "What's his name?"

"Victor Blacktongue."

Odd name. I wrote it down, hoping it wasn't some delusional fantasy of the crazy old coot. "And his address?"

He told me. I put the pen down. " You've got to be fucking kidding."

It was after midnight as my taxi pulled up in front of the 39th Street Bridge, a narrow, two-lane stone construction that started in Arcadia, crossed the Via Contessa Canal, and led into the Canal district. I over-tipped the cab driver and he sped off. I threw my duffel bag over one shoulder and a heavy gunnysack over the other and staggered onto the bridge, walking unevenly on the bricks. This quaint little bridge arched up and over the Via Contessa Canal like something out of a storybook. At the apex of the bridge, I stopped. I looked around and found I could see several deserted blocks in all directions. Lighting on the bridge was nonexistent, and I was navigating primarily by moonlight. I stamped my boot on the bricks three times, quickly. With my one free hand, I reached into my trench coat pocket for my iron horseshoe. Just in case.

I don't know what I expected, but I really should've known better. After a few seconds of waiting, I heard a horrible scraping of bone on stone to my right. I hugged the opposite side of the bridge as a clawed hand the size of a shovelhead wrapped itself over the stone guard rail and flexed cautiously. Twin red eyes the size of softballs peered at me over the knuckles of the hand.

"Victor Blacktongue?"

"Who goes there?" he rumbled in a gravelly baritone. The bag on my shoulder suddenly smelled like shit.

"I am Bowen, of Kentucky. I have need of your services."

Another hand joined the first one, and the troll hauled his massive frame out of the water. He was easily twice my height in every direction. Just when I thought he couldn't get any bigger, he stepped over the railing and crouched before me. I still had to crane my neck to look at him. The smelled of stagnant water and wet fur washed over me. The gunnysack kicked my shoulder. I sympathized.

The troll picked at the wart on his chin and said, "And what did you bring for poor old Victor, hmmm?"

I threw the sack down in front of him. Victor flicked the bag open with a huge finger, and the goat spilled out, along with that distinctive smell. I'd been away from the farm too long. I forgot that nervous goats shit like crazy. Victor didn't seem to notice. He caught it by a hind leg and lifted it into the air with an expression of delight. "Oh, that's very nice, very nice indeed!" The goat thrashed and bleated. Victor twisted its head off with the same amount of effort I use to open a bottle. I watched in fascination as he lifted the kicking carcass to his tremendous mouth and drained it of blood. He then cracked the goat open at the spine, pulled hunk after hunk of meat and bone out, and chewed noisily. That goat cost me the rest of my credit with Mama Wang. I hoped it was worth it.

"Now," he smacked his lips, "what can I do for you?"

"I want to talk to you about Teig Milligan."

"September 19th, 1927." He said around a mouthful of ribs. "Di Lessa's men found him with a truck full of their gin and decided to dump him in the canal for his trouble."

"So, they killed him?"

"Oh yes. I've lived in these canals since they were built. I know all of their secrets. I see everything."

"Victor Blacktongue, I need you to think back to that night.

You saw it. Were you close enough to hear anything?"

Victor cocked his head at me. "What are you getting at?"

"Did Teig mention his family?"

Victor wiped his mouth with the back of his hand and squinted up at the moon. "Hmm... Let me think..." His lips moved and his fingers twirled. "Yes! He did mention his family. Big one, too, I think." He stood up and swung his legs over the railing. "Come on."

"Where to?"

"I'll take you to where they killed him." He dropped out of sight. I peered over the railing. Victor had straddled the narrow canal on either side and offered his hand up to me. "Come on, then. Sit in the hand." I gingerly stepped over the bridge and settled in his palm, where his jagged, uneven nails pressed into the backs of my thighs. He lowered me so fast I thought I was falling. Instead, he dumped me into a small wooden boat that almost capsized. He brought his legs together and jumped into the water with barely a ripple. "Comfy?" he asked.

"As good as I'm going to get."

"Right." He started walking the canal, pulling the boat behind him. During my first week in San Cibola, I took a tour of the district on one of the big boats. Doing the canals at night, in a wooden dinghy being pulled by a talking bridge troll, was another matter entirely. We went down several narrow canals barely large enough for two gondolas, then he turned left and we were on one of the major waterways. Here Victor kept mostly underwater and hugged the far bank, away from the lights and sounds of the late night revelers. After a block, he pulled the boat under a bridge and leapt up onto the embankment. I got out as well. We walked for another block before Victor stopped.

"There!" He pointed to a small island in the middle of the

canal. It was maybe thirty yards square, with trees in the middle of the plot and benches that faced outward on all four sides. A low metal fence encircled the island. It was a nice spot for a picnic. "See that?"

"What is it?"

"It's a traffic circle for the boats." Victor made a light splash with his hand. "This is deep water. Di Lessa knew that. The west side of the island has a sloped groove all the way down, like a slide."

"What for?"

"Bodies! Stiffs! Corpses!" he said, irritation etched on his face.

"Victor, just tell me what happened."

He closed his eyes. "Di Lessa used to drop dead bodies off the docks. But then the Andaro people moved into the reefs and got a little testy when the di Lessa's former enemies started drifting into their homes, so di Lessa had to dump his bodies elsewhere. Di Lessa was building on the canal, so he added this little feature. I don't know what he had in mind for the island, but the Civilian Conservation Corps came in around 1936 and made it into a park. So, the di Lessas had to move their dumping spot again."

"And this is where they killed Teig?"

"Right. They drove up to that bridge there," he said, pointing to the one we parked the boat under, "and rowed out here on a little gondola they kept under the bridge for just such an occurrence. The whole way out he was begging for his life."

"His family? Did he mention children?"

"Yes. Of course, he was begging to Lily di Lessa, the most hateful woman in the world. I remember it clear as day. He said, 'Please let me live. I've got sons. And a daughter! She's sick. I need the money. That's why I did it.' And she said, 'You're breaking my fucking heart, you thieving Mick.

Don't worry, though. In two seconds, you won't have to worry about your family ever again.'" He stopped and looked at me. "She killed him herself. Shot him three times. They laughed while he died. Then her goons tied cinderblocks to his arms and shoved him over the side." He shook his head. "Damn di Lessa family."

"Victor, I need you to do something for me. I need you to bring Teig back up for me."

Victor stuck his toe in the water. "The odds are pretty good that the current pulled him out a long time ago."

"Victor, it's important to me. A matter of life and death, to be exact. My sanity depends on it."

"Oh, very well, but I make you no promises. What form of payment will you use?"

"Payment?" I yelped. "I brought you a whole goat!"

"That was the price for summoning me. If you hadn't brought the goat, I would've had to eat you. Trollish law. Completely out of my hands. Now, for labor, that's a separate contract altogether."

"Okay, okay, fine. What do you require for payment?"

Victor crossed his arms. "One favor."

I looked at the troll. His lined face was unreadable. He towered over me, tapping his forearm with his thumb claw. I looked around the canals for a minute, sizing the situation up. He had me over a barrel and he knew it. "Okay. One favor."

Victor extended his hand, and I took a finger and shook it. His laughter boomed through the canals. "A favor! Oh, happy day! Just you wait!" He dived into the canals without a sound, leaving me to ponder the size of the hole I'd dug for myself this time.

Victor was underwater just long enough for me to conclude that he'd stranded me in the middle of nowhere. I was lost in thought, trying to mentally retrace my steps, when his head popped up through the water. "Bring the boat, " he gasped, "I think I've got him."

Two-thirty in the morning. I walked from the 39th Street Bridge in Arcadia to the Founder's Cemetery, carrying my duffel bag and the shit-stained gunnysack filled with the rotting corpse of Teig Milligan. At least, I hoped it was. Victor was going from the memory of what his shoes looked like, along with the cinderblocks on the arms. My feet were killing me, and I was hot and smelly and hungry.

When I got to the cemetery, the gates were open. Caitlin was there, standing in the open gates, waiting for me. As I approached, she turned without a sound and walked inside. The graves were arranged in two separate arms of crooked spirals that started at the tombs in the middle and wound around one another. The Haves were buried in the front, and the Have-Nots were buried in the back. We walked to the back.

Caitlin walked up to two matching headstones, one small, one large. She pointed at the bigger stone. "Mommy's there." I checked the name and the date on the headstone to make sure. Apparently, the church took pity on her and gave her last rites anyway. I set the bag down between the two markers and dumped Teig's remains out. The stench rose up to gag me. I turned to Caitlin.

"Is this your daddy?"

Caitlin nodded, her eyes filling up with tears. "Thank you."

"You're welcome. Why don't you go lay down now? I know you're tired."

She nodded and dissolved into nothingness. I took my Bible out of my duffel bag and gave Teig his last rites. I then sprinkled the corpse and the two graves with holy water and blessed the ground. He wasn't married to Molly, but he was bound to the daughter. Let the womenfolk fight it out in the netherworld. Teig can watch over his kids.

I waited for a minute to see if Caitlin was satisfied. No answer came, but I didn't really expect one, either. Most ghosts were pretty selfish. Once you give them what they want, they're out of here. I wanted to pat myself on the back, but I was too relieved and too tired. I walked back into the Gaslight and hit Brewers Street, caught a cab, and went home to sleep for a week.

I took an extra day off, just to make sure she was gone. By midday, I was feeling my old self again. I dropped by Mama Wang's to thank her for the goat. She insisted that Ah Yin wait on me the whole time. I also dropped by the UNC computer lab and typed up the facts in the case for Thaddeus. I signed it and got it notarized by the librarian. When I dropped the document off, he read it and chuckled. "So Teig had a chippy on the side?"

"Yep. Had the girl out of wedlock and had to take some night work to pay for her. And what paid pretty good in those days?"

"Crime." Thaddeus clucked his tongue. "Poor old Teig. How'd you check all this out, anyway?"

"Through the daughter."

"DNA testing?"

Just to see what his reaction was, I said, "No, she was haunting me. If I didn't find her dad, she would've driven me nuts."

Thad's expression didn't change. "Ghost Walk, eh? Those'll get ya every time."

Year of the Hare

Ping Ping's was unusually crowded. Ordinarily, this little tavern off the the beaten path hosted a smattering of quiet alcoholics and the occasional Mah Jongg tournament. Today, it was wall-to-wall with happy revelers. The only reason I got a seat at the bar was because no one wanted to sit next to Monkey, or as he preferred to be called, The Great Sage, Equal of Heaven. Even though he claimed to have ten thousand different forms, the only thing I ever saw him in was that of a dirty, smelly, old man-sized simian. Still, I couldn't afford to be particular. The bar had been this crowded all week, and I was good and tired of it.

"Goddamn Chinese New Year anyway," I said to no one in particular.

Monkey turned to address me, his face resting in a gnarled hand. "Bowen, you stupid shit. It's bad luck to curse the New Year."

I tossed one of my charms out on the bar. "To hell with that. I make my own luck."

Ping Ping, the bartender, pulled it over to him and examined it. "Peasant magic," he scoffed. "You are lucky to be alive right now."

"Y'all are sweethearts. No wonder this seat wasn't taken." I drained my beer, pocketed my charm, and threw a ten-dollar bill on the bar.

"Hey, Bowen!" Monkey yelled. I turned around.

"What?"

He handed me a red envelope. "Give my regards to Chu Sheng Kai."

Lucky money. Chinese New Year custom. "Et tu, Monkey?"

He shrugged and smiled. "Hey, I've got a debt to work off." He bounded back to the bar. I stuffed the envelope into my trench coat pocket and walked out into the festivities.

Chinatown was cheerful mayhem. Everyone was in traditional costumes and every side street not on the parade route was jammed full of stages and spectators, vendors and wide-eyed patrons. The crowd was a full mix of ethnicities. The week of Chinese New Year was the single largest income generator for the district, as the spectacle brought in tens of thousands of tourists. The parade had just started, and the streets were crowded to overflowing. I walked the parade route, managing to stay ahead of the floats in spite of the crowd. The whole thing started at the Welcome Pagoda, ran all the way up Crane Street, and ended at the Garden of the Five Elements. There, at the park, the festivities commenced in earnest, including a fireworks display and a speech by Chu Sheng Kai. Afterwards, the whole district partied all night, or so I was told.

I could see the temporary stage erected in front of the small park. I could also see the Jen Long Security force everywhere. Some of them wore street clothes, while others stationed closer to the stage wore smart-looking suits with the corporate logo on the breast of their blazers. People were everywhere, tossing firecrackers and exchanging red envelopes and smiling. I made for the stage.

Two guards held a hand out to me. I showed them my battered letter. They looked at it, then each other. Finally, the hands came down and I walked through. My reputation preceded me.

"Sam!" It was Michael Chu. He wore his usual 3-piece tailored suit and smile.

I walked over to him. "Hey, Michael." We shook hands.

"Come on, you can meet some people."

He led me over to a cluster of people looking official and introduced me to them in Chinese. All I caught was "Sam Bowen" and "Ya Shen." I nodded, shook hands, and bowed as the introductions warranted. They all seemed real unimpressed with me. We went across the stage, popping in on each group, Michael introducing me proudly like I was some new pet in the family. Finally, I asked Michael, "What are you saying about me?"

"That you are my adopted brother, the youngest Chu in Father's family, and a great saver of lives."

"Oh, that's just perfect." We walked up to a small group near the opposite end of the platform. I knew one of the women standing there already.

"Sam, you know Jiang Shui, our second oldest brother." Said Michael. Jiang Shui was the second oldest son of Chu Sheng Kai and the head of Jen Long Security. Currently on my shit list, too. We had met once before, when Chu-San inducted me into his family, but we didn't get a chance to talk. He wore the blue blazer of the Jen Long and appeared to be in his mid-forties.

I cautiously shook his hand. "Hello. Will this outfit do?"

His smile became a frown. "What a rude greeting."

Michael stepped on my foot. "I apologize," I said through gritted teeth, bowing at the waist. "That was uncalled for."

Jiang's frown disappeared, but no smile returned. "Much better, Mr. Bowen."

Michael nervously stepped in between us. "And this is my wife, Kim, and our daughter, Elizabeth." His wife was

Chinese and gorgeous, dressed as smartly and conservatively as her husband. Little Elizabeth had her mother's looks.

"Hello, Mr. Bowen," she smiled warmly, no trace of an accent in her voice. "Michael told me so much about you. It's great to finally meet you."

"Same here," I said, returning the smile. I bent down to address Elizabeth. "Hi, I'm Sam."

"Call me Betty." She shook my hand.

I looked up at her mother. "The nickname changes every week," she explained.

Michael patted my shoulder. "And I believe you already know Mi Hei." She wore a black pants suit with the Jen Long emblem and favored me with an even glare.

I smiled at her. "Hello."

Jiang Shui put his arm around his daughter and turned to me. "Mi Hei tells me you are doing well in your research."

"Oh yeah," I replied. Mi Hei's expression changed, and a line of concern creased her forehead. "Mi Hei has been extremely helpful in my work. You should be proud of her."

The answer seemed to surprise them both. "Well...this pleases me greatly," he replied.

"Honey," said Michael, turning back to his wife, "I'm going to see if we can find Father. We'll be right back." He took me by the elbow and led me out of earshot. "What was that all about?" he asked.

"Ah, he sent me this." I handed him the crumpled letter. He scanned it quickly.

"Sam, he's the head of security for the family. This stuff goes out to all of us, so we will know what we are to do."

"Does that include telling me where to be and when? And telling me how to dress?"

Michael nodded. "In this family, this organization, yes, it does."

I looked at Michael for a long minute. He was the closest to my age, and with the exception of Chu-San himself, the most friendly to me. I decided not to press the issue just then. "Maybe so," I conceded. "I'm just not used to people I don't know ordering me around."

A swell from the crowd quieted us. The first of the parade floats was in sight. I felt a hand on my shoulder. It was Chu Sheng Kai.

"Ya Shen."

I turned and bowed. "Chu-San." I dug around in my pocket for the red envelope and handed it to him. "From the Great Sage, Equal of Heaven."

He took it with a smile. "That insolent monkey." He tucked the envelope into a breast pocket. "Are you enjoying the festivities so far?"

"Oh yeah, this is great."

"You wear your sincerity like a mask." He checked his watch. "The parade will take about an hour. You will not be needed here until seven o'clock. Why don't you wander around and take in the festivities?"

"Okay, sure," I said, grateful for the chance to make myself scarce. Jiang Shui walked up. He bowed to his father, who returned the greeting.

"You two have spoken, already, I take it," he said, indicating myself and Jiang. Chu-San turned to Jiang. "I trust everything is ready? I told Ya Shen he was free to wander until seven."

Jiang gave his father a look I couldn't read, then turned to me. "Here." He handed me an armband with the Jen Long logo on it. "This will allow you to pass through the security areas." I slipped it on over my trench coat sleeve. Jiang reached into his pocket and withdrew several red foil envelopes. "You will be given many of these. Lucky money.

Give in return. It is good for the family."

I looked at the envelopes. They bore the symbol of Red Moon Enterprises. "Right. Thanks." I faced Sheng again. "I'm going to eat. Do either of you want anything?"

Chu Sheng Kai beamed at me. "Thank you, no. I am fine." Jiang bowed demurely and left us. I shook my head.

Chu studied me. "You are displeased with my son, your brother?"

"I'm just not used to being given orders, is all. I've been my own man for too long now."

The old man stepped in close to me. "Ya Shen," he said, "as a member of my family, you have certain obligations. Chinese New Year is one of the few times we as a family gather together in a show of celebration...and strength. It is good for the rest of the family that you are seen doing what is expected of you." He glanced over at Me Hei, talking earnestly with Jiang Shui. "Unless, of course, you think you are getting along well enough on your own."

Of course, the old bastard was right. If all of the resources of his organization were going to open up to me, I had a few more hoops to jump through.

A tall, dark man in an Armani suit walked up to us with an entourage of men and one woman in tow. His bearing was noble, like old money. I backed up instinctively. Chu Sheng Kai and this man shook hands and smiled.

"Mr. di Lessa."

"Mr. Chu. Happy New Year."

So that was Mr. di Lessa. He didn't look anything like how I imagined a crime boss would look. I bowed to Chu Sheng Kai and left.

I walked back down to Sacramento Street, watching the parade on one side and the street vendors on the other. I passed by jugglers, magicians, puppet shows, and fortune-tellers. The float for the Buddhist temple drove by. It was a wooden platform with absolutely no decorations on it. Six monks sat in a lotus position and waved, while Master Jin Lei looked on with contentment and nodded to the crowd. Everyone was throwing red envelopes at the float. I threw one too and couldn't help noticing that Master Lei's feet weren't actually touching the platform.

The swarm of people around Zhu's Noodle Hut was unbelievable. The only thing visible was the red and yellow parasol over the food stand. I waited my turn. I finally caught sight of Zhu, looking more miserable than usual.

"Bowen." he muttered. "What, you come to kick me when I'm down?"

"Aw, Zhu, I'm just getting my dinner. You got any New Year's Specials?"

"Yeah, I got a special, all right. Five dollars."

"Done deal." I watched as Zhu threw several weird things into a big box and dropped in a wrapped crepe-like thing with chicken inside. "What the hell is that?" I asked.

"Happy Pancake. Good luck food. Five dollars even."

I handed him a five-dollar bill, and as an afterthought, handed him a red envelope. "Happy New Year, Zhu."

He looked at the envelope, turned it over, and caught sight of Chu Sheng Kai's company logo on the back. "Bowen, you bastard! Only you would spit in my face like this!" The crowd laughed good-naturedly. I dug into my food and strolled back towards the park in a much better mood.

I still had most of an hour to kill, so I took a left down Ventura Street and looked at some of the peddlers' wares. Some of them were actual Chinatown businesses that moved a selection of their wares outside their storefront. Others were weekend warriors or traveling salesmen. A few were outright carnies. I watched a magician in a full Mandarin costume pull threaded needles out of his mouth for a while, then I pawed through one of the many tables purporting to sell genuine Chinese alchemy. The guy behind the table regarded me through squinted eyes.

"What you look for, eh?"

"I dunno," I told him. "Just looking, mostly. Maybe a ward against evil."

The man squinted harder, making his eyes disappear outright. "Why a holy man like you need a charm?"

I glanced up at him quickly. "Holy man? I'm not holy."

He cackled at me. "In Chinese, you very holy." He waved his hands at me in wide circles. "Good color. Strong. Good heart. Good mind. Better than that old fool." He jerked his thumb at the Mandarin next door, currently performing the Chinese Rice Bowls trick, which is still included in most beginning magic sets.

"Buddy, you've got a better act than he does." I held up a pendant with a rabbit on it. "How much?"

"Twelve dollars."

I handed him a twenty. "Will you charge it up for me?"

The man grabbed the money, his eyes darting left and right. He put one hand on the necklace and made a focusing symbol with the other. He mumbled something in Chinese, and I felt static and smelled ozone. He handed me my charm and most of my change. I didn't kick about it.

"Thank you," I said. I slipped it on and felt its pull like a weak magnet. I turned to leave and ran into a Chinese kid, maybe twenty years old at the most, wearing a leather jacket. He looked at me casually, sizing me up. He was chewing gum. I said, "Whoa, sorry 'bout that," I said.

He nodded and moved away. I watched him walk through the crowd and noticed his elaborate design on the back of his jacket. In the center of a circle was the Chinese character for

"man." Around that were Chinese characters I couldn't identify. The kid was connected to the Blood Shadow Triad. I
breathed a sigh of relief for the bullet I just dodged.

I made for Crane Street, hurriedly finishing my meal. As
I rounded the corner to head back to Five Elements Park, I
caught a glimpse of someone standing in the shadows. I
couldn't tell if they were watching me or not, so I kept going
past them. It was about five yards to the crowd watching the
parade. I put my hands in my pockets and made for it.

As I pushed into the crowd, I heard a whine behind me.
Still moving, I looked back. A bare-chested Chinese man in
pantaloons had pinned to the wall a creature half man and
half rat. He yelled at the creature in Chinese, repeating a
single word over and over. Finally, the monster shimmered
and became a toothless beggar. Some bystanders clapped
and cheered, thinking it was all part of the festivities. Then
the crowd pushed me forward, and I lost sight of them. When
I worked my way back to the sidewalk, they were both gone.
I really missed my duffel bag. Fingering the junk in my pockets, I quickly walked the route back to the park.

More of the family had gathered. I didn't see Chu Sheng
Kai, but Michael was all over the place, glad-handing and
smiling, his wife and kid in tow. The rest of the family were
polite but not too cordial. I ascended the stage and stood off
to the side, watching the parade floats come riding by. It was
pretty standard stuff. Local businesses with flowers and lucky
symbols all over them. The Little India Business Association paid a shitload of money for the Avatar of Ganesh to
recline on their float. Lots of dancers in costumes. Several
finalists for the Miss Chinatown Contest rode by in convertibles. Bringing up the rear was the traditional Chinese dragon.
Not ten guys under a big kite, either, but twelve handlers
nervously escorting a real Chinese dragon. Around the

dragon's long neck was a wooden sign that read, "HAPPY NEW YEAR FROM RED MOON ENTERPRISES." I walked over to Michael and tugged on his sleeve to draw him out of the crowd.

"Okay, no bullshit, where did that thing come from?" Michael hesitated for a second. "It's a treasure-hoarder. My father knows it. He trades a walk for some item of antiquity from my father's collection." He looked at me as if daring me to refute it.

The crowd was laughing and jumping up and down. Fireworks were going off everywhere. The family was drifting together on the stage. Michael motioned to me. "Come on. It's time."

I took my place in the group, feeling conspicuous and out of place. The crowd quieted somewhat. Then our ranks parted, and Chu Sheng Kai strode forth. Everyone clapped and cheered. I watched the Jen Long bristle and scan the crowd. Chu Sheng Kai stepped up to the podium and began to talk to the crowd in Chinese. There was an English translation being broadcast somewhere in the park, but I couldn't really hear it from where I was. So I just stood there with my hands behind my back and tried not to look stupid. Michael had thoughtfully placed us towards the front, and I was suddenly aware of many eyes on me at once. The audience applauded and cheered several times. Chu finally gestured to us, and we waved to the crowd. More talking, more clapping, and then Chu Sheng Kai shouted something to the crowd and everyone went berserk. The lights dimmed, and then several rockets shot up into the night air from behind the stage. They exploded in shimmering arcs of gold and red. The fireworks display had begun.

Chu Sheng Kai turned his attention to us and spoke rapidly. The family dispersed, breaking up into little groups. I slipped off down the side entrance and tried to make my way back up the street, a job made more difficult by the fact that the crowd was going in the opposite direction. It took me ten minutes to walk a block. Finally, I gave up and took the first side street I came to.

Malenga Street was one of the narrow lanes that served as a commercial loading zone for the trendy tourists shops and restaurants in the neighborhood. People poured into the park from this street, but I could still walk without too much interference. I decided to make the block and get back onto Crane Street, behind the crowd watching the fireworks, then walk back to Ping Ping's and get snockered. I made a left and relaxed upon seeing even fewer people on this street. I walked quickly, paying no attention to my surroundings. That was a mistake.

I heard several sets of footsteps, really close behind me. I scanned quickly ahead, looking for an escape route. To my left, about ten yards away, was the mouth of an alley. I casually took it, relieved to see Crane Street and people at the end of it. I quickened my steps. I heard the feet behind me, still too close for comfort. Time to run. I broke into a sprint, wishing like hell I had my duffel bag with me. Something hit me high between the shoulder blades, and I went down, rolling forward as I did so. When I came up, I saw I was still twenty feet from the crowd. I turned to my attackers. Four young men in leather jackets. Blood Shadow jackets.

They fanned out like wolves, trying to surround me. My back throbbed from whatever it was that hit me. One of the tongs stepped into the weak light. It was the kid I'd run into earlier. "So, Gwai Lo, you are Jen Long now. Then you must know Lotus Street is off-limits to your kind."

What the hell was this kid talking about? "Look, son, I don't want any trouble. I sure as hell ain't no Jen Long."

They laughed. "Do you think we are fools? Your armband, Gwai Lo."

Damn. I told myself if I actually survived this to bump Jiang Shui to the top of my shit list. They were advancing. I matched them step for step. At this rate, I'd hit the crowd in no time, and they knew it too. The leader muttered something under his breath. Thin knives appeared in their hands. This was about to hurt.

They rushed me all at once. I ran forward to meet them, then tucked and rolled between their legs, the blades missing me by inches. When I got to my feet, I was facing the wrong direction, but I had worked my Bowie knife free.

"Now boys, we can end this right now. No one has to get hurt." I held the knife in front of me, loose in my fingers, and dropped into a fighting crouch. The kids paused for only a second. Another lunge from the group. I rolled left and grabbed a metal trash can and brained the Blood Shadow closest to me. He fell into the boy right beside him, and they both hit the pavement. I jumped over them and grabbed the leader by the throat, placed my knife against his jugular.

"Now, I don't want to do this, asshole, but I will. I just want to walk out of this..."

That was as far as I got. I felt a sharp pain in my abdomen and all the breath left me at once. I staggered back, shocked, and the leader lashed out with a kick that seemed to take forever to connect with the side of my head. I spun around and down, and then I was looking at the pavement. Get up, I screamed at myself. Everything felt distant and numb. I willed my arms and legs to crawl towards the mouth of the alley. Felt the asphalt and rocks digging into my hands. Okay, I'm moving again. I felt something hit my head once, twice, then I was lifted up onto my knees, and I felt something cold and sharp against my throat. Someone was chanting. The mouth of the alley was miles away. If I could get to my pockets, I might be able to set up a counterspell. I couldn't feel my hands or my pockets. The chanting grew louder, and I realized all at once this punk kid was going to kill me.

Suddenly, I was free. I fell onto my hands. Someone was framed in the light of the festivities. I looked behind me to see the leader trying to hold his throat together with his fingers to stop the cascade of blood. He choked and died and fell to the ground. The other Blood Shadows regrouped and charged past me towards my benefactor. I grabbed the closest one's heel and he went flying. I crawled on top of him and sat on the small of his back. I fished around in my coat pocket until I found my sharpened ash stick. I dug into the skin on his neck, leaving a pink welt, and drew a binding symbol. He squirmed and screamed and tried to knock me off. I whispered into the symbol, "Choke." Immediately, he started to gasp and retch. I looked to my rescuer to see if they needed any help.

Now I could see that my rescuer was a woman. One Blood Shadow was down, blood pooling up underneath him. The other was trying unsuccessfully to get his knife arm free. I didn't hear the bone snap, but his howl of pain explained the situation nicely. I watched, fascinated, as she twisted the forearm free from the elbow and lifted the useless limb holding the knife into the Blood Shadow's own throat. The howl became a gurgle, and he slumped in her arms.

She threw the body aside and turned to me. We stared for a long moment.

"You." Mi Hei and I said together.

She spit on the ground and started pacing. "Great, just great. Somebody says Jen Long is in trouble in the alley, and it's you."

"Well, I'm sorry you saved my life!" I yelled at her. "I

should'a let this sumbitch try to kill you too, I guess." I kicked the choking Blood Shadow at my feet."

"That's what you get for wearing that armband!" she screamed. "You are not one of us!"

"This armband was your father's idea!" I shouted back, noticing over her shoulder that a small crowd had gathered to watch the bloodbath after the fight.

"My father would never give that symbol to Gwai Lo like you."

"Ah! What the hell does that mean? These boys here called me that before you killed them all."

"It means, 'foreign devil,' which you are. And you're welcome for saving your life." She crossed her arms.

"Goddammit! I didn't ask you to save my life!" Just then, the crowd parted and a dozen Chinatown cops and six Jen Long marched through to secure the area. We were pulled deeper into the alley. One of the cops looked at my wounds and checked me for a concussion while another talked to Mi Hei about what happened. He wrote everything down, then came over to me for my side of the story. The Blood Shadow corpses were taken further back down the alley, away from the gawkers. The forth kid, still choking, was cuffed to a fire escape. The cop who took my story walked up to me. "You're Bowen, right?"

I nodded.

"They want you and her onstage now." His tone of voice suggested he didn't like playing the part of errand boy to someone like me.

I looked at Mi Hei. She wouldn't meet my gaze. "Thanks for patching me up." I said to the guy who taped my cuts. "Come on," I said to her. She followed without a word.

The fireworks were over and the crowd had thinned out only slightly. We pushed and prodded ourselves back to the stage. Something was wrong. Three Chinatown policemen were talking to Michael. Mr. di Lessa was talking to Chu. Jiang was barking orders and directing people. Michael spotted us and ran over. "Sam! You've got to help me!"

"Michael, what happened?"

"Elizabeth's been kidnapped!"

We pulled up to my apartment building. Mi Hei killed the engine and looked at me. "You live at Benny's Haunted Pagoda?"

"Don't you start on me, too." We hit the front door at a full gallop, and it banged loudly against the wall.

"Sam Bowen!" It was Benny, his torso sticking up through the floor in the entrance hall. "You be more careful with the building!"

"Sorry, Benny, I've got an emergency." I vaulted over him and made for the stairs.

"You always got an emergency!" he protested. "Oh, sorry, Sam, I didn't know you had a guest."

Behind me, I could see Mi Hei gaping at Benny, who was making an effort to smooth his hair and put on a smile. He rose up completely through the floor and stuck out a hand. I ran back down and intercepted.

"Benny, Mi Hei. Mi Hei, Benny. Don't shake his hand, we may need your arm later." I pulled her away, and we ran for the stairs.

Benny smiled and winked at me. "No need to explain, Sam, I'm not so old I forget the Art of the Bedchamber!" He gave me a thumbs-up.

"Oh perfect," Mi Hei said as we clambered up the stairs. "I finally get to meet Benny Wan, and he thinks I'm going to have sex with you."

"I'll straighten it out later. And what's the big deal, anyway? It's just Benny."

She chuckled to herself. "You don't know anything, do you?"

I stopped her short in front of my door and turned on her. "No, I don't know every single nuance and piece of history in Chinatown. I've only been here six months, and so far, everyone has been considerably less than helpful about passing on any information. But let's get one thing straight: I am not an idiot. You're on my turf, now. So do me a favor and cut me some slack, okay?"

"Fuck you, Bowen! This wasn't my idea. I was ordered to tag along and look after your clueless ass!"

"Hey, I don't want you here, either. I'm not used to having someone else to worry about. If you really want to help Elizabeth, and me, then give me a little room and let me do my thing. Okay?" We entered my room in silence. Me Hei stewed while I pulled out my duffel bag, relieved to actually have it in my hands again. She sat primly down on the bed and tried to look uninterested as I unpacked the pouch marked "Arizona." She watched as I laid out prayer stones in a rough Medicine Wheel on the hardwood floor.

"Those look like birds," she said, her curiosity finally getting the better of her.

"They are. All except this one." I set the roughly hewn carving of a cat next to the small brass brazier in the center of the wheel. "Open the window, will you?"

"Why birds?"

"Huh? Oh, these are my Spirit Animals. Totems. I don't know why, they chose me."

"What's all this for, anyway?"

"I need to sleep so I can go walking."

"What?"

"I'm cheating. Trust me." I dug through my "San Cibola"

pouch until I found the tanis leaves I'd bought last week and crushed them in my hand. That got mixed with some tobacco from the "Arizona" pouch and dumped into the fire in the brazier. When everything was ready, I turned to her. "Okay, I don't know how long this is going to take. I need to go into a deep trance, and I need you to guard me because I'll be totally unprotected."

She looked at me skeptically. "What do you expect to happen?"

"Dunno. But wake me up if I look like I'm in pain, okay? And don't touch anything, no matter what happens. Just go with it. Got it?"

I took my shirt off and sat down with my legs under me, breathing in the smoke and staring at the focusing stones, feeling their surface with my mind. It didn't take long. The tanis leaves were potent. I fell into a deep trance. Looking down, I could see my hands. I was grounded in the Dream-State.

An excited flutter came from the window. A raven slightly smaller than a Rottweiler sat on the windowsill. Mi Hei was a mere shadow on the bed.

"Hello, Brother Raven."

"Hello, Many Feathers." Raven cocked his head at me and hopped onto the floor.

"It's good to see you again."

"Is it?" Raven asked. "I would have thought you had forgotten us altogether."

"Not true. I have been just been preoccupied with my own quest," I answered, remembering to answer in the rhythm of the medicine drums.

"Only now you need something from me."

I stood up and looked behind me. My body was still on the floor. "No, not for me. An innocent. Caught in a war between two men. Blood enemies."

Raven paced back and forth, wings fluttering nervously. "And what would you ask of me, Many Feathers?"

"Nothing so much. Only deliver a message to Lynx for me."

Raven smiled. "And the message?"

I whispered it into his ear. Raven whistled. "That's a good one. Very well. I will take it to him."

"Thank you." Raven flapped his wings and was gone. I stood up, walked a few stops, and looked behind me for the silver tether that ran from the base of my spine to the middle of my sleeping self's forehead. Seeing it was always a bit disconcerting. I walked downstairs to wait for Lynx. Benny was at the front counter. He looked solid and tangible, a brightness in the muted world. Outside, the streets were surprisingly crowded. This was my first Spirit Walk in San Cibola, and, even though I knew about this city, I wasn't prepared for the number of beings out and about. I hoped it was just because of the New Year festivities.

"Many Feathers." I spun on my heel. Lynx came bounding up the street, four feet tall at the shoulder. I smiled.

"I no longer need to crouch down to look you in the eye, my brother," I said. Lynx sat down before me and assumed an air of contentment.

"This town is robust with magic, Many Feathers," he said, scratching behind his ear.

"Old friend, I need a favor. Something has been taken. An innocent spirit. I believe a great harm will come to her tonight. Will you help me find her?"

Lynx stopped grooming himself. "Why should I help you?"

I leaned against the railing on the steps of my building. "Because I am Many Feathers. That should be good enough."

"It isn't," Lynx said, turning away. "Not anymore."

"Wait!" I called out. "Please. Wait." Lynx stopped and looked over his shoulder at me. "I'm sorry."

Lynx turned on me, teeth bared. "Sorry? You think you can just borrow what you need from us and go? I have seen into your heart, Many Feathers. You are not like the other Whites. Why do you act like it?"

I hadn't counted on this. Lynx was genuinely pissed. "I-I- don't understand. How have I dishonored you?"

"By ignoring us."

"Forgive me, Brother Lynx, if I have not called upon you daily. As you know, I am still chasing answers to my own questions."

"But Many Feathers, you don't seem to realize that we can help you in your journey. You must visit the medicine wheel and consult the Sun..."

This was ridiculous. A totem jealous of another system of magic. Moreover, this was really getting irritating. "Look, Brother Lynx, I didn't ask you here for spiritual guidance," I said, forgetting my cadence in my anger. "I need your help or a little girl is going to die tonight. If you don't want to help me because I have turned my back on you, then fine. Don't help. I'll find her some other way." I turned to walk back inside the building.

"Sam, you owe me more than that," said Lynx.

"You're right. I do. And when I get the chance, I'll even our score. But right now, I have to find a little girl."

Brother Lynx sighed. "I see you're just as focused and driven as ever. All right. I will help you. What do you have for me?"

Thank God. I was counting on Lynx not being able to resist the chance to show off. My little speech about having other methods was a bluff. I closed my eyes and sent everything I could remember about Elizabeth to him. Lynx regarded the stars and sniffed the night air.

"She is close. Come on." He bounded off down the street. I ran after him, pacing myself because I knew that for Brother Lynx, "close" was always a relative distance.

We made good time through the back-alley maze of Chinatown, avoiding the bigger streets and cutting through the neighborhoods in the district. I got lost very quickly and had to rely on street signs. I couldn't even spot a familiar landmark. At least Brother Lynx didn't go from rooftop to rooftop. Eventually, he drew up short in front of a featureless warehouse. I looked at Lynx.

"She's in there," he told me. "Be careful."

"You're not coming in with me?"

"Heh. You're lucky I even brought you here at all, Many Feathers." Lynx bounded off.

I took a deep breath and walked through the battered metal door. Inside was your standard warehouse, filled with crates and boxes and forklifts. I could hear voices from somewhere inside. To my right was a set of metal stairs leading up to an observation deck and an office. Two goons in the office, speaking in Chinese. Blood Shadows. It had been too long since my last astral projection. I couldn't fly or hover, so I just moved through the office, careful not to touch either of them. Once on the other side, I had a great view of the layout of the place.

The Blood Shadows had built a separate area out of crates, maybe twenty-five feet square. Elaborate symbols were painted on the floor. In the center of the room was an altar, marked with straps for arms and legs and covered with dark brown stains. Three Blood Shadows stood around listlessly, fingering their weapons, smoking and talking. Elizabeth was bound and gagged on a small crate in the corner. She appeared to be asleep. I took a chance and ran down the cat-walk, threaded my way through the crates, and tapped her on the shoulder. She stirred, then floated slightly up out of her body.

"Betty." I remembered to use the nickname she gave me earlier tonight.

"Huh?" She looked up at me and almost dropped back into herself again. I grabbed her by the hand and held her in place.

"Betty, do you remember me?"

"Uh huh." She was groggy. Drugged.

"Listen, I want you to stay calm. I'm gonna get you out of here, you understand me? You be brave for me."

"O-okay."

"Good. Hang in there." I let her sink back into her body and beat a hasty retreat for the entrance. I crossed half the distance before I saw a shape descend from the rafters and land solidly in front of me, blocking my exit. He wore very elaborate robes with intricate gold embroidery and carried matching fans. His face was pale and gaunt and his eyes were mustard yellow. The ends of his long, thin mustache were beaded and seemed to move on their own, like jellyfish tentacles.

While I stood there gaping at both his costume and the fact that he could see me, he popped the fans open and said something to me in Chinese. Then his arm moved faster than I could follow, and an arc of blue energy flared out and struck me full in the chest. I fell back through the crates, which hurt more than the blast itself. The silver tether jerked tight and I was awake, back in my body and looking at Mi Hei. She was open-mouthed and held one of my journals in her hand.

"What the hell?" she asked. "Are you okay?"

"No, I'm not," I moaned. I rolled out of my sitting position, feeling the pain of the astral attack in my muscles, and staggered to the refrigerator for a drink of water. When I finished draining the bottle, I turned to her and gasped, "What the hell are you doing with that?"

"What? Oh, this." She closed the journal. "I got bored watching you snore, so I did a little poking."

I walked over to her and snatched the book out of her hand. "This is not for your amusement." I tossed it into the open duffel bag. "We've got work to do. I know where they're keeping her." I put my shirt back on and told her everything I saw about the neighborhood and the warehouse, even drew a few of the Chinese characters I'd seen during my Dream. She recognized the place. "We have to hurry. I only saw about a half-dozen men there, but there will be more."

"How do you know?" she asked.

"I'm pretty sure they're going to sacrifice her."

Mi Hei frowned. "Yeah, okay, but how do you know?"

I crossed my arms. "Look, I've been around, all right? I know how to spot a ritual sacrifice when I see it. Now, why would these Blood Shadows want to sacrifice a little girl?"

She thought about it for a second. "Sung Ti!"

"Who?"

"The king of the third level of Hell. This is about the feud!"

"Mi Hei, I don't know anything about what you're talking about. Please enlighten me."

For a second, a look of scorn flashed across her face, then she realized it was a fair question. "Okay, this is family business, understand? None of this goes into any of your journals or anything. When Wan Fei Ying..."

"David Wan? The leader of the Blood Shadow triad?"

"The head of the triad, yes. Don't interrupt. When Wan

Fei Ying was a young man, he had a disagreement with my grandfather over a woman. The way my father tells it, Wan Fei Ying was engaged to some local girl, a real catch, but he decided he would have a little tryst on the side with someone else. She found out about it and ran to Grandfather, who, um, consoled her, if you know what I mean. She was a virgin. The girl was to be his bride, you know what I'm saying? Well, Wan Fei Ying took this as an unforgivable insult, and the two have been fighting ever since."

"Okay, that explains the feud, but not the girl."

"Sung Ti is the king of the Third Hell. He punishes people who were guilty of unfilial behavior, disobedience, and disloyalty. Since it is the beginning of the New Year, many people sacrifice an offering to the gods for strength and luck in the coming months. But a loss during New Year is a bad omen and will cloud the whole year with bad luck."

I got the picture. David Wan's bold snatch and grab was the perfect way to strike a blow to the Chu family while strengthening his own position at the same time. This wasn't going to be easy. I grabbed my duffel bag, and we took off.

Mi Hei's car was sleek and black and a fetching example of Daddy's money at work. She drove briskly while I rummaged through my bag, and stuffed things in my pockets. She told me we weren't going more than twenty blocks, so I was trying to hurry.

"So, was all that stuff in your book true or just some fictional bullshit?"

I shot her a look. "No, it's all true. Why do you think I would make something like that up?"

"I don't know." We turned a corner, and she killed the lights. "So, why do all of that stuff? What's your point?"

I saw my opening and took it. "You don't know anything, do you?" I mimicked her tone and inflection from earlier.

"Ha ha. Not funny. Just tell me, before I lose my interest."

"Okay, here's the Cliff Notes version. When I turned sixteen, my family began dying off, one by one. Sometimes it was natural, sometimes it was accidental, and sometimes it was really weird. Uncle struck by lightning, brother mysteriously eaten by some animal, that sort of thing. Well, I did some checking and found out that my family was under some sort of a curse."

She nodded, her lips pursed. "So why aren't you dead yet?"

"The night is still young, don't tempt it. Actually, I'm the seventh son of a seventh son. I think it makes me the focal point of the curse. Anyway, what I'm trying to do is figure out who or what cursed my family and figure out how to remove it while I can."

"Why all the traveling, then?"

"I'm following an ancestor of mine that I think may be the originator of the curse. My Typhoid Bowen, or something like that. This ancestor, Jacob, was a real knockabout, and he went all over the place. So, I'm retracing his path and studying any and all local magic systems, bits of folklore, and mystical people that I find along the way. Eventually, I'll figure how what magic was used and hopefully be able to reverse it."

She nodded quietly. "That almost explains why I got stuck translating old family diaries instead of doing what I was trained to do."

"Sorry you weren't told about it before now. Your grandfather knew all about it. I just assumed he told you what was what."

The warehouse was a block away. Mi Hei rolled the car to a stop and killed the engine. "You ready?" I asked her.

"I think so. Just stick to the plan we outlined. No hot-dogging." I watched her open the door. "Aren't you going to call for back-up or something?"

"Later. This is my chance to prove to my father that I can take care of business."

"Oh no you don't," I objected. "This is my ass and Elizabeth's ass on the line here. Those guys have guns, a wizard, and God only knows what else. You call for back-up, or I'm not getting out of this car."

"I really don't like you."

"I don't care. Just make the call, so we can not like each other later."

She flipped open her digital phone, dialed a number, and spoke quickly and sharply into the receiver. I heard the street address and relaxed. The cavalry was coming. She hung up the phone. "Can we go now?"

"I've never seen someone so eager to get killed before," I said, getting out of the car.

Mi Hei didn't bother to answer. She popped open the trunk with a small control on her key chain and brought out a flat black metallic case. The lid flipped up at her touch, and I peeked inside. The interior was fashioned out of die-cut black foam. Standing out in sharp contrast was an assortment of knives, guns, electronic devices, and weird, Chinese weaponry that I had only seen in bad kung fu movies. While I marveled at the hardware, Mi Hei ducked out beside the car, out of sight. When she came up, she was wearing a simple black turtleneck and baggy black trousers. Over that was a Y-shaped harness with straps and pockets. She loaded a lot of gear, more than I thought the harness would hold, and then covered the whole ensemble with a black vest that hid most of the weapons. In the darkness, she was just a face floating in mid-air.

"Okay, I'll take the front, you go around the back," she said.

"Right." We separated in the darkness and I ran quickly to get in place before she did. The loading dock doors were cracked to allow the cool air to blow through, and I crawled on my belly to get under them. It took me a second to reorient myself. The crates and pallets were arranged along the walkways, so it was easier to move and harder to hide. I kept looking high and low for the wizard with the busy mustache. The second-story office was on the opposite wall, and I could see even more guards inside through the green glass window. It was almost time for Mi Hei's diversion. I grabbed a crate that allowed me a view of the front door, to the left of the stairs, and went to work on my spell.

I picked up a lot of really cool shit in Mexico. One of them was a very unique spell, given to me by the Zombie Killer Joaquim Tlomtec that he used for sneaking up on a bunch of undead and whacking them en masse. I set it up on the stairs, which would render anyone walking on them invisible to others. I wasn't real sure about the length of the shadow curtain, so I made sure to cover at least the open door at the top of the stairs.

Mi Hei either had great faith in my abilities, or she was a colossal idiot. The spell was barely in place before I saw the front door crack and her creep through. She didn't even look around once before heading straight to her right. I saw her put one foot on the bottom stair and promptly disappear. At least she was being quiet. I made for the sacrifice area in the middle with one eye peeled for the wizard.

I was within fifteen feet of Elizabeth when I heard someone's radio crackle and spit out something in Chinese that turned into a scream and a gasp. Immediately, several sets of footsteps took off in the direction of the office. Someone on the other side of the crate chambered a round. One guy left. He was watching the office. I slipped around the side of the crate and cracked the back of his head open with the handle of my Bowie knife. Elizabeth's eyes were open, and they widened when she saw me. She began to wiggle and thrash in her bonds.

"Betty, listen," I leaned in close, whispering as I untied her. "I need you to be very quiet, okay? We're gonna get you out of here, but you have to be real quiet. We're in a lot of danger, understand?" She nodded, and I undid her gag. "Okay, now we're going out the back." I picked her up, and we weaved back through the crates to the loading dock. I could see the office from here. The guards were shooting off the lock and the gunshots were deafening. Mi Hei was hanging off of the side railing, hand over hand, to come back in behind them. They didn't even stand a chance.

I lifted the door up so we could get under it. Once on the loading dock, I said, "Okay, Betty, let's see if you can stand." I set her down on unsteady legs, but they held. She took my hand, and we turned to go back to the car and wait for Mi Hei.

"Are you okay?" I asked, looking down at her.

"I guess. Sam, is that man with you?"

I glanced over. It was the wizard. He was blocking the way out of the alley. He flashed me a lecherous grin and pulled out the metal fans he had earlier.

"Betty? Listen carefully. I want you to go back to the big metal doors over there and go back under them and wait for me, can you do that?" She walked back under, and I slammed the door all the way down. I had bought the kid a few minutes.

The wizard walked towards me, slowly, confidently. I had all the time in the world to rummage through my pockets for the little clay pot I'd picked up in the Catskill Mountains. I threw it at his feet and watched the noxious green fumes billow forth, obscuring him completely. That sleeping potion would knock him out for twenty years if he so much as caught a whiff of it. Everything was still for three seconds. Then I saw a leg emerge, followed by an arm. The wizard stepped through the smoke, breathing deeply and laughing heartily. I started to panic.

He said something in Chinese, and then he was beside me, planting a foot in my gut. The impact knocked me off the loading dock, and I hit the ground with no breath left inside of me. I instinctively rolled forward, towards the concrete lip of the docks, and found both my breath and a discarded beer bottle. I smashed the glass and grabbed a handful. As I whispered the charging sequence, I could feel the glass biting into my hand. With any luck, my blood would help me with the potency.

The wizard landed without a sound and turned on me. I threw the glowing glass fragments and watched them streak unerringly towards his head. They never hit. The wizard waved a fan, and the shards melted into nothingness. I was so stunned, I didn't even see the kick. My head spun sideways, and I smelled blood in my nose. I couldn't tell if the high keening noise I heard was the onset of a concussion or Elizabeth screaming. This guy was going to kill me. I was out of fast magic. I needed time. He came at me again with a supple kick aimed at the other side of my head. I ducked under it, got to my feet, and ran like hell further down the alley.

As I ran, the meager street lights overhead and in front of me exploded and plunged the alley into darkness. Within seconds, the wizard was running beside me, first mimicking my effort, then reaching over to pinch my cheek as I ran. I stiff-armed him and he crashed into a dumpster with a howl of rage. I turned the corner and promptly regretted it. Dead end. I could hear footsteps behind me. I had no iron, no real firepower, and no hope. To my left was a large garbage can. I hid behind it.

The wizard came flying around the corner, his face twisted into a snarl. I jumped out from my hiding place and tackled him. We thrashed for a second, then he went down and I tried to get some leverage to punch him in the face. I finally managed to get my weight over him, and then he suddenly shimmered in my arms and I was holding nothing. Breathing heavily, I cautiously moved back into the dead-end and put my back to the wall. While I had the time, I used my knife to scratch a crude protective barrier between the two walls. Just as I finished, he reformed in front of me, his face a bloody mask of hate. The barrier wouldn't hold him for more than a couple of seconds, but that was all I would need. I reached into my pocket for my little talisman and slipped it over my head while he hammered against the spell wall with his fans. The barrier crackled and fell. He was five feet from me now, speaking Chinese in a sing-song fashion and holding the fans at strange angles.

I had one shot at this. I ran into him, full force, knife bared. He blocked the knife easily and whipped his fans across my face, my throat, my chest. The fans tripped through me six times in a second. The edges didn't cut flesh, but bitter cold coursed through my body, and I felt light-headed and disconnected.

Then I died.

When I came to, my talisman had exploded. It was a

simple soul-catcher, and not designed for such violent entry, but it served its purpose. However, I was in no shape to dance with him again. Even blinking hurt. The parts of my flesh that had touched the fans burned like fresh cuts. Those fans were not of this plane. I glanced down the length of my body to see the wizard walking away, his back to me. When he turned the corner, I tried moving. Nothing worked, so I laid there and quietly sang a song to the earth spirits, asking them for their protection and strength. I hoped they wouldn't be as petulant as Lynx and Raven. I kept the song going until I could stand up. This was borrowed time for me and I knew it. I moved as quickly as I could, singing the song under my breath.

The wizard was walking quickly, focused on getting to the girl. He was twenty feet from the loading docks. I knew Elizabeth was waiting for me on the other side of the door. I called upon one of the spirits to lock and hold the door. The wizard heard the metallic click and sprang forward, hammering on the doors and yanking upward on the handle. It held, but not for long. I put my hands on the ground and whispered quickly, quietly, and drew the earth magic up around me like a cloak. The energy washed over me, filling out my psychic wounds. The wizard turned, eyes wide, and went for his fans, trying to quick-draw them. I shouted the command word, and the earth magic became a column of spirits that shot from my hands and sent him into the metal doors with a thunderous crack. The spirits pinned him in place, in spite of his frenzied cries and chanting. Elizabeth screamed from behind the doors. I hobbled over to him, scribbled a permanency sigil on the blade of my knife using some of my blood, and embedded it in his throat. The spirits left all at once, and he collapsed in front of me. I took the fans and shoved them in my back pocket.

Elizabeth was still screaming, and now I could also hear gunshots. I pulled the other door up. She was crouched off to the side, head down. I dove for her and pulled her behind a crate. Half of the warehouse was on fire. I could barely make out Mi Hei through the haze, still on the stairs. The cloaking spell had worn off, and she was crouched about half-way up, emptying her gun into men as they ran into the room. With strength I didn't have, I fished out a prayer stone from my pocket and heaved it at her. It bounced off the wall and clattered to the ground. I almost caught a bullet for my trouble, but she pulled her aim just in time. I motioned for her to get to us. She waved her gun, fired three more shots, and vaulted over the railing.

She ran through the smoke, her mouth covered, and we burst out onto the loading dock with great gasping and heaving. Elizabeth was crying. I picked her up and held her as she cried. Mi Hei was bleeding and holding her side. We limped back to the car in silence. Something exploded in the warehouse, a muffled sound that sent a tremor through the ground. No telling what it was. Sirens sounded very close. Mi Hei reached into her purse and pulled out her phone. She hit a single button.

"Daddy? We need a pick-up, now." She gave the address of the warehouse, then pushed the phone closed with her jaw.

I was incredulous. "You mean, they weren't coming to get us?"

"No. I called time and temperature. Get in. I'm bleeding to death."

I looked at Elizabeth, curled up in my arms. "Good," I said.

By the time Chu's clinic treated us all for cuts, bullet

wounds, smoke inhalation, and psychic wounds, it was dawn. Michael and Kim were beyond grateful and cried and hugged both Elizabeth and me. Jiang Shui just frowned at us. Hell, I would have kept my nose out of it if Michael hadn't begged in front of the whole family for me to help them. Jiang Shui wouldn't even look at Mi Hei. She had crossed some line, in spite of our heroic effort. During all of the hubbub, he walked over to me and said, "You did a good job tonight. Here is a check for the hours you've worked, plus commission."

I looked at the check. Six thousand dollars. Enough to live on for at least three months. I pocketed it and nodded thanks. He shook his head and walked off. I didn't know it then, but I just failed a test. Jiang Shui expected me to refuse the money, since this was a family matter. I didn't quite see it that way. I used up a quantity of magic in that fight and still almost died. I also conveniently neglected to tell anyone about the fans I'd snagged.

Mi Hei caught holy hell for endangering Elizabeth and me. I caught holy hell for endangering Elizabeth and Mi Hei. Then I told them my version of what happened. Mi Hei caught a fresh batch of hell for not following my suggestion and calling for back-up.

Later, when we were alone, Chu Sheng Kai told me he was pleased with how things turned out. I asked him about possible repercussions to our little jaunt. All he said was, "We have a saying in San Cibola: 'The walls of Chinatown are high.' Not that any of it matters to Wan Fei Ying. He is now fighting his war on two fronts." I had no earthly idea what he meant. He sipped his tea contentedly, then leaned in close. "It will only get worse for you from here on. You have been seen with my family. Do you understand now what you have done?"

"Yeah, I think I do. But that's okay, I can handle myself."

"I thought you would say something like that." He passed me a thin red leather book with rice paper interiors. "Perhaps you can make some use of this." I opened the book. It was several spells and formulae, all translated into English.

"Thank you." I bowed and stood up to leave. "Chu-San? There is one other thing."

"Yes?"

"I would like to learn Chinese."

He smiled. "To aid you in your studies?"

"That. And to be able to understand the names they are calling me."

He threw his head back and laughed. "I'll see what I can do."

Family Business

When Chu Sheng Kai told me he had Fox trouble, I didn't know exactly how to take that. Now, looking down from the fire escape, it made perfect sense, although not in the way he meant it. She was beautiful. She wore a simple black outfit in keeping with her chosen activity, and even with distance and darkness, I could see that she filled the suit out in the best of ways. She had classical Chinese features that seemed to stand out on her face, like a painter's idealized picture of a courtesan. Her long, wavy black hair was pulled back into a ponytail, to keep it out of her eyes while she picked the lock on the door of my adopted father's warehouse.

It took me long enough to find her. I spent the last week showing up five minutes after she'd broken into various Red Moon businesses and them. Chu and his sons were livid. They asked me to capture her, using any and all means at my disposal, and bring her to Chu. Alive. The night before, I decided to go on the offensive and took to patrolling the darker side of Chinatown, hoping to scare her up. It was blind luck that I found her as quickly as I did.

I was loaded down with spells, having taken Chu Sheng Kai at his word. I used some standard sorcery to mask my scent completely, mute all sounds around me in a five-foot radius, and render myself invisible to dogs; as an afterthought, I tossed on something called Quickstepper in case I had to give chase. The last one was a bit of a gamble, as any hastening spell can be tricky to work. All movement you perform is sped up exponentially, but your body is unprotected by the spell. So you can punch someone and it'll more than likely kill them, but it will also shatter your arm because your fist is moving at sixty miles per hour. You can't even walk normally; you have to employ sort of a hopping tip-toe. Concentration is essential.

She was still working on that lock. No doubt a Jen Long invention. I debated the merits of capturing her right away or waiting to see what she would do. With extra caution, I navigated the fire escape to the alley and stood behind her, about fifty feet away, and watched her work. I could have nabbed her right then, while her back was turned. Something about Chu's description of the girl bothered me. He stressed that she was an actual Fox. She didn't look supernatural, but in Chinatown, that didn't mean a damn thing. Chu warned me that she would be tricky. Eventually, caution won out over just grabbing her and I decided to test her, in case she was a shape-shifter.

I pulled the trisk out of my back pocket. The handle was flat and made of wood and fit in my hand just so. Three tines were embedded in the handle like a broken comb. One tine was made of wood, one of silver, and one of iron. All I had to do was gently scrape her and see if she had a reaction to any of the materials. Proud of my decision to use my head, I crept forward and was behind her in one second. If I did this right, I could scratch the back of her neck and back up out of the way before she turned around. I slowly, cautiously, inched my hand forward, completely mindful of the amount of force I was using.

Suddenly, the air was filled with the smell of ozone, and all of the spells I'd so carefully cast earlier that night were yanked off me. It felt like someone had torn my clothes off all at once and left me standing nude in the alley. The woman gasped and turned around and looked at me like I'd come from nowhere, which, technically, was true. I was still moving slowly, completely stunned by what just happened. I dropped the trisk without thinking. She stared into my eyes for a long second, then smiled and grabbed my arm. I could only watch as she brought my forearm to her mouth and bit through my sleeve into skin and muscle. I screamed, and she let go, her mouth bloody. She winked at me and pushed me hard in the chest. I lost my footing and fell flat on my back, the wind knocked out of me. She literally ran right over me and out of the alley. I rolled over and looked up, trying to find her, but it was too late. Blood flowed freely from the bite. It hurt like a son of a bitch. With my good arm, I clawed in my pocket until I came up with a small cell phone. I flipped it open and hit autodial.

"What?" answered Mi Hei on the other end.

"Officer is down."

"Are you dying?" She almost sounded hopeful.

"No, but I've been bitten. Come get me."

"Your wish is my command, Foreigner."

She hung up. I sat up to bleed more comfortably and wonder how the hell she managed to pull that little stunt with my spells.

It took some time to patch me up. Mi Hei drove me to the Knights of Malta hospital, famous for their "don't ask, don't tell" policy. They irrigated the wound, stitched me up, gave me a tetanus shots, and sent me on my merry way with a prescription for antibiotics. The entire procedure took about two hours, and Mi Hei chastised me the whole time for having the Fox in my sights and letting her get away. Once we were driving again, Mi Hei asked, "Where to now, Great

White Hunter?"

"Home."

"You're not giving up already? It's barely midnight!"

"Do you have any idea how long those spells take to cast? If I got started now, it would be four hours at the earliest before I could go out again. Besides, I'm out of over half the shit I need to cast them. I'll go pick up some more tomorrow, then we'll try again in the evening."

"Meanwhile, this Fox continues to make an ass of the family."

"I'm sorry, but I didn't count on the spells fizzling out like that."

"Maybe you're losing your touch."

I didn't say anything to that. She stopped the car in front of my building and gave me just enough time to get clear of the door before she sped off into the night. No doubt to try and stumble across the Fox herself. Headstrong woman. I trudged up the stairs to my small flat, crawled into bed, and went right to sleep.

The morning came far too soon. This was the week before finals at UNC, and my services as a tutor would be invaluable. With effort, I forced myself to get up and get ready. I caught the bus just right and was walking across the commons, duffel bag slapping against my thigh, by 8:00 a.m. I popped into the administration office to check my mail, just in case I had missed a letter from the college or the few business contacts that I don't want to give my home address to for one reason or another. Polly was at the receptionist's desk, slowly pecking out something on her computer.

"Hey, Polly," I said, breezing by the compartmentalized wooden cabinet to my mailbox in the corner. Faculty had little plastic engraved plaques; TA's and guests had their name written in magic marker on masking tape. A single white envelope was waiting for me.

"Hey, Sam. Missed you last week. Oh, that reminds me, someone was asking for you."

"Really? Who?"

Polly continued staring vacantly at the screen, her long brown hair occasionally falling in her eyes, only to be removed by a quick horse-like toss of her head. Apparently, if she lost contact with the keyboard, all of the words on the screen would go away. "Don't know. He said he was an old friend of yours, come a long way to see you."

How odd, I thought. Who else knew I was here, besides the Armitage Foundation? "Did he leave a name or number?"

"No. Asked for yours, though. When I wouldn't give it to him he got pissed off...e...r...v...i...c...e. Got it."

"What did he look like?" The letter wasn't from Armitage. The postmark was San Cibola. Typed address.

"Taller than you, kinda thin. Blonde hair. Kinda round head."

"So, in other words, anybody." The letter was probably from the mystery man, then.

"Yeah."

"Thank you, Polly, you've been helpful." I left her to her pecking and walked to the study hall.

The students kept me late. Not that I minded, the extra hours just meant more money. I still felt a little woozy from the bite and the antibiotics. About the time I started to get irritable and cranky, I realized I had worked through lunch, so I shooed the kids away and hopped the bus for Chinatown. Zhu's Noodle Hut was fast becoming my comfort food when I'd had a hard day of it. Right then, I needed a bucket of lo mein and chicken before I did anything else. On the way, I opened the letter from my mystery man. Inside was a single sheet of paper, a typewritten sentence spaced neatly in the middle of the page:

YOU WILL PAY FOR YOUR CRIMES.

Ah, students, I thought, wadding the paper up. I tossed the note into my duffel bag to show to the dean of students later. Probably some kid who got a bad grade in Freshman Comp and thought I should've written the paper for him. At least, that's what I tried to believe, as I thought about who I might've angered since my wanderings in California.

I stepped off the bus, stunned. The cart was there, but not Zhu. He was always there, twenty-four seven. Now, no Zhu. My stomach was screaming for food, and I felt a headache coming on. I walked to Mama Wang's instead and let her pamper me. After stuffing myself on dumplings and fried rice, my stomach shut up, but my head still hurt. I walked back to my apartment for a quick nap before chaining myself to the lab for the rest of the day.

I opened the door to Benny's Pagoda House and said, "Hey, Benny," automatically. When I got no answer, I walked back down the stairs and looked at the front desk. No Benny. Weird, I thought. He's always here to greet everyone. It didn't make any sense. I walked the three flights to my room slowly, pondering the significance of both Zhu and Benny being gone from their usual posts.

Before I could turn the doorknob to my flat, it swung open of its own volition. Surprise gave way to shock as I stepped into my room. It had been cleansed. I could feel it. Completely and spiritually, according to the rites of consecration. No witchcraft or black arts could be done from here for at least a week, maybe more. I went through the room; nothing was taken or missing. I rooted through my duffel bag, relieved that I thought to take it with me, and pulled out a sprig of fairy's breath. I said a little cantrip and waved it around in the air. It wilted and turned to dust in my fingers. So much for that. Someone had very thoughtfully fucked with my conjuring abilities and left. Then I remembered my self-opening door.

I stepped back out into the hall and felt a chill crawl up my spine that made my heart race. Something was in the hall with me, and it had to be Benny. He opened the door for me to show me that he was still around. I just couldn't see him. I'd been supernaturally blinded. A vicious spell, makes the eye gloss right over everything not of this earth, even readily visible entities like Zhu and Benny. I had learned a blinding spell from a rogue sorcerer named Larkin. His specialty was dirty work, and he used the blind spell to get close to other sorcerers in order to surprise them with a magical ambush. It was the only thing that spell was used for. Someone had it out for me.

After calling in sick for the rest of the day, I caught the SCAT to Arcadia and took a bus to the Pocket Shop. Ian Rosewood was behind the counter tinkering with a watch when I walked in. "Hi, Sam," he said without looking up. The place was empty.

"Ian, how you doing?" Ian recently suffered a heart attack and forced all of his regular patrons to deal with his partner, Deedle, for the week he was recuperating. I'm not sure who got the worse end of the deal, us or him.

"Fine, knock wood." He did so.

"I need to stock up." I said.

"Help yourself."

"Thanks." I walked back to the back wall with full shelves running the length of the store, took a quick look around to see if anyone was watching, and flipped the catch that turned a section of shelves into a door. Inside was a well-stocked assortment of magical devices, wards, spell components, and charms. Ian's selection wasn't the most complete in the city, but it was slanted towards professionals that did field work. I went slowly through his stock, completely refilling my arsenal. On a whim, I grabbed Ian's last garland of nightshade, that being the key ingredient in a blinding spell. If I could figure out who was messing with me, then maybe I could turn the tables on them.

I brought my armload of goods up to the counter and let Ian sort through it all. He cheerfully rang everything up, obviously pleased with the amount of money I was about to hand him. He fingered the nightshade thoughtfully. "Damnedest thing," he said.

"What's that?" I asked.

"Well, I stock a lot of stuff back there that I never used, would never use, you know what I mean? I try to be complete."

"Right."

"This," he said, indicating the nightshade, "is hardly ever used. I stock it, throw the old stuff out, get more, and keep it fresh all year. I maybe sell two of these things in a year."

"Yeah, so?"

"This is the second one I've sold this week."

My heart sped up. "Really? Anyone you know?"

"Nope. New guy. At least, I've never seen him before."

"What did he look like?" I winced, hearing the desperation in my voice, but Ian didn't catch it.

"Taller than you, blonde hair. Kinda skinny. He knew what he was talking about. Said he knew about my special stock, so I let him buy some stuff."

"Okay, Ian, without getting you involved in my business too much, I think this guy is gunning for me. Can you remember what else he bought?"

Ian put his forearms on the counter and leaned in. "Now, why would I want to go and stick my neck out for you like that, Mr. Bowen?"

"See that total in the register? I'll double it."

Ian chuckled. "I was kidding. I can see you're serious, though. Let me see..." He rummaged under the counter and came up with a scrap of paper. He scribbled a list of things down, pausing at the end. "I think that's it. Come to think of it, you two have the same tastes."

I took the list and handed Ian his money. "Listen, if he comes back in, can you tell me what he buys? I need as much information on this guy as I can get." Ian looked doubtful. "Please?"

"Okay, but only because you're such a good customer here. And as long as you respect my one rule of engagement where this matter is concerned."

"What's that?"

"Don't duel in my store, or I'll kick your teeth in."

I wrote down my number. I still needed some dirt on this guy. He was close to me, I was sure of that. I just needed to ask people the right questions. Questions. Suddenly, inspiration struck me. Spiritualism 101. On the way back to Chinatown, I stopped at the discount store and bought some chalk and a small chalkboard.

Back at my building, I walked around the desk in the front lobby and sat down on the dusty stool. Without disturbing anything, I set the chalkboard and chalk on the front counter. With no real hope that this lame stunt would work, I said, "Benny, I know you are here. I can't see you or hear you because someone is working powerful magic against me. I need your help. Will you help me?"

I held my breath and waited. For a minute, nothing moved.

Then the chalk leapt to life and squeaked out some marks on the board.

"YES SAM."

"Has anyone been in my room in the past day or two?"

Benny wrote, "I DON'T KNOW."

"Okay, what about recently? Anyone strange hanging around?"

"NO."

That wasn't a good question. What did Benny define as strange? If I wanted information, I would have to be specific. "Benny, have you rented any rooms to anyone lately?"

"YES."

"What did he look like?"

I watched the chalk start to sketch a head, then erase it. It sketched the beginning of a face, then erased it. Benny wrote "SHIT," then erased it. I swore, too. I could have used a visual. Benny wrote, "LIKE YOU. BLONDE HAIR. GOATEE. TALL."

It figured. Same guy. "What apartment did you give him?"

"401."

The bastard was right on top of me. I erased Benny's scribbles and said, "Benny, I'm going to go get some answers. Will you be a lookout for me?"

"OKAY."

"Thanks."

I left the slate and chalk on the desk and ran up the stairs, pausing only long enough to toss my stuff in my room, then continued up to the fourth floor. After no one answered my knocking, I tried the door. It was locked, but that was a minor obstacle. I grasped the doorknob and pulled with all of my weight in the opposite direction, toward the hinges. There was a muffled click, and the bolt snapped free of the slot.

God bless Benny and his shoddy workmanship. Or this guy's overconfidence. I had replaced the lock on my door during the first month I lived here, and a fat lot of good it did me. The door swung open, and I cautiously stepped inside. The room was furnished like mine. In addition to the rickety table and chair, bed and dresser, and feeble recliner, the mystery man had three suitcases with airport tags on them and a ratty-looking backpack. I methodically tossed the room, looking for something that would tell me who I was dealing with. The nametags were missing from the luggage and he left no identification anywhere. The backpack was full of spell-casting paraphernalia. I noticed we carried a lot of the same materials.

Okay, I thought, if we're so alike, where would I hide my important papers, the things I didn't want anyone to find? Well, I was pretty sure he didn't have a wall safe, and it would have to be some place reasonably secure. Unfortunately, there wasn't any place secure in Benny's pagoda. I pulled the throw rug aside and looked at the floor for loose boards. Sure enough, he had sawed a four-board panel out, about a foot and a half square. Benny will be pissed, I thought, as I knelt down and pried the trapdoor up.

Paydirt. In the space between the boards was a small stack of books, the top one clearly marked "Journal." Copycat. I started for it and was summarily punched so hard in the stomach that I landed on my ass.

Something was moving in the room. I had a vague impression of the air being displaced in front of me, nothing more. He apparently had a guardian of some sort, and with me being magically blinded, I had no way of knowing what I was up against. The books were about five feet away from me, but with an invisible something between us, I wasn't going to chance it. The sentinel was magic, which meant that right then, I was at a distinct disadvantage. It was time to get out of there.

I left the apartment and walked quickly to the SCAT station and caught the downtown train. Ten minutes later, I was safely seated at the bar in Doyle's, one eye on my double bourbon and the other on the entrance behind me via the mirror behind the bar. Silas leaned in, flipping his ever-present bar rag.

"Evening, Sam. You look like a man in need."

"Silas," I said, never taking my eye off the door in the mirror, "do me a favor, will you? Cut me off at two of these, but keep something that looks like bourbon coming instead. And can you get me a meatloaf sandwich? I may be here a while."

Silas grinned. "Coming up." He slid back down the bar to effortlessly, quietly, tend to his other customers. I relaxed slightly to watch the doormen. Patrons came and went. Some regulars came in through the private entrance that led to the rest of the club. But all newbies would have to come through that door. There was no way around that. I waited. My sandwich came, and I ate it mechanically. The third time Silas refilled my glass, it was watered down Coke instead of bourbon. Thirty minutes went by.

Finally, I noticed a slight altercation at the door. Good thing, too. I was on my tenth flat Coke. I chanced a direct look at my shadow. He was tall and blonde with slightly long hair and feathered bangs. The veins on his arms stood out as he gesticulated wildly. He had a neat little goatee, dyed a darker color than his hair. The Italian bouncer watching the door was unfazed. Then the man leaned in close and whispered something to him. The bouncer considered it for a moment, then finally nodded him through the door. I got a brief but clear look at his face before it passed into shadow

142

and then I had to quickly drop my eyes. He had spotted me. I polished off two more Cokes, winked at Silas, and paid my tab. Silas asked me in a voice that was exactly one notch too loud, "Sam, you want me to call you a cab?"

"No thanksh." I waved him off.

He nodded. "Be careful, then."

"Shure."

I walked unsteadily to the door, my eyes on nothing but the door. I could feel his look as I crossed the room, but I didn't dare return it. Once outside, I again walked quickly to the SCAT station and went straight back to Chinatown. On the way back, I replayed his face and tried to see if I knew it. There was something familiar about him. I had seen him before, I was certain of that. Looking at him made me feel very uncomfortable, like I'd forgotten something important. I thought about it until my stop, then pushed it out of my mind and ran back to my building.

I said hi to Benny, who banged the slate on his desk for a reply, then bolted up to my room, locked the door behind me, and got to work. I unpacked my fresh spell components and laid a Protective Rune on the door. It wasn't very strong, but it would be enough to slow or stop him until I could cold-cock him a good one.

I sat down in the recliner and waited. After an hour, when it became apparent that he didn't follow me directly home, I went to the bathroom. I came back out, a little disappointed that I couldn't lay my hands on him, and took up my post in the chair. Eventually, I fell asleep.

I am some sort of dog, and I am being hunted, driven through a forest by men on horseback. I can smell them, along with my fear, which has a sharp, metallic smell, like blood. I dodge arrows and stones, but they are coming closer and closer, and I am getting tired. A Chinese man appears in the path before me and beckons. "Come here, little one. Quickly!"

I jump into his arms, and he dives into the hedges on the side of the trail. The men all ride by, the hooves of the horses cracking the ground beneath them. I turn to the man, and he looks at me and says, "You don't know your own nature. You are smarter than you think."

I ask, "Why are they trying to kill me?"

He says, "Because you deserve to die." *His hands tighten around my throat. I am clawing with my back legs, trying to rake flesh, but his grip is tight.* "Honorless thief!" *he hisses. I can't breathe any longer...*

I woke up in the chair, head cocked sideways, half twisted around in my own shirt. The rune on the door was still in place. Nothing was disturbed. I spent an uncomfortable night for nothing.

After a long, hot shower, most of the cricks in my neck had been reduced to a dull throb. I needed breakfast, coffee, and a change of scenery. All of this waiting around was making me skittish.

The best thing about rune magic is that it's all very sensitive. Even before I pulled my door open, I saw the rune shudder. As the door opened, it hit me that something was coming for me, and I let go of the doorknob, caught the doorframe, and pushed myself backwards, away from the door into the room. Thundering hoof beats made the walls vibrate, and I saw a huge spectral horse gallop through the hallway and do considerable damage to the walls and doorframe as it passed by. The noise faded, and I heard doors open all through the building. I stuck my head out into the hall. There was a set of fused horseshoes lying on the floor, by the stairs at the end of the hall. A crude gate. A matching set was arranged on the opposite end of the hallway. That horse had my name on it. It would have trampled me to death or carried me back to where ever it came from. Pieces of the mystery were falling together quickly. I left the building and made a beeline for UNC to check my hunch.

I called the Armitage Foundation from the teacher's lounge and talked to my advisor, Professor Daniel Galloway. We chatted briefly, and I had to bite my tongue from blurting out what I wanted from him. Finally, I gently asked him if he could do a field agent cross-section for me. I outlined what I needed from him, and he told me he'd call me back in an hour. It took almost two.

"Sam? Daniel."

"Hey, did you get it for me?"

"Yeah, I did. Listen, Sam, it's, uh..."

"What's wrong?"

"First of all, we never had this talk, you know what I'm saying?"

"Loud and clear," I said. "Why is that?"

Galloway was uncharacteristically nervous. "Well, I cross-checked your check points in Mexico and Texas, and to be honest, I was a little surprised. I mean, we have agents all over the place, but..."

"I'll wager more than one of us went through Bastrop, though."

"Yeah, you were right about that. Listen, Sam, I don't know what's going on, but you understand, the Foundation does not condone combat dueling of any sort..."

"Dan, what are you talking about? Who else went through Bastrop?"

There was an audible pause. He sighed heavily, and said, "Travis Caufield."

•

I stood outside my building, sick to my stomach. Benny's Pagoda House looked strange and distant to me. I couldn't go in, and I didn't really want to. He would have something waiting for me. Travis would. Of all the people to track me down and find me, it had to be him. I was completely cornered. He wouldn't give up, either. I was completely out of options. Well, not completely, but I was reluctant to use the ace up my sleeve. So I stood outside my building and stared at it, hoping for an answer that didn't involve my patron. After about an hour of stewing in my own juices, I hadn't come up with any answers. I adjusted my shoulder strap and started walking. The walk to Chu's house was just over a mile, and I was determined to take my time.

The walk felt good to me. I knew where I was going, knew every shop along the street. Vendors that I frequented caught my eye and nodded to me. I was becoming a part of the neighborhood. After three blocks, I became aware of another set of footsteps. This was it, then. I kept moving through the crowded streets, like a shark, making no sudden moves but keeping my momentum. In a short time he caught up to me, matching my pace easily with longer legs.

"Travis Caufield," I said, my mind racing, "Been a long time, huh?" Up close, he looked pretty bad. His hair was obviously dyed blonde, the goatee betraying his natural mousy color. Back when I knew him, years ago, he was three years older than me and looked like Ichabod Crane. Never a handsome man to begin with, he now looked like he'd spent a lot of time on the road, face first. Premature wrinkles showed around his eyes and mouth. His eyes were hollow and bloodshot. I knew what those signs meant. Black magic. He had been walking in the shadows for a while.

"Mr. Bowen."

"It's Sam, Travis, Sam. I lived in your home, remember?"

"I remember, Sam. Let's cut the crap, okay? You know why I'm here."

"No, I really don't, Travis. This is some old, settled shit you're bringing up here."

He walked beside me, his hands in his pockets. He had an imp with him, presumably his invisible guardian from yesterday. It hovered between us, a foot-long humanoid with a barbed tail and wings. It leered at me as we walked.

"Who settled it, Sam?"

"The police, for one."

"That's bullshit. Don't talk to me like I'm Norman, Sam."

"You used to be Norman. What happened to you, anyway?"

"My sister died!"

"Don't shout, I know. I was there. And get that fucking imp out of my face or I'll hammer it flat."

"Huh. How pleasant." He made a clicking sound with his tongue and the imp retreated to his opposite shoulder, where it lifted its tail and waved its ass at me while braying high-pitched laughter.

"Thank you. You want to tell me what you want with me?"

"Isn't it obvious? I want you dead. A life for a life." He clicked his tongue. "It's a shame that cat burglar didn't finish you off the other night. Would've saved us both a lot of trouble."

That explained what happened to my sorceries. "So, this is some revenge game, then? I'm surprised, really. Does your father know about this?"

"Yeah, he knows. He didn't think it was a good idea at first, but I talked him into showing me some stuff. I got into the Armitage Foundation a couple of years later on Dad's reputation and proceeded to piece together your trail and follow you."

"This is wrong, Travis. You can't really believe I had anything to do with..."

"Sam, my father is one of the foremost folklore historians in the world. Did you really think he wouldn't find out about your family curse? I mean, shit, Sam, he knows everyone at Armitage!"

Ever since the Armitage Foundation asked me for my personal occult history, I've regretting giving it to them. The records are sealed but can be opened if you grease the right palms. Or ask the right people the right questions. "No, I figured he'd know about it, but I don't think that had anything to do with Harriet's death."

"You're serious, right? Now, let's just look at the facts for a minute, okay? Everyone in your family is dead. You said yourself you think the curse is a love and marriage curse, designed to keep you from having children, and that it will eventually kill the bloodline."

"Yeah, I thought so then, but it's just speculation. I don't really know—"

"Point number two. My sister was trampled to death by her own horse. The horse she raised from a colt. That horse never threw her, never hurt her before. Suddenly, six months after you two fall in love, the horse goes berserk and throws and tramples her."

"Travis, you're making a big assumption."

"Am I? That horse never recovered. She moped around waiting for Harriet to show up. She got sick and died, and no one knows why."

"What a load of—"

"My father did some tests and found that the horse had been touched by the a magical energy of some sort that he couldn't identify. So, therefore, me showing up here and demanding my pound of flesh should make perfect sense to you."

"You're nuts." That last piece of info shook me up a bit. If I lived through this, I resolved to try and make peace with Dr. Caufield so I could find out what the results of his tests were. "No, really, you're frigging crazy. You followed me for nine years to get your revenge? Why not just walk up to me with a gun and blow my head off?"

"If I use sorcery, Norman will never convict me. Besides, you had at least two years and a couple of disciplines on me, there was no way I could get close to you with a gun. That's why I decided to follow you and learn what you learned. It's funny, too, Sam. You know you've pissed off a lot of people in your little walkabout. Some of the folks I visited had some really interesting things to say about you."

"Really." Here it comes, I thought.

"Oh yeah. The Derrington sisters, for example, were under the impression that you were interested in becoming an initiate in the Order of the Yellow Circle. So they gave you some pretty powerful spells, and then you were gone the next day."

"That's not quite how I remember it."

"No, it wouldn't be, would it? Then there's Hans Van Gulick. Remember him? I think he called you the 'last great hope for geomancy.' That is, until you ran out on him and took his spell books with him. He's still got a bounty on those books, you know. Then there was Vasquez and Elario from Texas, Gideon Chessler in Florida, and that medicine man from the Navajo reservation..."

"Yeah, okay, I get the point. So, what, you've added their little gripes to your own private vendetta?"

"No, but a lot of them were only too glad to give me

counterspells and wards to interrupt the things they taught you. Others pointed me to some diametrically opposed wizards. It was pretty rewarding."

I had taken all from him that I intended. It was time to see if he could be rattled. "That Ghost-horse gag you pulled was a big tip-off. I learned that type of summoning in— "

"Bastrop, Texas, I know. It was clumsy, but I was shooting for poetic justice," he said proudly.

"Yeah, you're a regular knight in shining armor. Look at you. I didn't recognize you because you dyed your hair. You even dress like me now. Face it, Travis. You want to be me. And I think I know why."

"Preposterous." I heard the tension in his voice.

"You never liked me, were always jealous of me, because deep down inside, you wanted her for yourself. She never liked you much, and I suspected it was because you were hung up on her in some weird way. That's some sick shit, Travis, and you can't let it go even after all this time. Well, this sympathetic magic bit you've got going is not going to be able to show you what she felt like in my arms, so you might as well go on home. My memories of Harriet are my own, and I intend to keep them that way."

His lip quivered between anger and grief. "You-you-bastard! How dare you?" he sputtered.

It was time to press the advantage, to see just how far off his game I could push him. "God, Travis, if you're really mad, just take a swing at me. But don't posture. You look even more pathetic."

The quivering lip went away. His eyes became cold. "You deserve your curse. Every bit of it. I'm glad your family is dead. The sooner you die, the sooner your miserable line can get to the task of becoming topsoil for my children."

Shit. I was hoping to rattle him enough so I could sprint.

I don't think he realized what our destination was, and we were getting close. "So, you want a duel, then?"

"No, I just want you dead."

"Can I give you a piece of advice?"

"I don't think you have anything I don't know, but sure."

"Never get up close to kill a man when you can do it from a mile away." I elbowed him in the stomach and the face and ran like hell. I hoped the pain would distract him, but I wasn't counting on it. The pain wouldn't have distracted me.

I heard him say something, and then the imp was in front of me, laughing and trying to sting my face. I grabbed my duffel bag by the ends and pushed it into the imp like a nylon shield. It squealed and dropped out of sight. Something in the bag must not have agreed with it. In the back of my head, I made a note to figure out what it was later and write it up for the foundation.

Chu Sheng Kai's estate was about a hundred yards away. The guards saw me coming and dropped into a fighting crouch. I jerked a thumb over my shoulder and gasped, "That guy back there is trying to kill me." I slid to a stop just inside the gate and turned to look. Travis trailed behind me by no more than two hundred feet. The imp shakily followed him.

They drew pistols and pointed them at Travis. Travis smiled, and a ball of flame shot from his head and caught up their guns and fused them together. They didn't stop, reaching for their back-up weapons as another ball of flame shot between them heading straight for me. I threw up my hands, but the flame never reached me. Chu had a strong magical shield around his house, and apparently I was just inside of it. The energy arced in every direction and dissipated. Travis swore, but now a new pair of guns were trained on him by the two security men. He began another spell.

Footsteps rushed by me in twos and threes. Reinforcements. I breathed a sigh of relief. The guards would cut Travis down and remove this problem forever. As I watched the stand-off, Chu appeared at my side. "Ya Shen, what is going on?"

"Master Chu," I said, "it is a very long story."

"Then make it a short one." Travis now had a dozen weapons pointed at him. The guards were screaming in Chinese, and Travis was screaming in Lemurian and gesticulating wildly. The imp hid behind his master and gave the guards the finger.

"He wants to kill me because he thinks I had something to do with his sister's death."

"Did you?"

"No. I was in love with her."

"If that is your reason for lack of involvement, it is a poor one. One can be in love and still kill their lover."

Arcs of yellow electricity spun around Travis' upraised hands. The guards were shouting furiously. Chu stepped in between them, and half the pistols dropped immediately. Travis stopped chanting, the yellow energy evaporating as he stared at the sixty year-old Chinese man in a red silk smoking jacket and bare feet. Chu raised his hand in a dismissive gesture, and the guards pulled back. Everyone holstered their weapons.

"Who are you, who would chase my adopted son to my house and slaughter him in front of his family?"

Travis dropped his arms. "Travis Caufield, sorcerer and agent for the Armitage Foundation."

Chu was unimpressed with the pedigree. "I am Chu Sheng Kai. This is my home. These are my children. If you have a grievance with one of them, then you must come to me and we will discuss it." Chu beckoned with his hand. He wanted Travis to take tea with him.

Travis didn't believe it, either. "I don't trust you. You'll get me inside and kill me."

Chu's shoulders tightened and contracted, then he relaxed them. "I give you my word that no harm will come to you as long as you are within 300 feet of my property."

Travis scratched his goatee and kicked his foot against the curb. "Okay. That's fair."

Chu motioned us both inside. I walked ahead of Travis, not looking back. I had no idea what Chu was planning. As it turned out, I'm sorry I went to him at all.

We got inside the house, and Chu ushered Travis into the sitting room. I started to follow, but he cut me off. "I will speak to him alone, Ya Shen. Go wait in the library."

"Sir, I'd rather not. He wants me dead, and I'd just as soon have this over with."

"Then wait out here. But I will speak to him alone." He shut the door in my face. I sat down on the floor of the entrance hall, legs crossed, and tried like hell to figure out what they were saying to one another.

They spoke for over an hour. My legs fell asleep waiting for them to come out. When the door finally opened, Travis came out first, shoulders slumped. He looked at me with an expression that I to this day cannot fathom. As near as I can figure, it was a mixture of triumph and pity. Then he was gone out the front door and Chu was standing over me.

"We will talk in my office, please."

I was in real trouble.

With Chu ensconced behind his massive desk and me in the wing-backed leather chair, he turned on me with an anger I've never seen. "How could you bring him here? To my home! This is not my affair, and you have made it my affair by bringing him here, Ya Shen."

"Hey, whoa, I wasn't wanting you to jump in the middle of this..."

"Yes, Sam, you did. That is why you came here, seeking sanctuary. You knew the Jen Long would protect you, and if not them, then me. You are shameless!"

"Okay, I was coming here to keep him from killing me, but I never asked you to get involved."

"And what would you have me do, Sam? Do nothing and have him tear through my loyal guards? Or cause a public disturbance that would reach the newspapers? Or maybe I should have let him kill my adopted son."

"I hadn't thought about that." I confessed.

"No, of course not. You haven't thought very much about this whole situation. Did it ever occur to you that his position against you may be completely legitimate?"

Something told me not to lie to him at that moment. I met his gaze. "Yeah, I've thought about it."

Chu nodded in satisfaction. "And what did you decide once you had considered it?"

"Well, I didn't want to hurt anyone else, so I've more or less stayed away from any potential romantic partners for the past eight years. I mean, I still don't know how this goddamn curse works. Maybe I am the focus for it."

"Don't turn this around so that you feel sorry for yourself. You have disappointed me greatly. Not only have you endangered the lives of your adopted family, but you have taken advantage of my resources, and you still have not lived up to your part of our agreement and apprehended the Fox-Spirit for me."

I stood up. "So what do you want? You want me to go, is that it?"

"No. I want you to think about your actions and what they have done to other people. In your greed for the truth, you have hurt many people. Those people would now do you an evil turn, to restore balance to their spirit. This will drive you out of balance, and you will have to atone for what you've done."

I wasn't buying any of this. "Okay, I'll think about it."

"Why don't you think about it while you hunt the Fox?"

"Sure. Right."

"I do not wish to see you for some time."

That hurt more than if he'd punched me in the stomach.

"Fine." I stood up and walked to the door. "For what it's worth, I never meant to hurt you. I was just doing what I could to solve my problem."

"I don't think you meant any harm. That you haven't once thought about someone other than yourself is what saddens me."

"So, what do I do about Travis?" I asked him.

"I took care of it."

"How?"

Chu smiled. "I showed him the future. I showed him what would happen if he continued on his course to kill you. Then I showed him what would happen if he let you live. Think on his decision, and realize it's not too late to change your fate." He turned away from the door.

I walked home in silence, pissed at the world. I kept working everything Chu said around until my rationalizations for my actions made sense. Mostly, I thought about the look in Travis' eyes. He saw something of my fate, and I didn't like it one little bit.

As I neared my building, I could see Zhu hawking noodles at his appointed corner. My sight was back. I should have been thrilled, but at the time, all I wanted was the bourbon that waited for me in my magically-sterile flat.

Bad Blood

I stumbled into the lobby of my apartment building, leaving my left boot on the stoop in the process. The tear in my shirtsleeve caught on the handle of the door, ripping it completely free from my arm. Another turtleneck ruined. I was running out of work clothes fast.

Benny Wan took one look at me and opened his mouth to speak. I silenced him with an upraised hand. The steps leading up to my apartment were a million miles away. I made for them, walking unsteadily. Something ground together unpleasantly in my left knee.

As I dragged myself upstairs, Benny stuck his head through the wall, his face following me as I climbed.

"Still hunting the Fox?"

I nodded.

"Still no luck, huh?"

I shook my head.

"Getting any closer?"

I held up my clenched fist for his inspection. "I got a handful of her hair tonight."

Benny clucked his tongue at me. "Not a nice thing to do."

"Who do you think got the worse of it?" I asked him, indicating my ruined clothes. "Benny, I've seen her so much this past week, I'm starting to think of our little outings as dates. When I finally get my hands on her, I think I'm going to kiss her first, then I'm going to kick her perfect little ass."

"You're bleeding." He pointed at my face. I touched my nose and my fingers came away with two maroon dots on the tips.

"Yeah, I've been getting nose bleeds a lot lately. Haven't gotten them before."

Benny clucked his tongue again. "Bad magic. Be careful, Sam." He faded back into the wall. Benny was always pretty cryptic like that with me. He loved to subtly remind me that he knew more about the goings on of Chinatown than I did.

I finally made it to my flat, let myself in, and walked straight to the shower, shedding clothes as I went. The shower knocked all of the dirt and most of the kinks out of my body. I watched the water run off me in brown, gray and red rivulets. Halfway through it all I remembered the hair in my hand and gingerly wrapped the tangled wad in a dry washcloth. That would be my ticket to finding her, I thought. I stood under the hot spray for another ten minutes, then trudged to my bed and collapsed.

The phone rang and wouldn't stop. I was determined to ignore it, but Ms. Tipplethwaite in 303 wasn't. She started banging on my wall with something heavy, most likely her prized cast iron skillet, and screaming, "Meester Bowen, you answer your phone this instant!"

I was too tired to recall that cantrip for thickening a person's tongue so that they couldn't speak, so I answered the phone mechanically while I searched my memory for the spell.

"H'lo?"

"Ah Sam, I was about to give up and assume that you had started your day like the rest of the world. How nice to be consistently surprised by your antics."

Alex Crowe. Great. "Alex," I said, straightening up with a wince. "What time is it?"

"It's exactly ten-thirty seven, young Mister Bowen."

"Jesus. Well, Alex, I can assure you that I've only had about five hours of sleep. I'm not indulging, here, just because school is out." Ms. Tipplethwaite continued to bang with her skillet. I slapped the wall in answer to her incessant clamor.

Alex made a noise in the back of his throat. "No doubt some interesting occult cipher has your attention." He continued without letting me speak. "Sam, are you free for lunch today? At the house?"

"Uh, sure. What's up?" More banging and screeching from the other side of the wall

"I have a matter of some...importance to discuss..." he sighed. "Listen, it's about Jennifer. Can you be here at eleven-thirty?"

"Sure, Doc. I'll see you soon."

"Fine." He hung up.

I heard the thump again and leaned into the wall, cupping my hands like a megaphone. "Ms. Tipplethwaite, I've got it!" I yelled.

She thumped the wall a final time. "Well! There's no need for that kind of noise."

She was damn lucky I forgot that cantrip.

Alex and Sophie's daughter, Jennifer, was only a couple of years younger than me, and was an absolute knockout. The fates were kind and gave her as little of her father and as much of her mother as genetically possible. Unfortunately, the trade-off for all of that natural beauty was the worst luck in the world with her personal relationships. I saw Jennifer date a couple of fast-talking types in red convertibles who used her for sex. I watched her come home more than once covered in bruises. She even brought a woman home once, which gave Sophie fits. Jennifer had spent so much time in therapy that she could diagnose other people's problems (with great accuracy) inside of five minutes. Then she married Robert Stonehill, a fellow Neighbor more or less in the same line of work as me, who somehow forgot to mention to her that he had two other wives. Sure, they lived apart from each other, separated by dimensional barriers, but marriage is marriage. Alex got the whole thing annulled and somehow managed to keep it quiet. That was last year. Jen hadn't gotten much better since then. Alex tried to set us up a couple of times, but I'd always managed to avoid it. She needed me in her life like a shark needs a steak knife.

Now Alex wanted to talk to me about something involving his daughter. Another favor, most likely. I hoped it wasn't more rough stuff. I just didn't have the strength, and frankly, I was a little too old to be beating up her current bad-idea-for-a-suitor.

I took a taxi to get there, not wanting to be late. Most people would have worn a jacket, or at least khakis, when doing lunch at Dr. Crowe's house, but I was something of a special exception and could get away with blue jeans and a nice pullover shirt. Sophie answered the door and greeted me with a hug, but I could see in her eyes that she was worried about something. She let me in, and I smelled the familiar odors of Alex's pipe and Sophie's garlic-strewn kitchen. Together we walked through the sitting room where a selection of the Crowe library stood impressively against one wall, the living room with more of the Crowe library and various object d'art from around the world, and the study, where the only books on display were the ones Alex himself had written. When we finally walked into the sparsely decorated dining room, I spied Alex sitting at the end of the long, dark table, pouring a glass of wine from the carafe in front of him. He had on his tweed sweater with the patches on the sleeves, covering a plain white oxford shirt. His jeans and loafers were carefully worn. Alex had a bad habit of running his hand through the distinguished gray mane of hair on his head in an effort to smooth it down. It never worked. Lines of concern creased his tanned face, but he put on a smile for me and stood up as I entered.

"Sam."

"Alex." We shook hands warmly. I took the seat next to him while Sophie melted into the kitchen. He scooted the glass of wine in front of me and I took a sip. "Okay, what's up?"

Alex waved his hand at me. "Please, let's at least make an effort to have a normal conversation. First, tell me what you are working on that has you keeping such late hours?"

"As much as I'd like to tell you about it, I can't. It's personal business for Chu Sheng Kai."

Crowe nodded. "Ah. I see. Well, it's nice to know your loyalty is still above reproach." He smiled wryly at me. "Then perhaps I'll just launch into my tale. I suppose I should tell you as a matter of routine that this is private, personal family business."

"Understood. As always."

"Thank you, Sam. Actually, I knew I could trust you. You're the only one I can turn to who understands Jennifer's...history."

Sophie brought in dishes of roast chicken breast, pasta in marinara sauce, steamed vegetables, and bread. She patted my shoulder as she walked back to the kitchen and we lost ourselves in the food for a few minutes. Finally, Dr. Crowe folded his napkin, refilled his glass, and started to talk.

"I don't have to tell you about Jennifer's notorious lack of coping skills, a gift from her mother's side of the family, no doubt," he said with a wince. "Well, she's been fairly unhinged since this whole thing with Stonehill and the marriage and so forth." He gave me an even glance. "Sorry again about sending him to you. I basically tried to cut a deal to insure that he wouldn't come around again. I didn't mean to involve you."

Alex had recommended me to Robert Stonehill to do some legwork for a case he was working on. The incident ended in me almost getting my head pulled off by Morrigan, the former Celtic goddess of war. It wasn't until after all of it that I found out about Stonehill's involvement with Jennifer. As soon as he had paid me, I severed my ties with him, which left us on less than friendly terms. Realistically, the choice between the Crowe family and a bigamist, Neighbor or not, was no choice at all.

"It's okay," I said, still eating. "I got paid pretty good for the work, so it wasn't so bad. All things considered, it was probably the easiest job I'd done in a while."

Dr. Crowe nodded absently. "Well, Jennifer was reaching out for something, anything. She's been on this religious kick the last few months. Wouldn't tell us anything about it, but she seemed happier. Then one night about two weeks ago, she came in late. I heard her moving around in her room, and then she left again. She hasn't been back since."

I stopped eating. "Not at all?"

"No phone call, no letter, nothing." Alex leaned in. "Listen, I know this isn't exactly your field, but do you think you could look into this?"

"Alex, if she's been gone this long, you need the cops."

He leaned back. "Absolutely not. I can't involve the

police. Not about this. It would destroy me. Sophie doesn't see it my way, of course."

"Sometimes, I think she's the smart one in this house. I don't want to be the doomsayer here, but what if she's in trouble?"

His eyes flashed. "Then I would hope that you would get her out of trouble, Mr. Bowen."

I spent the day at the Crowe house, talking to Sophie at great length about what Jennifer was into for the past three months. She had apparently met someone in her Survivors of Abusive Relationships therapy group named Emily Brown. They became friends, although Alex and Sophie never met her. Through Emily, Jennifer found out about an organization called "Herself." It was a woman's only empowerment group. That's when Sophie noticed the change in Jennifer. She seemed more positive, more strong. More self-assured. Jennifer would only give vague answers to questions about the group. Dr. Crowe thought it was a cult. Sophie didn't know what to think.

I checked out Jennifer's room and found only one thing that might be able to help me: a scrap of paper pushed under the phone, written by someone not Jennifer:

Em B.
555-1212
Call me!

I wrote down the number and told the Crowes not to touch anything else in the room. Just in case.

I stayed for dinner, and afterwards, Alex gave me a ride home. As I got out of the car in front of my building, he leaned over and said, "Sam? You won't involve anyone else, will you?"

"Not if I can help it." I smiled. "I'll do what I can."

I went up to my room and tried the number. An answering machine clicked, then a young woman's voice said, "Hello, this is Jill. Em and I can't come to the phone, but if you leave your name and number, we'll get back to you. Or if this is an emergency, you can page me at 555-7006. Byeee." The machine beeped. "Hi Emily, my name is Sam Bowen. Please call me back at 555-8050, I need to talk to you about Jennifer Crowe. Thank you."

Two minutes later, the phone rang. I picked it up. "Hello?"

"Hi, is this Sam Bowen?" A young woman's voice.

"Yeah, is this Emily?"

"No. This is Jill, her roommate. Well, ex-roommate."

"Jill, do you know where she is? I need to talk to her."

"Are you a cop?"

"No. But I need to find Emily. It's real important. I'm looking for a friend of Emily's and I think she's the only one who knows where she went."

Jill hesitated for a minute. "Okay, I think she's still working at Stashes. I don't know. But listen, if you talk to her, tell her I still need that hundred dollars, okay?"

"Will do. Thank you."

Stashes was a diner that tried really hard to be a restaurant. I loitered around the counter until I found Emily, a short, buxom girl with long blonde hair tucked up in a hair net. When a table in her section cleared out, I took a seat. She walked up a minute later with silverware and water. "Hi, what can I get you tonight?" The smile punctuated her apple cheeks and dimples. Very all-American.

I made eye contact, smiled, and said, "Can I have a few minutes?" I brushed her hand with my fingertips, which were coated with a peculiar ointment, as I took the water from her.

She mumbled sure and backed away, suddenly uncertain. The salve on my left hand was step one. I poured some of the water in an empty coffee cup and mixed it with a packet of dried herbs I'd prepared earlier, held my nose, and drank it down in one swallow. It tasted like rotten licorice. Emily came back a minute later.

"Ready to order?" She had regained her composure.

"I have a question about the fish?" I held the menu away from her; she automatically stepped around behind me to view the item I was pointing at. I moved it away from my body, and she leaned in. "Is this prepared with bread crumbs or flour?" As I spoke, my breath struck her in the face. She recoiled like she'd been slapped.

"It's flour," she said automatically.

I handed the menu back, careful to brush the spot on her right hand where I'd touched her earlier. "Thanks. I'll just have some coffee."

She staggered off. Normally, I wouldn't use that type of control magic, but time was of the essence. I needed information quickly and didn't want to have to strong arm it out of her or bring the police in. Emotion control is dangerous business because it's blind chemistry. You don't really know how much of a certain thing will work on a man or a woman. Especially women.

When Emily returned with my coffee, her eyes were shining. "Here you go. I brought you cream and sugar. Do you need anything else?" She looked at me pointedly.

"Yeah," I said, "I know this sounds crazy, but you seem really familiar. Do I know you?"

She smiled.

Curiously enough, she related that she didn't know me but would very much like to. As we walked back to her place, I let her talk about whatever was running through her head.

It was a lot of static. Stuff about how she never had done anything like this before, and how she couldn't explain the electric connection between us. When she mentioned something about Callie being right about the cosmic attraction to men of the sacred yoni, I perked my ears up. "What's that?" I asked.

She grabbed my hand. "Well, I'm not supposed to tell you, because it's sacred and secret. But my belief system is the Order of Herself. We're a Sapphic order that distills the Estrus and the Yin and rechannels that energy into a usable form for the new Millennium."

"Wow," I said, and I meant it. "Sounds like a lot." A lot of crap, I thought to myself.

"Oh, you have no idea. I mean, what are the odds of us meeting like this?"

"It's magic," I told her. She smiled and nudged me with her elbow.

Later, at her apartment, I played with her hair and asked her questions under the guise of getting to know her and thanked God she kept the cheerleader body up. Eventually, I asked her about her belief system again. I expected her to be reluctant to talk about it, but she opened up. I found out about their spiritual guru, a woman named Callie, who taught them of the joys of love, sex, and death. Many of the women lived there as initiates chosen by Callie herself. She told me a lot. Halfway through it, she frowned.

"Em, what's wrong?" I asked.

"I have a headache," she said.

"Does that mean you don't want to do it again?"

She giggled and nudged me with her elbow. "No, silly, I mean for real. A real big one."

I sat up. "Where does it hurt?"

She thought about it for a second. "Right in the middle of my head."

I rubbed her temples, and she settled back down in the crook of my arm. "Mmm, that feels nice."

"Is your church here? I mean, is it local, or is it national?"

"Oh, it's here. Local. Callie isn't about material gain. She's into helping people. Well, women."

Eventually, Emily fell asleep. As soon as she was snoring, I put on my clothes. Her headache had me worried. It meant that Emily was already under some kind of control. My spell started a small chemical war in her brain. I didn't think Emily was evil, just a little misguided. Okay, a lot misguided. I ran through her personal papers, her mail, and her address book. It took some doing, but I eventually found a flier under her bed for a bold new direction in the future of women. The address was in Spanishtown. I took it and left quietly.

The next morning, I took the SCAT to Spanishtown and walked until I found the Herself House, a converted mission repainted in Earth Mother beige and green. The sign outside the heavy wooden doors said:

WOMAN'S CLINIC
BY APPOINTMENT ONLY.

I walked right inside.

The foyer was filled with plants and warm light from the stained glass windows. A mousy woman sat behind a wood and metal desk, typing on the computer. She looked up, locked eyes with me, and swallowed her gum.

I gave her my best professional smile. "Good morning! I'm Gabe Kaplin, I'm here to see Callie."

She shut her mouth slowly, then said, "Um, one moment please," and picked up the phone. She hit a button on the bottom row and spoke quietly into the phone. Then she turned to me and said, "I'm sorry, Mr. Kaplin, she doesn't have you in her book. Would you like to make an appointment now?"

"Yes, for today. As soon as possible." I kept the smile up. She got back on the phone real quick. When she hung up, her jaw was set.

"Please take a seat." She indicated a knock-off doctor's office chair in the hallway off to the left. I sat down, my duffel bag in my lap. After a ten minute wait, the door at the far end of the hall opened, and a woman came sauntering out, her black business heels clicking imperiously on the tiled floor. Her hips and breasts were ample, carefully concealed behind a smart gray business suit. Her dark complexion stood out against the gray, her exotic features difficult to place in any ethnic group. Her dark hair was done up in a conservative bun and went well with her fashionable horn-rimmed glasses. As she got closer, she smiled at me and held out her hand. "Mr. Kaplin, I'm Callie. What can I do for you?"

"Hi, Callie." I took her hand and shook it. Her skin was soft and smooth. "I'm a researcher for the Armitage Foundation. We are an altruistic consortium that specializes in religion, philosophy, and the anthropological sciences. We're doing a big write-up on alternative treatment methods for the millennium, you know, a light and upbeat piece."

"I see." She was wearing a musky perfume that was quite distracting.

"Well, I've heard some nice things about this place, and so I thought you could give me the nickel tour of the place and give me some information."

"You seemed pretty insistent with Bethany just now," she said evenly.

"Deadline." I shrugged and smiled.

"Ah. Well, if you've heard anything about Herself, then you no doubt have heard that it's a woman-only center."

"Sure, sure, I don't want to intrude on any sessions."

"No, I mean, really, you aren't even allowed in the building."

"Really."

She nodded severely, then her face brightened considerably. "But, given the nature of your piece, if you keep flashing those baby blues at me like that, I may be forced to make an exception." She took my hand in hers, chuckling. "Come on, I'll show you my office and the visitor's center. Then we'll talk about the programs we offer, and if we have time, I'll buy you lunch." I followed in a daze, completely caught up in the moment, my own lie, and my hand in hers. We talked in her office for a couple of hours, then broke for lunch. While eating, I developed a screaming headache and had to cut our time short. This irritated me, because Callie was talking to me about the rape-recovery program and its 90% success rate. I was fascinated and spent the whole trip home thinking about all the good that the institution did and what a boon it was for the community.

Brother Lynx comes through the door and nudges me awake with his nose. "Come on, Sam," he says, "get up."

I jump out of bed and look at him. "What are you doing here?" I ask.

He replies, "Aren't you looking for something? Am I not the Finder-of-Things?"

He turns and walks out into the hall. I follow, and we are suddenly on the streets. It's dark and deserted. The sky is the color of a bruise. As we walk, I can see people half in shadow now, screaming in pain and anger. We're in Spanishtown and I can smell the ocean. At the end of the street, between Oceanview and us, is a large, black building, broad and squat.

"She has your number, Many Feathers," Lynx said to me.

"Who, Jennifer?"

Brother Lynx says, "No, her."

I look at the building and see Callie. Her hair is loose and blows freely about her head. She is naked, and her skin is colored a deep, rich red. She moves towards me with a curious sidestep, weaving through the screaming people to get to me. I feel my desire for her well up, along with a cold chill.

She reaches out to me, but stops just short of my face. "You are already marked," she says.

"Marked how?" I reply. Lynx nudges my right arm and licks me with a rough tongue.

"Little walker," she says, "you are strong. I should have been more direct with you." I step forward and begin a song of protection, calling out to Brother Owl. She laughs. "Spirits do not bother Callie," she says. "Only flesh."

I look at her, scared and excited all at once. "I don't understand."

I turn to ask Brother Lynx what is going on but he is walking away. "Sorry, Many Feathers, I can go no further."

I look back at Callie. "Why does he fear you?" I ask.

She takes my head in her reptilian hands and says, "Let me show you." Her mouth closes over mine, and a thick, hot tongue forces its way past my lips, down my throat. I'm choking. I can smell blood.

I woke up. The pain in my head was severe, but I was thinking clearly for myself again. My nose was bleeding. I went to the bathroom and cleaned myself up, looking at my face in the mirror. "Ask for healing," I said out loud, looking into my own haunted eyes.

I walked back into the living room and made a crude

prayer wheel on the floor, stripped, and sang a purification song. During the song, I asked Brother Raven to show me the truth. He obligingly sent me a series of images from his point of view. I saw myself asking questions to Callie, and her being evasive. I saw myself get angry and demand to see the rest of the building. She waved her hand and whispered things to me. Then we went to lunch, and she suggested that I write a glowing article that praised the clinic but discouraged men from seeing the place. That's when my headache started. She bought my story about me being a journalist, so she planted a suggestion that was incompatible with my real self.

I finished my song, calm and determined. The headache was gone, and I felt refreshed. As I dressed, I realized that Callie was no ordinary cult leader. I would need help getting in there. It was time to do a little research.

The rest of my day was spent running all over the Financial District, first to the hall of records, then to the county clerk's office at city hall, and finally to several of the UNC libraries. By the time I was through, it was after 11 p.m. I had a ream of photocopied pages and a sinking feeling in my gut. There was absolutely no way I could do this alone, and unfortunately, there was only one person I could ask for help. I hailed a taxi.

"Where to?" the wraith behind the wheel asked.

"Doyle's."

"Is this some kind of joke?"

Robert Stonehill was seated at the bar table that doubled as his office. His face hovered somewhere between amusement and contempt.

"No, I'm very serious. I wouldn't be asking you for help if it wasn't important."

"Or if it wasn't about Jennifer."

I shrugged. "I'm not going to apologize for it, Rob. But even if she weren't involved, you are the only guy that can get me in."

Stonehill held up a hand. "Hold on, I may not be able to get you in there. It's possible, not probable."

"But you'll help me?"

Stonehill sat back. "I never said that."

I leaned in. "May I sit down? Please?"

He waved his hand at the chair I was leaning on. "Sure, be my guest."

"Thank you." On cue, Rosemary appeared with a bourbon for me. Astounding service at Doyle's.

Stonehill leaned in, enjoying himself immensely. "Now, let's see, how did you put it to me a few months back? 'Any further association, professional or otherwise, is unlikely.'"

"Okay, what do you want from me? An apology?"

"For starters, yes. You gave me a big speech about my personal life, and now you're trying to capitalize on that same personal situation."

I took a deep breath. He wasn't making this easy, and that was pretty fair, but I still wanted to kick his ass. "Okay, Robert, I'm sorry. I was wrong to bring up your personal life."

Stonehill nodded. "That's good. Well, Mr. Bowen, I accept your apology, but I'm afraid I can't quite make myself extend the hand of friendship to you."

I looked him in the eyes. "Then I'll hire you." I dug around in my pockets until I came up with my checkbook. "I'll hire you to get me inside the building, watch my back, and get me out again with Jennifer." I wrote out the check as I talked and pushed the whole thing over to him. "You'll see that it's the balance of what I have in the bank. This is all I can give you. Please help me."

Stonehill took the checkbook in hand and glanced at it. "It's funny, you know, but I really do have two fees for my various services. I have the fee for nearly everyone that I deal with, and it's rightfully exorbitant, as I am putting my precious neck on the line. Then I have my fee for friends, which is considerably lower, you know, as I am doing basically a favor for a friend..."

"In other words, it's not enough."

"Not even close."

I sighed and looked down at the check. "What will that get me, then?"

Stonehill considered it for a while. Rosemary came and refreshed my drink. Finally, he focused back on me and said, "I'll get you inside. After that, you're on your own."

It wasn't what I wanted, but it would have to do. I debated telling him what we were walking into and decided against it. He wasn't going to be around for long, so why bother, I told myself. I finished my drink and stood up. "Okay. Can we do it tonight?"

"It's your nickel."

"Great. I'll meet you there at 2 a.m. Okay?"

"I'll be there."

I went home to get ready.

Stonehill was waiting for me when I got there. I recognized Silas, the bartender from Doyle's, driving the car. Stonehill stepped out of the vehicle as I walked up. "You ready?"

Stonehill nodded. "Just to make sure we understand the arrangement here, I am going to get you inside that building," he jerked his thumb over his shoulder, "and nothing else. No back-up, no rescuing, nothing else. Are we clear?"

"Crystal."

"Okay, follow me and do exactly what I do."

"You got it."

We turned, trench coats flapping in unison, and walked toward the Herself building. I let Stonehill lead, and he took us around the side to an alley that ran directly behind the building and accessed a small parking lot filled with cars. He ducked and weaved through the cars in the dim light, and I had to hurry to keep up. We walked around to the opposite side of the building, close to the wall, then he stepped through a door and vanished. By the time I realized that there was no door in front of us, I had followed him. There was a crackling in the air, like I was passing through someplace pristine, then I was inside.

We were standing in the corner of an immense, empty room, what had previously been the chapel but was now converted into something worse. The ceiling was high, domed, and painted with complicated patterns. Stained glass was imbedded in the dome, sending colored moonlight across the floor at odd angles and in distracting patterns. Pillows lay strewn about the floor, knee-high in some places. The back window of the converted chapel held a stained glass portrait of a four-armed goddess in a dancing pose. In front of the window, on a raised dais, was some kind of padded table in an inverted -Y shape, elevated at a slight angle. Painted scenes of women locked in passionate embraces were etched in the adobe walls, colored in mute tones. Thick, heady perfume hung in the air. It was Callie's scent.

"This place is bigger on the inside," I whispered to Stonehill.

"Yeah, I think I know the guy who set all this up," he replied calmly.

"Bullshit."

Stonehill shrugged. "Suit yourself. Do you know where Jennifer is?"

"Theoretically, yes."

"Theoretically?"

"Well, according to some plans I found, and from what I was able to piece together, she should be in one of these six doors." I pointed to the evenly spaced vestibules nestled between the erotic murals. "Wait here."

I ran from door to door, occasionally tripping over wads of pillows, pulling open each door. The rooms were identical: a small bed, a dresser table, a wire-frame wardrobe, and a trunk. All were unoccupied. "Shit," I said out loud.

Stonehill walked over. "What?"

"She's not here. I don't get it."

"Did you try that door?" He nodded to the altar at the front.

"What door?"

Stonehill walked up and touched the stained glass and vanished. Sometimes I really hate that guy, I thought, stepping through the doorway. Before I had a chance to adjust to the transition, I felt his hand over my mouth. Then I looked past him and saw what was going down.

It was a small room in comparison to the one we just left. Brass braziers sent clouds of strange incense into the air, filling the room with a dusky haze. Bright tapestries of every color adorned the walls, visible between four pillars that held up another domed ceiling painted in a twilight motif. Callie was in the room, sitting naked and cross-legged on the floor. Surrounding her were six women, one of them Jennifer. They wore red robes tied in place with black sashes. Callie was chanting in a dialect that I didn't know. The women were glassy-eyed, swaying to the chanting like wheat in the wind.

Stonehill leaned in and whispered softly, "I know who

that is."

I took his hand away from my mouth and said, "So do I."

"Are you stupid, or just insane? Did you think you could take on a goddess all by yourself?"

"She's not half the goddess she used to be. Besides, you wouldn't help me, remember?"

The chanting stopped. We looked over as the six women opened their mouths, spitting out a torrent of thick, dark blood. It splashed over Callie and she moaned ecstatically and rubbed it into her skin until she was deep crimson. The women knelt down, blood dripping down their chins, and Callie kissed them each in turn, licking the blood off their faces.

"Jesus," Stonehill whispered.

"Not hardly."

"Did you have a plan?" he asked.

"Well, it didn't account for this. I'm open to suggestions."

"Look, by just standing in this room, talking to you about this, I have gone way beyond our original agreement. If you want to retain my services, it's going to cost you."

"What?" I growled.

"I want a blank check from you, for research work on a case to be named later. No rough stuff, but the next time I call you, you will drop what you're doing and work for me until my job is through. That, plus I want a public apology from you, at Doyle's."

I wasn't in any position to argue or barter. "Okay, sure." We shook on it. "Now, what do you have in mind?"

" I have a little experience with her, so why don't you go back through the door and wait for Jennifer to come out? When she does, grab her and head out the front door. Get in the car, get her home."

"What about you?"

"Like I said, we have a certain history. Don't worry about me."

I stepped back without another word, but kept my ear to the door. I could only dimly hear inside.

Stonehill stepped into the room and said, loudly and clearly, "Hello, Kali. Quite a set-up you've got here. What name are you using this time? You've only got, what? A couple dozen left?"

"Stonehill, you grievous prick," Kali spat. "Get the hell out of here."

"Blood magic, Kali. Not nice. What are you up to? More world domination? Or are you and the old man fighting again?"

She clapped her hands. "Leave us, my disciples." I heard rustling, and pressed myself against the wall. The women filed out, one by one, walking slowly. The third one through was Jennifer. I pulled her aside, my hand over her mouth. She struggled, and I pulled her into one of the pools of light. We were both bathed in an amber glow. She looked at me, then her eyes focused, and she collapsed into my arms. The other women filed into their rooms, still dazed.

I shook her lightly. "Come on, Jenn. Wake up."

"Sam?" she mumbled, squinting her eyes. "What're you doin' here?"

"Jenn, we've got to go. You're in danger."

"...Okay...if you say so..." I helped her to a standing position and we walked to her room.

"Get dressed," I told her. She complied mechanically. Under the bed I found an empty duffel bag and emptied the contents of the trunk into it while Jennifer slipped on some jeans and shoes. We crept out of the vestibule, hand in hand, and tiptoed to the double doors that I knew would lead to the main hall. They swung outward soundlessly. We were look-

176

ing down a long, wide hallway that in no way resembled the hall I had walked down earlier that day.

"It's bigger on the inside," she said.

"Yeah, I got that." We started down the hallway. Doorways were evenly spaced every thirty feet, to the right and left. I tried them all and found many of them locked. Other rooms held supplies or were empty altogether. The corridor stretched ahead into inky darkness. As we walked, the double doors behind us followed. Jennifer noticed it too.

"What is this place?" she asked.

"An reinterpretation of mythic Kalighat."

"What?"

"Your guru is an old Indian Goddess. Kali. The creator and the destroyer."

Jennifer was slowly becoming her old self. "That statue that came to life in the Sinbad movie?"

"Sort of. Yeah, she is the four-armed goddess, usually depicted with black skin and a long red tongue, but she has a multitude of forms. There is the Raksha-Kali, the protector, the Shyama-Kali, the Maha-Kali, and the Nitya-Kali..." I stopped talking and walking.

"What?"

"Nitya-Kali. Endless Time. This building is an extension of her." I turned around and walked back towards the double doors. "Come on."

"We're going back there?"

"No, I don't think so." I opened the double doors, and we strode inside. The room was now dark. I took Jennifer's hand and held her in place for a minute so that our eyes could adjust. That was our mistake.

The room was hexagonal, high domed, and decorated in a similar fashion to the worship hall. The air was thick with the smell of bodies in close quarters. Strewn across the floor was a host of naked women, their limbs slack and unnatural. A great quantity of blood was pooled up on the floor, yet none of the women appeared to be injured or dead. Several robed acolytes moved among the women, kneeling between their legs. I stood there in shock and confusion, taking it all in until it hit me. They were all menstruating. The acolyte's mouths were full, and blood trickled from the corners of their mouths. They were harvesting. The full implication of what I witnessed sank in. I turned to Jennifer, but she had joined her sisters on the floor in a swoon. I guess she got it, too.

I threw her over my shoulder and pushed the doors open again. New hallway, a short one, ending in a circular alcove. Two corridors on the left, two on the right. Jennifer was pretty heavy, so I left the duffel bag by the door, walked into the corridor, and looked down. There, in intricate colored tile, was a mosaic depiction of Kali. Her arms were at full extension, and each hand held a different object. Going clockwise, from the upper left, she held a sword, a severed head, a pair of large needles, and a flower. Her face was smiling, with the tip of her long tongue sticking out, but she in no way looked friendly. This was a test. The arms corresponded to the corridors in some way, I was sure of that. The key to the puzzle was knowing what form of Kali this represented.

The floor buckled and rolled like a bedspread being unfurled. I hit the stone floor hard, Jennifer on top of me. I watched the walls and floor in front of me ripple, then return to normal. Something told me that wasn't a usual occurrence. Stonehill must have really pissed her off. I didn't want to think about the alternative explanation. I took the closest left-hand passage, the flower path. How bad could flowers be, I reasoned.

Visibility was limited to roughly twenty feet in front of and behind me. I noticed another vividly painted tableau on the left-hand wall. As I quickly walked, the scene played out for me. A group of Indians were burying someone, evidently a holy man. They said prayers over him and Kali appeared and pushed him into the ground. The Indians laid garlands of flowers on the holy man's grave and backed away. Then a man stole into the graveyard and dug the holy man up. He pocketed some of the finery that was buried with the dead man. Suddenly, Kali appeared and unleashed two jackals on the man. They tore him to bits while Kali watched....

I stopped. Behind me, in the darkness, I heard several sharp clicks on the stone floor. They stopped, too. I resumed walking...then stopped quickly. More scrabbling. A low growl. Shit. I turned and saw twin pairs of yellow eyes shining in the dimness.

"Jennifer, are you awake?" I said.

"Huh?" She stirred. "Sam...Oh God, the blood...I...she...made me..."

"Listen, we're in trouble. Can you walk?"

"Uh, yeah." I set her down. "Where are we now?" she asked.

"In deep shit. On second thought, let's run." I yanked her arm, and we took off with the jackals in close pursuit. They gained steadily, effortlessly. There was nothing I could throw at them that would stop them or even slow them up. I was completely outclassed here. One of the jackals snapped at my heel. I almost tripped. It wouldn't be long, now. Up ahead was a dim light, growing brighter as we ran towards it. Jennifer began to falter, so I scooped her in my arms and pulled her along. I chanced a look back over my shoulder.

The jackals had vanished. We stopped running, hands on our knees, and tried to catch our breath.

"I don't get it," she wheezed. "Where did they go?"

"I don't think we want to know." I kept my eyes on the

black end of the corridor as we resumed walking towards the light. "Come on. We need to hurry." I urged her forward. The light grew brighter still. Finally, we came to an open door. I peeked around the corner. It was the main hallway I had sat in earlier. From this door, I could see the wooden double doors but not the front desk. It was a chance we would have to take. "Get ready," I whispered. "Let's go!"

I led out through the door, Jennifer on my heels. Someone was at the desk, but we were in motion, running full-tilt for the door. I heard a shriek behind us and glanced back. Bethany, the mousy receptionist, stood up, contorting and flailing. Her face lengthened and creased in unnatural ways. Then her body shuddered violently, and it was Kali standing in front of us, naked and holding her side in pain.

"I hate putting on new faces," Kali said. "Damn Robert Stonehill and the horse he rode in on."

I turned to Jennifer and whispered, "Run. Get out of here."

"No! I'm not leaving you here!" she said.

"Jen, go, please! There's a car parked down the street, waiting on us. I'll distract her. Go!"

She took off. I stepped forward between Kali and the door to cover her retreat. Kali didn't seem to notice. "Mister Bowen, do you have any idea how thoroughly you've fucked up everything?"

"Look, I don't want any trouble. Personally, I don't give a damn what you do, but I was asked to help a friend out, and that's what I did. I tried to play nice, but you thought it would be easier to screw with my head."

She spit on the floor. "Please, don't pretend to be innocent. The only reason I don't pull your heart out now is because you are already marked by another."

"What?"

She looked surprised, then smiled. "Oh, you didn't know.

That's amusing, a learned person like yourself not knowing his own soul."

I stepped forward. "Tell me."

"No."

I pulled a flat, green, palm-sized gem out of my back pocket and held it up. "Tell me, or I'll take this place apart."

Kali bristled. "What? Is that a threat? In another time, I would already be sucking the marrow out of your bones, bathing in your blood."

"Yeah, but the time is now. We are here. And I will scatter the collected energy in this place to the four winds if you don't tell me what the hell you're talking about."

"Mister Bowen, you can die with that question on your lips." She smiled, then shimmered, and I was staring up into nine feet of ebony, four-armed, red tongued goddess. Make that three arms. The lower right side was missing, a bloodless wound. Stonehill's work, no doubt. She was still pretty, even as she charged at me, baring fangs and brandishing her sword. I dropped the gem on the floor and spoke a few words in careful, phonetic Mandarin. The floor buckled under Kali, and she screamed. I saw a disembodied silver hand pick up the gem. I decided it was time to get the hell out of there.

Kali flailed out at me, flinging her sword, but I was in motion and through the door. I felt the whole building shudder as I slammed the door closed behind me and leaned into it. A thunderclap tore the door apart all around me. I ducked and ran, trying to get as far away from the door and Kali as possible. She didn't come through. The old mission continued to shiver and warp, and I saw blue energy race through the mortar and stone. Four different beings flickered in and out of the building, a look of glee on their faces. Cracks appeared in the adobe. I backed up further as pieces of the building caved in, sending dust and debris out into the street.

A scream welled up from the building, and, as the door fell down, I caught a glimpse of Kali, looking at me with full and generous hatred. She was fearsome and erotic all at once. I looked into those eyes, and every part of me wanted to march into the crumbling Herself building to be with her, even if it meant my death. Then dust and more falling mortar obscured my view, and she was gone.

I found Jennifer wandering down the block aimlessly. Silas' car and Stonehill weren't in sight. I had no money, so we walked all the way from Spanishtown to Chinatown, that being the closest point of sanctuary. As we walked, I wondered if Stonehill made it out of there. I decided it was best if I didn't mention Stonehill's involvement to Jennifer. She'd been through enough. I did have time to ponder what Kali had said and realized I had heard it before in my dream. I couldn't decide if it was another reference to the curse or something else. It was possible, however unlikely, that somehow Chu Sheng Kai had spiritually tagged me. I couldn't figure out why he would do that. It wasn't his style. As my building came into view, I decided to sleep on it. I was never good at thinking when I was tired. I touched my lip and noticed my nose was bleeding. Again. Time to have that looked into as well, I thought as we climbed the stoop.

We were both completely exhausted by the end of the hike. Jennifer told me she wanted to take a shower, so I showed her where the towels were and collapsed into my easy chair. After twenty minutes, I went to check on her and found her in a fetal position in the tub while cold water splashed on her. I picked her up, naked and shivering, and put her into my bed. She reached for me and held me and asked me to help keep her warm.

I climbed in next to her, and she tucked herself into my side and whispered thank you into my ear. Then we kissed.

We kissed a lot. I'm not really sure how it happened, but we found each other in the dark and discovered that we weren't completely exhausted after all.

The phone was ringing. I answered it. "Hello?"

"Mister Bowen."

"Alex." I sat bolt upright in the bed. Jennifer followed suit. He didn't sound happy at all.

"Sam, I am going to ask you a series of questions, but first I am going to tell you a little story."

"Alex, listen, I—"

"Shush. I got a call this morning from a very worried Robert Stonehill, who asked me if I had seen you. Then he asked me if I had seen Jennifer. Then he told me this very interesting tale about how you hired him to help you recover my daughter, and when he got to the part about the church collapsing, I decided to become very worried."

"Listen, sir, I—"

"I said, shush. Sam, yes or no. Is my daughter there?"

"Yes."

"Is she all right?"

"Yes."

"Good. Her mother and I are on the way. Have her outside at the door in twenty minutes." The phone went dead. Jennifer saw my face and got up to get dressed.

Outside, she tried to calm me. I knew why he was mad. Jennifer had no idea that I'd involved Stonehill; she thought I was worried about us sleeping together. I was, but it was a distant second to what Dr. Crowe was going to say about my choice of help.

The car pulled up with a jerk, and the whole family embraced. Sophie thanked me with her eyes and Alex damned me with his. The women climbed into the car. Jennifer mouthed "Thank you" through the rear window. Dr. Crowe stood in front of me, arms crossed.

"Why him, Sam? Of all the people in the world you could have broken your promise to me with, you had to pick Robert Stonehill."

"I know you probably won't believe me, but he was the only one who could have helped me. As it was, I think he destroyed the temple by himself. He saved me and your daughter, sir."

"Yes, he did, and it makes me obliged to the man. I don't want to be obliged to that man, Sam, I would rather he ceased to exist altogether. And why didn't you bring her home last night?"

"I was broke. I had no money. This place was closer. She was in shock."

"You could've called!"

"It was the middle of the night."

"It's my daughter!" he thundered, all scholarly composure gone.

I looked at the ground. "I'm sorry."

He turned and walked around to his car door. "Sam, I'm grateful for your rescuing my daughter...but I'd rather not see you for a while. Don't call. Don't come around. Stay away from Jennifer." He got in the car and drove away. Jennifer looked at me through the rear window. I watched her disappear, then went back inside to get drunk.

Follow a Hunch

Her kick was technically perfect: fast and low, right in the solar plexus. It pushed the air out of my lungs and knocked me backwards, right off the rooftop. I had a lot of time to think about the beauty of that kick before I slammed into the fire escape. The impact stunned me for a moment, and I swore because it meant I'd lost her yet again. When I got my sight back, the Fox was standing over me. Her expression had changed in the six weeks that we had gotten to know one another. Her eyes were hard, dangerous. The playful smile was gone. It wasn't fun for her anymore. I tried to move but was still woozy. My arm was completely numb. She knelt down over me, looking intently at my face.

"I'm not going to go away," I said, spraying blood from my battered lips. She picked up my arm, the same one she took a bite out of, and sniffed it curiously. Then she stood up and gracefully vaulted down the fire escape. By the time I rolled to the edge to see her, she was gone. That woman would be the death of me yet, I thought.

I grabbed the metal railing for support and stood up. My damaged arm had a pinched nerve but was otherwise unharmed. Damn lucky, I thought, eyeing the rooftop some twelve feet above me. On the way down the fire escape, I felt something warm touch my neck. Blood, I thought wryly as I examined my fingertips. Maybe I wasn't so lucky after all. By the time I reached the ground, I could barely walk. It was hard to remember where Mi Hei parked the car. I took a wild guess and started stumbling. There were some lights, and someone screamed. Then everything went gray. It took me five minutes to realize I was looking at the ground. I laughed at my stupidity, and then everything went black.

A gentle hand touched my forehead. I opened my eyes. I was in the guest room in Chu Sheng Kai's estate. It was where they would take me whenever I was hurt or sick. Lately, it was once a week. Chu's nurse, Ying Bing, was working on me. She smiled when I opened my eyes.

"Hi," I croaked.

"Concussion," she replied. "Not too bad, but you need rest. Drink this." She handed me a cup of green tea. I drank it.

"It will make you sleep..." That was all I heard.

I stayed there for three days. Mi Hei came by to tell me how stupid I looked with my head wide open, lying on the street like that. Nice girl. Michael Chu stopped in as well and brought home-cooked food and a change of clothes. On the third day, before I left, Chu Sheng Kai stuck his head in the door. Normally, he would check on me every day. This delayed appearance meant something was up.

"Ya Shen, my son," he greeted me.

I inclined my head. "Master Chu. Thank you once again for taking care of me."

"Wounds received while in my service are my responsibility." He paused. "And we have seen much of you lately, have we not?"

"I'm not sure I understand what you mean."

"It is merely an observation. You are having difficulty capturing the Fox for me. I wondered if you required additional assistance."

"I see. So, in other words, I can't handle the job, so let's bring in some ringers. Is that it?"

Chu pressed his lips together. "I am sorry, Sam. I didn't mean to offend you. But you must look at it from my point of view. I asked you for this almost two months ago, and you still can't bring her to me."

"Hey, she's not vandalizing your businesses anymore! Isn't that enough?"

"I need her, Ya Shen. She is in the employ of an enemy and carries something very important to me. If you can't do it, then I will happily assign the Jen Long to this task. I don't wish to see you hurt any more...or perhaps even killed."

I was good and pissed now. "Look, I'm very close to getting her. She's been magically tagged. I don't know where she goes in the day, but I can pick her up every night with a simple spell. It's just a matter of time. Don't worry."

Chu Sheng Kai nodded silently and left me to my fuming.

I insisted on walking home. At that point, I wouldn't have taken any more charity from him on a dare. As I walked, the scenery changed from neighborhoods to city streets, and I thought about what it was that Chu wanted with the Fox. He obviously felt she was working for David Wan, but why all the interest in a supernatural cat burglar? Or better still, why not just hire one of his under the table hatchet men to take care of her? Why throw me into this? It was because of my talents, but even with spells, artifacts, and some dirty fighting, I was having a devil of a time bringing her in.

By the time I reached Zhu's Noodle Hut, I had worked up a healthy appetite. As I approached, Zhu took one look at me and burst out laughing. "Bowen look like he lose a fight with polar bear!" he howled.

"Yeah, yeah, you old pig. Why don't you sling noodles

and shut up? What's good today, anyway?"

Zhu adjusted his "I Heart San Cibola" cap on his head. "It's all good, you white devil. What size?"

"Two larges. An order of lo mein and half garlic chicken, half chicken with orange sauce." As he worked, I closed my eyes and concentrated. The chain around his ankle, clamped to the sidewalk, was just barely visible to me. "So, when do you get set free, anyway?"

"That's for me to know and you to worry about, Round Eyes."

"God, you're a sweetheart, Zhu." I handed him money.

"Hey, don't blame me for your troubles." He gave me two cartons in a paper sack.

"What troubles?" I helped myself to chopsticks and napkins.

"Oh come on, Bowen. Everyone knows the Fox is making a fool of you."

I looked him square in his red eye. "Everyone, huh? Well, do you have any sage advice for me?"

Zhu shrugged. "Not really. I hope she kicks your disrespectful ass." He smiled an evil smile, showing uneven teeth. "Fortune cookie?"

Normally, I took a pass on Zhu's fortune cookies. They were hand-made, like the rest of his food, and without a doubt the best fortune cookies I had ever eaten in my whole life. The problem was Zhu's messages. The demon in him came through with some of the most dire and awful predictions. I have a couple of them saved, like "THAT LUMP YOU FOUND IS CANCEROUS" and "BET YOU DON'T KNOW WHAT YOUR WIFE IS DOING WITH YOUR FRIEND RIGHT NOW." Tourists loved them. I didn't. Nonetheless, something made me take one and toss it into the sack with my food. "Sure, thanks."

188

"Go to hell." he shot back. I walked quickly to my building.

Benny Wan greeted me with, "Sam, you okay? Someone says to me you died three days ago!"

"Do I look like a ghost to you, Benny?"

"You all look alike to me," he said with a wave of his hand. "Here's your mail and your messages."

"Thanks." I took the stack from him and leafed awkwardly through it on the three-story climb. One of the letters was from the Armitage Foundation. Thank God, I thought, it was probably my stipend. I was operating on less than a hundred dollars cash right now. I tore it open. It was a single sheet of paper with no check inside, a letter to all field agents stating that they were currently working on rebuilding the computer after an industrial saboteur destroyed the hard drive. Their backup systems were approximately two years out of date and there would be a slight delay in sending my stipend. Shit.

Once inside my apartment, I threw the rest of the mail on the bed and hurriedly unpacked my food. My drinking options were water or bourbon, so I combined them in order to keep from having to make that call and fell into my meal with gusto. As I ate, I thought about ways to stretch my money in order to stay alive. Benny would let me slide on the rent, if necessary. I could rely on Chu's houseboy, Su Yun, and the cooks at the Chu estate to keep me in meals. Alex Crowe was right out. Maybe Ian Rosewood was good for a meal. I made a small list in my head of people I could touch for food, then itemized all the rest of my expenses for the rest of the month. It left me with exactly thirteen dollars. I ate until I was full, then scraped the extra chicken onto the noodles and stuck it all in the fridge, to save for dinner.

I refilled my glass, then cracked open the fortune cookie.

While I crunched the pieces and marveled at Zhu's culinary talents, I read the fortune:

FOLLOW A HUNCH.

I turned it over. Lottery numbers. Follow a hunch? What was dour about that? And come to think of it, why did he go out of his way to offer me a fortune cookie? He never had before. I turned the piece of paper over and over in my fingers. Follow a hunch...I closed my eyes and drank deeply of the bourbon. Zhu was trying to tell me something. Listen to my heart. I should suspect something, but what? Maybe...something about the fox. No. Something about Chu.

I put on my street clothes and grabbed my duffel bag, not knowing quite what I was doing. Time to act instinctively. I can't believe I'm heeding the advice of a demonic fortune cookie, I thought, pulling the door closed.

Zhu seemed surprised to see me walking up to his cart again. "Hey, no refunds!"

I didn't have time for the banter. "Zhu, where can I go for a translator spell? I want to be able to understand Mandarin."

Zhu chuckled. "There is an alchemist on Hutchinson Lane. Yun Guan. Tell him I sent you."

"Thanks." I walked away with Zhu's laughter following me.

Hutchinson Avenue was a three-block cul-de-sac just north of the Asian Market. In the heart of Chinatown. Here the businesses were smaller, less obvious by their blank storefronts, and there were seldom any signs at all, much less in English. I asked a couple of old ladies for Yun Guan, and they yammered at me and made protective signs with their hands, but eventually I figured out which door to try.

The shop was dimly lit and smelled terrible. A cacophony of odors battled for dominance, and no one was making head-

190

way. On either side of me were wooden shelves filled completely with glass canisters. Inside was everything from ginger and salt to strange chips of tree bark, mushrooms, roots, and hundreds of things I couldn't identify. Out of all of the things I've seen in my travels, I recognized maybe two dozen plants in the place. Everything else was totally foreign to me. In front of me was a low wooden counter, and behind that counter I could see even more shelves full of canisters and clay pots. Twisted vines and drying roots hung from the ceiling so I had to duck my head upon entering. I walked up to the counter and looked around, then hit the hand bell I found there.

A door slammed, then another, and I heard shuffling footsteps, followed by a string of Chinese. The old man was at least seventy years old. He wore a dirty black smock, deeply stained with plant juices and other less recognizable fluids. His head was bald, save for a small crest of white hair that started behind his ears and hung in strings around the base of his skull. He squinted up at me, regarding me with some suspicion.

"Yun Guan?" I asked.

He nodded.

"Hello, I was sent here by Zhu. He said you could help me."

The old man's face broke into a crinkled smile. "Ah, you are Sam C. Bowen!" he said in a pronounced accent.

I frowned. I didn't like my reputation preceding me like that. "What? Did Zhu tell you I was coming?"

"Yes, yes, Zhu Kuei Wu has spoken of you often. Not many like you in Chinatown, hmm?" He indicated my blonde hair and fair skin.

"Right. I need your help. I am looking for sorcery that will let me understand Mandarin."

The old man clucked his tongue. "How long?"

"I don't know. A week?"

Yun Guan crossed his arms and stared at the ceiling. "Read, speak, or both?"

"Both."

"Okay, wait right here." I started to ask him about payment, but he was already gone. I cooled my heels for about fifteen minutes, then he reappeared with a full teacup. "Okay, you drink this, count to ten, then let me know."

I took the cup. "How much is this going to cost me?"

Yun shook his head in disapproval. "Zhu Kuei Wu didn't tell you...so sorry, but...he tells me only to trade for favor with you. You owe me a favor now, yes?"

I sucked in a breath. "What did you have in mind?"

He shrugged. "I don't need anything now. Maybe one day I need someone to take a potion to Little India, or maybe someone has a book for me and you go get it. Fair?"

I nodded. "Sure, okay." It wasn't the first time I'd done business by barter, but it was the first time an imprisoned demon negotiated the fee. Zhu and I were going to have a long talk about that, later. I drank the cup full of foul tea and almost gagged. My mouth tasted like metal, and my tongue was totally numb.

"Breathe in through your nose." He instructed. I did so and felt a tickle up in my sinuses. My ears were ringing. "Now breathe out through your mouth." Exhale. "And again." The tickle and the ringing subsided, only to flare up every time he spoke. "Can you understand me now?"

"Of course. Your accent went away."

Yun smiled. "Look at my mouth and tell me what you see." I burst out laughing. The voice I heard through the ringing in my ears in no way matched the movements of his lips. He was dubbed. Badly, from the looks of it. Yun rolled his eyes. "Yeah, yeah, I know, 'My kung fu is superior.' I watch those movies at the Royal Theater too, you know."

"I'm sorry, it's just that..."

"Never mind, Mister Bowen, I get the joke, too. Now get out of here, you're running away all of my good customers."

Still chuckling, I walked out into the street to explore my new world.

I took the long way back to the streets I knew, marveling at all of the businesses that suddenly opened up to me. There was an outstanding number of brothels that I resolved to go explore as soon as my money showed up, in addition to bookstores, markets, occult shops, healers, and general five-and-dime stores. Many of the buildings held a number of family businesses all grouped together that included restaurants, clothing stores, and other common establishments. None of that mattered, as I could now finally read what was what. I know I looked like a tourist as I walked down the street, but I couldn't help smiling and laughing. I was so used to the symbols over my head not meaning anything, and now I could actually read words, weird approximations of English, but I could understand them. Occasionally, a word would appear on a sign that there was no English equivalent for, so my brain would translate it into Latin. Suffice to say, it took an hour to make the fifteen-minute walk to Chu's place.

The guards had long since stopped giving me the "who goes there" business and let me walk right in. I walked up the front gate, reading the characters over the arch of the doorway: Honor, Respect, Family. Good to know. I had thought it was more decoration. I knocked and waited for Su Yun, the houseboy, to answer. He bowed.

"Ya Shen, I am pleased and surprised to see you again so soon."

"Yeah, thanks, Su. I wanted to get some more research

done. Is Mi Hei around? Or Chu-San?"

"Master Chu is at a meeting. He will be gone for many hours. Mi Hei is in the exercise room."

"Thanks," I said, breezing by him. I made straight for Chu's library. It was connected to his office, and in the past few months, I had been told to help myself to whatever I could find in there. Mi Hei was in the gym at the end of the hall, working out to some sort of hip-hop dance mix. Good. I was about to break a few house rules and wanted to know if she planned on suddenly sticking her head in the door to check on me. I shut the door to the library behind me and went to the door to Chu's office. It was locked from the inside. I knocked, just to be sure, then jimmied the lock and stepped inside.

Chu kept a nice wall of books behind his desk, largely for show, but I suspected there was more to it from the moment I saw them. Very few of the books had writing on the spines. The few that did seemed to be poetry collections and books on the living Tao. Standard stuff. I scanned the top shelf quickly and found it to be an impressive collection of Chinese erotica. The rest of the books wouldn't be so easy to figure out. I sat down in his chair and took a few deep breaths to clear my head. Then I started to visualize what I was looking for in an abstract form. I mentally put those pictures into a bag and sealed it with the mark of Brother Lynx. This mental Mojo bag may or may not be bullshit, but it's something I have done for as long as I can remember, and it has frequently led me to the right books on the first try. This time, it took much longer. The translator spell was working overtime to keep up with me. I went down the shelves, touching books randomly, pulling some off of the shelves to see their covers, and thumbing through others. After an hour, I had a stack of seven books to examine. I hurriedly took them back to the library and set them down on my table. From there, I made another pile of innocuous books to disguise what I was reading, and started taking notes.

It took me the whole week. In the day, all day, I stayed in the library and wrote furiously between Chu's frequent absences. It was a real pain in the neck to have to keep spiriting the books in and out of his office, but I managed to do it without getting caught. I kept Me Hei busy translating some spells for me and marveled at her potty mouth now that I could understand what she was calling me. The translator spell gave me a ferocious headache and made my eyes water, but I whipped up some home remedies to take care of the side effects and kept scribbling.

At night, I gave chase to the Fox but never closed in. I just kept the pretense up for the family in order to learn more. It cost me a lot of sleep and roughly two pints of blood through my nose. By the end of the week, even the Fox sensed something wasn't right and made to approach me. I sent some spectral wind her way and she backed off, confused and angry.

As mad as she was, it paled in comparison to what I learned about Chu Sheng Kai. I found several personal journals that went back as far as seventy-five years in the same crabby hand. These journal entries gave a lot of personal family information and history. Definitely the kind of thing you don't want outsiders to see. I also stumbled across something called *The Book of the Years*. Inside the book were ledger entries with various people's names, addresses, and monetary amounts paid to them. In the notes column were simple descriptions like "Restaurant" or "College." Beside every name was a parenthetical number between one and five. Fives were rare, ones were common. With a little searching, I located Mama Wang's name, as well as her dead husband's name, and quite a few others I had met in Chinatown.

Once I figured out what the ledger was for, I did some cross-referencing and found a bunch of spells I wasn't supposed to find, along with detailed information about my intended quarry, the Fox. The whole thing made me sick. My translator spell wore off before I was really finished with the books, but I had learned enough. I spent the last night in meditation, mulling things over, rather than chasing the Fox. All it got me was another goddamn nosebleed.

I am running through the streets, low to the ground, and I am joined by large, red and brown fox. She runs with me for a while and then asks me to stop. She comes up and licks my face, and I can smell her very strongly. She wants me to go with her. Go where, I ask, thinking it strange that the dog talked, yet the woman never said a word to me. To my home, she says. China.

We start running again, only this time, much faster. We are running straight for a fog bank sliding in low over the streets. The fox jumps up through the fog and disappears. I follow, only to find I am standing on top of the fog, which feels like a soft, wet pillow beneath me. The fog lifts us up and has become a cloud. The fox walks over to me and says, thank you for helping me to live...

I woke up with blood all down the front of my T-shirt. It was morning. I got up, changed clothes, and started the walk to Chu's house.

He was waiting for me in his office, looking stern. "Ya Shen. You didn't go hunting last night."

"No, I didn't."

He didn't move. "May I ask why?"

I leaned forward. "Okay, I'll tell you. For starters, I'm not a murderer and I will not be an accomplice to a murder."

For one second, I saw surprise register on his face, then

the mask was back up. "What are you talking about?"

"I'm talking about the fact that you are a lot older than you look, and I'm talking about how you go about doing that."

He instantly whipped his head around to stare at the books behind him. "You came into my private office like a common thief? What have I done to deserve such disrespect?"

"It's nothing personal. I needed answers that I didn't think you would give me. I thought there was more to this than a simple grudge between you and David Wan."

Chu shook his head, disgusted. "You have betrayed my trust in you. I cannot believe that you would go behind my back."

"And I can't believe that I've aligned myself with a life-stealer! How can you do that to your own people—"

"You are in a position to judge no one!" he thundered, rising from his chair. "Did you once, in your arrogance, ever stop to think that these people may have willingly given up a year of their life? For the chance at making their dreams come true?"

"Spare me your sales pitch. You shorten people's lives in order to make yours longer. You want to do the same thing to the Fox because she's over 500 years old. You can take more from her, and it won't be missed."

"Yes, that is true. And then I will not take any from my people for a long, long time."

I hadn't considered that, but it was too late. "I won't do it."

Chu's face froze. A look came over him that made me question my decision. One muscle in his cheek twitched as he spoke. "You deny me?"

"Yes."

"You fool! You know nothing! You read a few sentences in a book, you think it makes you an expert on me, my family? The family you are a part of? I have given you my library, my trust, my resources, my family name, and you would now deny me?" He made a visible effort to compose himself. "I can see they were right about you. They tried to tell me, but I just wouldn't listen. You are just like all the others. Ignorant. Pompous. You don't even know when you have been infected with magic."

"What are you talking about?"

"The Fox bit you, did she not? Are you having nosebleeds now? Strange dreams? You are becoming like her, you fool."

I felt hot anger boil up in my stomach. I knew right away that he was right, and I was an idiot not to have put that together. "Why didn't you tell me?"

"Why didn't you ask me? You didn't even know she was a shape-shifter until you read it in my books. I would have told you. In fact, I tried to warn you, but your pride and arrogance kept you from considering that I might know something about it."

It had been years since I'd been talked to that way. "You should have told me what you wanted her for."

"Why? It's none of your business. Part of our arrangement, as my adopted son, was that you do things for me when I ask them of you. Our deal did not include a detailed explanation of my motives. And yet, you still didn't ask me directly, but you take the answers from me. How insulting. You are completely without honor."

His face was red and dangerous. I'd had enough of this, anyway. "You know what? Fuck this. I don't need it." I walked out with him screaming my name.

There is nothing worse than drinking to get drunk at two in the afternoon. I really needed to do it, but I didn't want to go to Ping Ping's and endure the insults of Monkey and the

198

other regulars. The last thing I needed was jibes about being Chu's errand boy. I went instead to Parasol Liquor, where I could buy booze to take home and be as pitiful as I wanted to be. With two fifths of bourbon in a brown paper bag, I went straight up to my room and sat in my chair, turned to face the window.

As I drank mechanically, I thought about the chances I'd made, the resources I'd squandered, and the opportunities I'd blown since coming to this town. Chu and the family figured heavily through it all, either in spirit or in deed. Chu was one of maybe three people in that family that didn't hate me. Everyone else would be happy if I just went away and never came back. Somehow, I got myself caught up in this situation, and I had completely lost touch with my real mission: figure out what happened to my family.

The first fifth didn't last very long at all.

When I saw her looking in my window from the fire escape, long dark hair blowing in the breeze, I thought I was dreaming again. She stepped in and walked right up to me, as beautiful as ever, wearing her ever-present cat burglar suit like a second skin. Looking down at me, she jerked her head back in the direction of the window. It was a very dog-like gesture. She smiled, did it again, and then squatted down to look me in the face.

It finally hit me through the bourbon soaked fog. She was here, in my apartment. The chance to square everything up with Chu, the cause of all my problems, was looking at me like a dog that wants to go outside and play. All these months of chasing her and she just walks right in. I had to laugh. She joined in. I had no idea of what to do with her. No matter how I played it out in my head, someone would lose. If I brought this girl in, there's no telling what Chu would do to her. If I let her go, I ran the risk of permanently severing all ties with Chu and his resources, and I still badly needed answers to my questions. She touched my arm at the spot where she'd bitten me, and a patch of coarse, red-brown hairs sprung up under her fingers. I could sense her loneliness, her hopefulness. I could smell it. And I could sympathize with how she felt because I felt it, too.

This is not good, I thought. She would have me join her, I was certain of that. And a part of me wanted that, if only to continue to have some sort of interaction with her. But the larger part of me screamed at the absurdity of that thought. I was off the path of my personal journey so far that I had no clue what to do. So I went with the only choice that has never once betrayed me. I chose to help myself. I looked at my alarm clock and saw that it was after midnight.

The Fox made the head tossing gesture again and smiled and nodded. I came up hard and fast, catching her under the chin with my boot. She lurched backward, howling in pain. I jumped on her and hit her three times in the left temple. The third tap made her eyes roll up in her head, and she slumped to the side. I shook her to make sure she was out, then got off of her and got to work tying her up with a length of clothesline. Then I called Mi Hei, waking her from a sound sleep, and then I brewed some coffee and splashed cold water on my face. By the end of my second cup, she was waiting for me outside the building, impatiently honking her horn.

Mi Hei shook her head as she drove. "You're already in hot water. This is just going to make it worse."

"Mi Hei, you don't know shit. For once, just shut up and drive."

Her eyes narrowed, and she opened her mouth to yell at me, but the knocking in the trunk started up again. She turned the radio up louder to drown it out and fumed to herself.

As we pulled into the driveway, I noted the time on her dashboard. 2:03 a.m. We stopped, and I popped the trunk. Mi Hei and I carried the securely trussed Fox to the door, and I rang the bell. There was movement in the house. I looked down at the Fox. Her eyes were large and sad. I tried not to think about it.

Su opened the door, rubbing his eyes. I picked up the Fox. "Wake Chu. I've got something for him."

Su gaped. He smiled and ran down the hall. Mi Hei walked in around me and stood with a hand on her hip in the entrance hall. Chu appeared shortly, dressed in pajama bottoms and a red smoking jacket. I stood the Fox upright.

"Can you take her influence out of me?"

He paused a second before answering. "Yes, I can."

"Do you have some way of keeping her captive when she changes back into her true shape?"

"Yes."

"Then, I propose that we do this thing now, while she is in her were-form, and sort out our personal business later."

Chu studied me intently, his arms folded. He turned to Mi Hei. "Call your father." And he walked back to his study.

I looked at Mi Hei, who was fiddling with her cell phone. "What am I supposed to do with this?"

She shrugged. "Go to hell, Bowen. I don't know shit, remember?" She dialed Jiang Shui's number and spoke into the phone. I took a seat to wait.

Thirty minutes later, Jiang Shui strode through the door, sparing me and the trussed-up Asian woman on the floor the barest of glances on his way to Chu's office. Mi Hei was gone, and the Fox and I were alone. I crept down the long hall and put my ear to the office door. It was tough to make out what they were saying.

"...told you he was dangerous..."

"...much good...not like this..."

"...brought her to me...mean something..."

"...would have agreed with you...had visions for a while now..."

"...what I thought?"

"...will save the family..."

"...betrayal...deceit..."

"...dealings with devils..."

"...family...honor..."

"...punish...any of us..."

I crept back to the foyer. They talked for another ten minutes or so. When the door opened and footsteps walked down the hall, it was Jiang Shui that stuck his head around the corner.

"Bowen, bring her to the library."

I picked her up and followed Jiang. Chu had cleared away one of the tables. I set her down on it. "Will this hurt her?"

Chu glanced up at me. "No, we are just turning the bite inside out to take her essence out of you." He nodded at the chair. "Sit here. Take your coat off."

I did as I was told. Jiang took my arm and laid it across her stomach. He and Chu joined hands over us and began to chant. Chu said things in Mandarin that Jiang duplicated. The Fox began to thrash on the table, and Chu held her steady as Jiang made a pulling motion over my arm.

The pain of the bite came back to me and set my arm on fire. No skin was broken, but I could feel something leaving me, like a string, traveling the length of my shoulder and out the little scar. I clenched my fist and gritted my teeth. Jiang stopped pulling. My whole arm felt dead. I was suddenly very tired. Jiang held his hand over her head and dropped it down. She reacted violently. Jiang held her steady. Chu reached into his pocket and withdrew some gray powder, which he sprinkled over her face. "Sleep," he said. She nodded off almost immediately.

I felt a surge of anger well up again. Still withholding stuff from me. I could've used that in my hunt, I thought. Then I saw the looks on their faces and swallowed that thought. Jiang spoke to me. "We have a lot to do. You don't. Stay in the guest room tonight. We will talk tomorrow."

I was too tired to argue. I nodded and went to bed.

I checked my nose the next morning. No bleeding. My arm was still numb, but moveable. I put on my pants from the night before and a clean T-shirt from the closet and walked to the dining room. Su smiled as he came from the kitchen, bearing food on a tray.

"Ya Shen, they are on the veranda, waiting for you."

"Thanks."

I followed him out. The morning was cool and bright, and Chu's garden was in rare form. He and Jiang sat at the table, both looking tired. At Chu's side was a large bamboo cage, decorated with red ribbons and iron disks with Chinese characters on them. The Fox was inside, pacing and panting. She was reddish-brown with a white breast and pointed ears. This was her true shape. It was very hard to wrap my mind around the fact that this was the same woman I'd been chasing for two months. I shuddered at the thought, even as a wave of affectionate sadness passed over me. The fox in the cage could have been me, were it not for the two men sitting at the table. I joined them. "Good morning, Jiang Shui, good morning, Master Chu."

"Good morning," they said formally. Su served us tea and left.

"I wanted to thank you both for taking care of me last night, and I want to apologize for my actions."

Chu raised his eyebrows and said nothing. Jiang sipped his tea. "Mr. Bowen, what makes you think that will make it all better?"

"What?" I took a sip of tea to cut off the expletive that leapt to mind.

"Do you have any idea of the gravity of what you have done? Never mind, I can see that you do not. What you have done is unforgivable, inexcusable."

"I find it hard to believe that I can't make it right with Chu in some way."

"No, not just Father, you have insulted the whole family." He was talking calmly, no trace of anger in his voice. I wanted him to yell at me, so I could get upset, too.

"Look, Jiang-San, I really am sorry. I have been a total asshole lately. It's my fault. But I can fix this, I just know it."

Now Chu spoke. "Do you remember our deal? Not the family obligations, but our business arrangement? Well, I will address you as your adopted father first. Thank you for bringing me this gift. You have provided me with strength to endure the attacks of my enemies and I am very grateful. Now, as to your apology, I will accept it. But you must make amends." He paused to drink his tea. "As your business partner, I am asking the following of you. Leave this house and do not come back until you learn humility. I want you to bring me proof of your humility."

I was sick to my stomach and confused. "Proof? What proof?"

"You will know it when you have found it." And with that, he turned away.

I looked at Jiang Shui. He nodded, satisfied. There wasn't anything left to do. I got up, stuck my hand in the cage, and scratched the Fox behind the ear. She licked my hand. My coat was still in the library. I retrieved it and started the long walk home.

The Kindness of Strangers, First Refrain

Chu kicked me out a week ago. My money ran out yesterday. I don't remember much after that.

I walked on shaky legs, lost in the neon lights and unintelligible chatter of the street. This all looked familiar, but I had no real idea of where I was or where I was going. I kept tripping over my feet, stumbling into other pedestrians, who would yammer at me and push me away. I swore at them each in turn, throwing out curses indiscriminately. Eventually, I found a gentleman who knew what the phrase "cocksucker" meant, and he hammered a fist into my gut and another into the side of my head. I turned to follow the spin of it all and ended up on the sidewalk. There was a pool of darkness in front of me. I crawled towards it and hugged myself and watched the people walk by. A spell came to mind, but I couldn't remember what it would do. I sat there, my back against the cold bricks. I thought about the last meal I'd eaten.

Michael Chu had met me in Germantown, which was as far away from Chinatown fundamentally as we could get. He sat down opposite me, eyeing the patrons in the café warily. "Sam, I'm not supposed to be talking to you."

"I know, Michael. Thank you for coming." Our eyes met and he looked away, embarrassed. He owed me, and we both knew it. I wasn't afraid to call that marker in if I had to.

The waitress appeared and took our order. I picked the

large shepherd's pie, which would fill me up with room to spare. She left and came back with water, which I gulped down.

Michael frowned, concerned. "You okay?"

"Yeah, just a little hungry. Listen, I wanted to talk to you about your father."

"Sam, I can't—"

"Just listen. I know you two don't always get along, but you're the only one I can talk to about this."

Michael drummed his fingers on the table. "Yeah, and that's precisely why you shouldn't take any advice I have to give. Do you have any idea what a controversy anglicizing my name was?" I shook my head. "He wouldn't even speak to me until I agreed to run the Cultural Center. Hell, Sam, I still have relatives that deny my existence. See, I was the black sheep of the family, until..."

I watched him swallow the rest of that sentence. "Until me, right?"

He shrugged apologetically. "Sorry, Sam. But you are the adopted son, which makes you second-class in the family's eyes. Plus, you're white. And now you are being difficult." He smiled. "We aren't the easiest people in the world to get along with."

"Who, your family or the Chinese in general?"

He shrugged again. "Take your pick."

Our food showed up, and we talked around bites. "What about this quest I am supposed to do? Prove my worth, or something like that."

Michael's eyes met mine. "He said humility. Prove your humility. And to be honest, Sam, I don't know how you're going to do that. For us, it's pretty simple. We live with the pecking order every day. You, on the other hand, are going to have to alter your thinking completely."

206

"Great. So, tell me what I need to say."

Michael shook his head. "It doesn't work that way. I can't tell you what to say, and even if I could, the old man wouldn't believe it for a second. He can see your heart, you know."

"Well, shit, Michael, I'm up against a wall here!" The waitress made to refill my drink, but I waved her off. "Can you give me at least a hint of what I'm supposed to do?"

He sat back and rubbed his eyes with his thumb and forefinger. "Geez...okay...in his eyes, you are an obtainer. You get and do things for him. He would expect you to bring him something tangible. I think. What tangible thing means a lot to you?"

"My duffel bag, but he wouldn't want that, would he?"

"I doubt it. Shit, Sam, maybe he does want an apology. I don't know. If I thought I could help you, I would. Really. Look, I'll keep thinking about it." He stood up and reached for his wallet. "I gotta go, man. Here, pay for us with this." He handed me a hundred dollar bill. "And keep the change."

I looked at the bill. "Thank you, Michael."

"Forget it." he smiled. "You're family, right?" He looked around quickly. "Just do me a favor and lay low until you and Dad can sort this out, okay? Hang in there, buddy." He patted my shoulder and was gone.

That was three days ago. I took the money and stretched it out as far as I could, which meant buying the generic label bourbon and a lot of stops to Zhu's Noodle Hut. Yesterday, I decided I needed some company and went to Ping Ping's, where I succeeded in doing what they quickly dubbed "Bowen's Hat Trick." I threw a drink on Monkey, got the crap beat out of me, and got kicked out of the bar.

I went to Doyle's to drink and eat, mainly because Rosemary, the best waitress in the bar, had been comping my meals of late. Not that I cared, I would take what I could get. I showed up still drunk and was quickly hustled out the back by Fu Yan, the alcoholic bouncer. For a guy pushing sixty, he had strength like you wouldn't believe. That and the way he was holding my wrist and shoulder, which made it really easy to direct me wherever he wanted me to go. As he released me into the alley, he said, "You disgrace your family here with your presence. Go sleep it off."

"What the fuck is it to you what I do or where I drink, old man?" I yelled at him. He stood there in the door, arms crossed, looking very not drunk at all. I yelled at him for a few minutes more, expressing my distaste for him and others like him. He never made a move towards me. Eventually, I ran out of steam and turned away. He whistled at me and threw me a gourd. It was full of liquid.

"What you do with it will decide your fate." And then he turned and walked back inside. The gourd contained rice wine. I drank it all on the way back to Chinatown. By the time I hit the Welcome Pagoda, I was completely tanked. The late night neon lights blurred together, making me dizzy. I concentrated on making my feet work, keeping them on the sidewalk. Every time I looked up, there was another strange face looking at me. I yelled inarticulately at them, and they all disappeared. A wave of nausea and fatigue suddenly descended over me. Home, I thought, I've got to get home. Pagoda House. Benny the ghost. I had stayed away from the building out of embarrassment, but now I was past the point of caring.

Someone bumped into me, sending me caroming into the street. There was a flash of lights, a blaring horn, and then I was down. That wasn't fair, I thought, I didn't even get to throw a punch. I laughed at my humor, sitting in the street with my legs out in front of me like they were broken. Hands grabbed me and lifted me up, put my legs under me. I could see it was a man and he was worried about something. He kept asking me questions that, for the life of me, I could not understand. "Why don't you fuckin' talk right?" I yelled in his face. He pushed me away, and that meant down, too. When I came up, his back was to me as he walked away. I planted a kick in his kidneys, yelling my head off. He turned, holding his back, and made threatening motions with a cell phone in his hand. I knocked it away and leapt on him.

By the time I had my hands around his throat, we had drawn a crowd. Something hit me in the face, which brought big flowers of pain behind my eyes. I tried to crawl through the crowd, but they started kicking me and hitting me. I felt bruises and knots form all over me, and there was a light dancing behind my eyes. I kept crawling until I hit the alley, then made for a hole in the stack of garbage cans and curled up. They kicked the cans and screamed things at me for a few minutes longer, and then left me alone. I hurt. But if I could get to my room, I could fix myself up. I stood up, started walking, and blacked out.

A sharp, strong smell, close to my face, woke me up. Urine. I didn't stop to wonder if it was mine or not and crawled away from it. I was in an alley. No telling which one or where.

From your hands and knees, all alleys look pretty much alike.

It was daytime. People and cars bustled and shuffled beyond the mouth of the alley, and I got up and staggered instinctively towards it. Home, I thought, I still have to get home. My body still hurt, and my face felt heavy. I stank. I was sick, hung over. It was all too much to bear at once. Benny might look down on me, but at least I'll get some of these bruises taken care of.

The street beyond the alley looked totally familiar, but I couldn't place it. I was in Chinatown, that much was certain. I took a wild guess which direction my apartment was and started walking, staying close to the buildings, avoiding people, who paid me zero attention in return. I walked and walked, looking for something I knew. I was tired, weak. Without really realizing it, I had left Chinatown completely. I swore and started looking for the Welcome Pagoda that served as the tourist's gateway to the neighborhood. When I couldn't find that, I sat down to rest, ready to cry.

My back up against the building, head down, trying to think, it didn't even occur to me how that might look until I heard a clink between my legs. A quarter. Dropped by one of the passers-by, a neat-looking man in a casual business suit. I took the quarter and threw it at him and yelled, "Hey! Keep your money, I ain't no goddamn bum!"

He turned towards me, still walking, "Yeah, right, you look inna mirror lately?"

Shit, I thought. I had no idea what I looked like. In my addled state, the only place with mirrors that I could think of was Spec's the lighthouse bar in Oceanview. But if I didn't know where Chinatown was, how would I ever find that? Hopeless.

As I sat there, feeling sorry for myself, I became aware of someone standing over me. I looked up into a field of white, topped by a human face. He was tall, maybe 6'2", wearing a white suit, white vest, white pants, white shoes, right down to his buttons and accessories. His friendly face was long and broad, and he bore a shock of jet-black hair that threatened to curl if it grew so much as another half-inch. In that get-up, he looked like a cartoon Southern colonel. When he spoke, his voice was deep and without an accent.

"Friend, you look like you are in a world of shit."

210

Great, I thought, that's just what I need, another religious nut. "I'm fine, really. Don't trouble yourself."

He squatted down. "From the South? Missouri?"

"Kentucky." Impressive deduction on his part, but not impressive enough for me to hand my soul over to him for salvation.

He nodded to my appearance. "As bad as you look, you don't seem to be a professional at this."

"I'll be fine."

He shook his head. "Southern boy like you doesn't even know that pride is one of the seven deadly sins of man?"

This guy was not going to drop it. "Who are you?"

He smiled, stood up, and fished out a business card. "Cadillac Arlington Nicholson." He squatted back down and handed it to me. "But call me Caddy. Please. No, really. I hate C.A. and I hate the way Cadillac sounds. You?"

It took a moment for the question to sink in and find meaning. "Sam C. Bowen."

He shook my hand. "What's the 'C' stand for?"

I made a face. "Corbie."

He laughed. "Son, that don't even come close to beating Cadillac Arlington." He shook his head. "Can I give you a lift somewhere?"

I thought about this odd duck and his won't-go-away attitude and the fact that I had no clue where I was right then. This was a weird situation, but I wasn't adverse to a little help. "Yeah, that'd be nice." I told him. As he was helping me up, I asked, "So, what's your angle?"

"Your nose is broken. Hold still." He put his hands on either side of my face and, before I could stop him, reset my nose. I howled and swore for a minute while he looked on. "Better?" he asked.

My face no longer felt thick, only sore, and it was a lot

easier to breathe. The pain was galvanizing, and my head was a lot clearer. "Yeah, much. Thanks. So, about your angle?"

"Don't you believe in altruism?" he asked.

"Not really, no."

"Are you hungry?" he asked.

"Starving."

"Come on. We'll talk about it over some food." I followed him to his car, a huge 1962 Cadillac, the long boat with the fins, fire engine red, completely tricked out and cherry. He noticed my look. "I tried to distance myself from it, but I found that people expected me to live up to my name. So, I embraced it."

I opened the door and sat down gingerly, aware of my appearance. As Nicholson started the car, I flipped the visor down and looked in the mirror. "I look like hammered shit," I said. My left eye was black, and I had a multitude of nicks and scratches all over the right side of my face. My nose was red, puffy, and now had a hell of a lump across the bridge. The rest of me was dirt and grime. We drove a block before he said anything.

"So, where to?" he asked.

"Chinatown."

"You want to eat Chinese food?"

"No, I want to clean up a little bit first, so if you could just swing by my place, I can—"

We stopped for a light. He looked over at me. "Sam, I know you don't know me from Adam, but I'm gonna ask you to trust me here for a second. Can you do that?"

I sized him up again. "Okay," I said cautiously, pretty confidant that I could get away from this guy if I had to.

"I'm pretty good at figuring people out. Part of my job, you see. Just let me talk for a minute, then you can tell me

212

how full of shit you think I am." We started moving again. "Ordinarily, you're a pretty resourceful guy. You take care of yourself, you don't get in anyone's way. Self-made, self-reliant, right?" When I didn't say anything he pressed on. "Something tells me you just ran into a string of bad luck. In between jobs right now, you had a couple of bills come due, something like that. So, you did what you could, but it wasn't enough. Now you're feeling sorry for yourself. You have no friends or family in town, and you are on your last buck or two. How'd I do?"

"That's close, close enough, I guess."

He smiled to himself, nodding thoughtfully. "Ordinarily, I would not have stopped to help someone such as yourself, because either I had other business or had enough to worry about myself. But today, I have come into some luck of my own. I have two big business deals to complete out in Trinity, and they will keep me flush for a long time."

I looked at him. "All I need, really, Mr. Nicholson, is a ride to Chinatown and maybe some food if you can spare it..."

"Caddy, call me Caddy, please. No, Sam, you need more than that. You need to change your luck. And I want to help you do that. Will you let me do that?"

"What exactly do you have in mind?"

He laughed. "This ain't no pick-up, son. But I can help you, if you let me. I want to help you. Who knows? You may be able to do something for me down the road. I may be in miserable straits and have to rely on the kindness of strangers."

I sat up straighter. The last time I had heard that phrase was almost a year ago from Chu Sheng Kai. It stuck with me ever since. The *Gone With the Wind* reference notwithstanding, it bought him a little more time. "Okay, I'll accept your help. But no charity, okay? I'll pay you back. Deal?"

"It's a deal." He smiled and stuck out his hand again. I shook it and actually felt the deal cement between us. He had a salesman's handshake.

He drove into Spanishtown and pulled up at the Pacific Vista hotel. I knew of the place but never had the occasion to go there. It was swanky, way more expensive than I had seen in a long time. My appearance caused some concern amongst the staff, including the tall, nervous man behind the counter. He viewed me with obvious distaste as Caddy picked up his messages.

In the elevator, I had a chance to look at myself in the full-length mirrors. I looked like a bum. I didn't even know myself. Caddy noticed my embarrassment. "Don't worry. We'll fix that, too."

The door opened at the penthouse level, and he steered me to the Southern Suite, an opulent example of excessive living straight out of the movies. "First thing is to get your-self cleaned up," he said, clapping me on the shoulder. I made a beeline for the bathroom and spent thirty minutes getting myself right. I stood under the hot water and worked the knots and kinks out of my body, then lathered myself up and rinsed twice. When I finally emerged, I found shaving supplies and a first aid kit on the counter. That took another twenty minutes. Finally, I took a good long look at myself in the mirror. I looked like me again. Felt like me, too. I looked around, but my clothes were gone. I panicked for a second. This is exactly what I was afraid of.

"Hey, Caddy, I need to get dressed, man," I said loudly through the door. When I didn't get an answer, I opened it a crack and saw garment bags hanging on the knob. In the room, I could hear him talking on the phone to someone, so I pulled the clothes into the bathroom and gave us both some privacy.

It was a black suit with hint of gray in the weave, stylishly cut, with a black tie and some black dress shoes, polished to a mirrored surface. I dressed slowly, pondering the implications of these gifts. The suit fit perfectly, even the shoes. I almost didn't recognize myself yet again. The color reminded me of the last time I wore a suit, the day I buried my parents. I looked back in the mirror and saw myself looking very young again, even though I felt extremely old.

I walked back out into the room. Caddy was hanging up the phone. He turned around, smiling. "How'd I do? I guessed on the size."

"Damn good guess. It all fits." I looked at the phone behind him. "So, what do you do, anyway? I mean, is this your line of work?"

He shook his head and grinned. "Nope. Just got an eye for clothes. I'm in sales and marketing, what else?"

"What else what?"

He spread his hands to indicate the whole room. "What else can get me all of this?"

I could think of about a dozen things right off the top of my head, but I knew what he meant and nodded with him. "Well, I'm clean and dressed. Now what?"

Caddy headed for the door. "First, we eat. Then, we drive. Come on."

We had dinner in the hotel restaurant, with service so complete that it was almost intrusive. The type of places I normally eat, my service stops when the guy at the counter hands me my change. I spoil myself at Mama Wang's, when her horse-faced daughters refill my water glass. This, however, was almost too much.

I ordered the beef lasagna with garlic bread and a salad, and Caddy followed suit. He also selected a bottle of red wine. The waiter's eyebrows shot up, so I knew it wasn't cheap. They brought us appetizers and bread, and I dug in heartily.

"You might want to save some room for the meal, Hoss," Caddy said good-naturedly.

"Don't worry, Caddy, I'll clean my plate." Then to change the subject, I asked, "So, what do you do?"

He waved his hand dismissively. "I do the boring shit. I get people the things they need to make other things work. I rep nine different companies, vast conglomerates, with global ties, and fill out a bunch of orders and see that things get from point A to point B on time." His eyes twinkled as he smiled. "But I do it on commission."

"Well, here's to commission." I raised my glass.

"Brother, you said it." We touched goblets and drank. The wine was heady and strong. Nice change from cheap bourbon. I drained my glass and poured myself another.

"Okay," I said, "You still haven't given me a straight answer. Why are you doing this for me?"

"I told you, I am in a position to help you out."

"Bullshit. Give me the real reason."

He started to speak, stopped himself, then started again. "Look, Sam, what do you need to hear? What can I say that will allow you to trust me?"

"No one does anything for free...and you being a salesman should understand exactly where I'm coming from."

He nodded appreciatively. "Okay, that's true. Then let me say that I am speculating on your future. I think you will be of great use to me some time from now, and I want to establish a line of credit and a relationship with you right now, so you will be more inclined to help me later. Okay?"

"Fair enough. I just wanted to know where we stand." I drained my goblet again and poured another glass.

216

Caddy looked me right in the eye. "You drink too much, you know."

"I don't, either," I answered automatically. "I go for months and months drinking socially or not at all..."

"Yeah, and then you make up for it by binging and boozing until you are thrown out of your perceived reality. It's a defense mechanism, Sam. You're throwing walls up, for some reason." He took a sip of his wine. "But you do drink too much." He shook his head. "And they call it 'demon alcohol.' Heh. Devil had nothing to do with it. It's all man's fault, yes sir."

I wanted to be mad at him, but something about what he said got into my brain and wouldn't let go. I fell silent, thinking about it until our food came. It was the best lasagna I'd ever had, and our conversation revolved around that very fact as we ate. Finally, I pushed my plate away, stuffed.

"Well, that was just fine. Thank you, Caddy."

"My pleasure," he said. The waiter came by with the bill, and he signed it to his room. "It's about time to motor. You ready?"

"Now where to?"

He grinned, showing a lot of teeth. "Trinity."

I'd never been to Trinity, but everyone knew about it. All of the locals rolled their eyes at the prospect of a little Las Vegas strip set up on the Indian reservation, but they secretly said they had a blast when they went there. For tourists, it was a chance to do something almost normal while visiting San Cibola.

We rode out to Trinity with the top down, and it felt great to be moving so fast for once. We got plenty of looks in that car, dressed as we were, and more than a few stares from pretty women.

"God damn, I love this car." Caddy said to no one in

particular. "So, Sam, tell me your story."

"Okay, what do you want to know?"

"Well, for starters, what do you do?"

I hesitated. What do I tell him? Certainly not the truth. He couldn't handle it. I opted for careful omission.

"I do research for a living, and I'm writing a book on the side. My employers are back East, and they send me money and supplies from time to time. Mostly, I work out of my house, taking contract work as it comes."

He nodded. "Sounds a little risky to me. I mean, no steady income and all that."

"Normally, it's not. And, as you pointed out, I am real good at living by my wits. But I hit this patch of bad luck. Due to a computer error, my check got delayed. And I don't have any more work lined up, because of a falling out between me and a couple of...clients."

"Life can be a fickle bitch sometimes," he mused.

"Yeah. Anyway, I had everything going just right, and then all at once, it took a tumble on me. So now I have no money and no means."

"You thinking about giving up?" he asked.

I turned to face him. "What makes you say that?"

"The way I found you. You decided to give all of your control over to the world and let it decide what to do for you." He kept his eyes on the road as he talked, but it still felt like he was looking at me. "Look, Sam, I'm a people reader. It's a big part of what I do, and I am damned good at it. And you can trust me when I tell you that you have a lot more to do before you hang up your spurs. I know you must have an end result to your personal plans, you just got caught in the bullshit. You lost your way on your path. Hey, it happens to all of us. But that's no reason to get all loopy and stupid." He paused, reached for a pack of cigarettes, shook one out, and lit it.

"You will continue to be your own worst enemy until you figure out what it is that's making you so unhappy." He blew a smoke ring that was instantly consumed by the wind.

"That's a lot of pop psychology, there, Caddy. You sell those motivational tapes or something?"

"Yeah, I do, as a matter of fact. But can you say anything I've told you is wrong or off-base?"

I thought about it for a second. "No."

"Okay, then." He smiled, and offered me a cigarette. "Want one?"

"Never started."

"Good thing, they shorten your life."

We drove down the strip of casinos, bathing in the colored neon that got gradually brighter in the setting sun. The evening breeze came with us and cooled everything down about fifteen degrees, which made for very pleasant driving.

The Timberlands Casino was the most gaudy, most cater-to-the-tourist casino of the lot. The theme was log cabins and teepees, cowboys and Indians. The hotel itself was fairly small and normal looking, but the casino out back looked like it was built with oversized Lincoln logs. Having spent several years among the native cultures of America, I was offended for them. As we turned into the parking lot, I asked Caddy, "Your business is here?"

"Yep." He swung into valet parking, and the two attendants in Sheriff's outfits were mighty impressed. He handed the lead kid a twenty dollar bill. "Mind my hoss, Hoss. Don't let anyone breathe on her."

"Yes, sir!" The kid eased into the seat and pulled the car out of sight. We walked inside the hotel and through the spacious, tacky lobby. Caddy leaned into me. "Look, Sam, do me a favor and wait just outside the casino entrance for me. I won't be a minute."

"Is your business in the casino?"

"Sam, my business is the casino."

I pondered that cryptic remark as he turned away and walked over to a group of three suited men, all natives from the reservation. I heard him say, "How y'all doin'?" in that accentless voice, then the noise of the casino overtook all conversation. They talked for a few minutes, laughing and smiling. One of them nodded to me, and Caddy said something to them that made them all nod and look over. I nodded back by way of a greeting. One of them handed Caddy something, and he turned and walked over to me. "Listen, this is going to take a bit. I get these complimentary lines of credit from them every time I come here, but I never use them. Why don't you take these and go have fun?"

I started to protest, but he pushed five chips into my hand. "Please, I insist. Go on, I'll come get you when I'm done."

"Okay," I said, waggling a finger at him, "but I'm considering this as part of the loan."

He grinned. "Whatever you want," he said, as he turned and walked back to the group.

I looked down at the chips as I walked into the muted light of the casino and my heart gave a leap. Five one hundred dollar chips. Shit. I debated on just putting them in my pocket and walking back into the lobby to wait, but I quickly realized that I had in my hand a chance to square myself with Caddy, Benny, and anyone else for that matter. With renewed purpose, I started looking for something to play.

The slot machines were right out. Succubae, all of them. That left Blackjack, a game I've always hated; Baccarat, a game I didn't understand; the roulette wheel, which couldn't possibly be worth anyone's time; and craps. Those tables were in the middle and I occasionally heard shouts of glee as something happened. I knew more about craps than any of the others, so I made a space for myself at one of the busy tables and took a look.

The board was amazingly complicated. I stood there for a long time, watching the table, the dealers, and the other players. It took a while, but I eventually got a sense of what the game was and how it worked. After that, I turned my attention to the other players and copied the most conservative player. The guy I was following would bet on the point, then place a second bet on the next roll. Finally, he would throw out small chips onto the "hard way" rolls: double twos, double threes, double fours, and double fives. He was hitting better than 60%, so I took his game plan and ran with it.

The problem was, I kept getting crazy. I'd get up a few hundred, then start betting wild...and losing big. Three times I got down to around two hundred bucks and had to nurse it back up to my original stake. The guy I was following kept gradually collecting more chips, while mine gradually dwindled.

Finally, I was way down, with under forty bucks in chips. The guy throwing the dice was in dire straits, and he'd been throwing like shit all night. He rolled...the point was four. A tough one to make. Without thinking, I threw out my single twenty-five dollar chip and said, "On the hard way."

The dealer slid my chip over into the appropriate box and repeated the bet. The dice flew...two twos. Everyone went nuts. The dealer looked at me and before I could stop myself, I said, "Let it ride." Even the guy I had been copying all night shot me a look. Dealer said, "Pushing the hard way," and dropped his eyes to the board.

The dice rolled, bounced and fell. Two twos. The other players exploded, clapping and shouting and patting me on the back. The dealer handed me a stack of chips and said, "Nice bet, sir."

"Lucky break," I said.

"Yeah, for him," said the guy I'd been copying all night. "You had no luck left so you took some of his."

For the first time, I really looked at the guy. He was Indian, in his mid-forties, wearing Bermuda shorts and a Hawaiian shirt. At his throat was a single black feather on a leather thong. "Excuse me?"

He leaned over so only I could hear him speak. "Like most everyone, you think luck works only for you. Luck never works for you, only for other people. You see what I'm saying? It's perspective. You obviously had some sort of system that was working, but then you started feeling 'lucky,' right? That's when you started losing. And you of all people should know better." He placed a bet on the come line without looking and kept talking. "I was you, I'd walk away now before the Spirits notice you have something that does not belong to you. And change your skin. It is not you." He raked in some chips and proceeded to ignore me.

I started to reply, but a friendly hand clapped me on the shoulder and I turned around. "How'd you do?" Caddy asked. I looked back at the man but he was gone, save for the feather on the empty chip tray. A raven feather. Was my spirit guide here? I looked around, but didn't see him. I shoved the feather into my pocket, intending to ask him about it later, and moved away from the table.

"C'mon, I'll show you." We walked to the change booth, and the cashier gave me just over two thousand dollars for my little pile of clay chips.

Caddy whistled. "Not bad, not bad at all."

I turned to him, money in hand. "Here's your original stake back, and here's for the suit and the meal." I handed him well over half of my winnings. The rest was going to square me on rent with Benny.

Caddy tried to hand me the money back. "Look, you should keep this, you need it much more than I do..."

"No, don't start that shit. You agreed to a loan, I'm just paying you back right now instead of later. Please, Caddy, I insist."

"But it's too much! I can't..."

"Then factor in for gas money." I looked at him evenly. He hesitated for a minute, then smiled and ruefully pocketed the money.

"Okay, okay," he laughed. "We're even-steven. Now, let me take you to breakfast."

"Breakfast?"

He tapped his watch. "It's six a.m. You've been gambling all night, Hoss."

"Jesus. Felt like maybe two-three hours."

"Pretty wild, huh? That's just how they want it."

I shook my head, suddenly very tired. "Actually, I'm bushed. Mind just dropping me off?"

"You got it. Let's go."

We stopped at a Burger King and got Caddy a coffee and some French toast sticks, which he ate deftly while he drove. I asked, "So, did you finish your business?"

"Oh yeah," he said, patting his breast pocket, "Got the contracts right here. They signed their life away to me."

"You cutthroat," I said.

"Brother, you better believe it." He looked at me from the corner of his eye. "Say, Sam, I've been thinking...would you like a job?"

"I don't know..." I started to say.

"No, really, I'm serious. You want to come work for me? I have tons of calls to make and frankly, it's nothing you can't handle instead of me. You'd be like a field agent. You're young, smart, and personable. Plus, you have no idea what kind of benefits I can offer you."

"You mean, you'd be my boss?"

"More or less. I'd hand out your assignments, you would go close deals. I'll get you a car, some plastic for traveling, you name it. I'll set you up."

I watched him as he talked, and something dangerous flickered across his face that I couldn't read. Something wasn't right with this situation, but I was too sleepy to see it. It occurred to me that I'd spent most of my time in Caddy's company either working off a drunk or groggy. My judgment was completely clouded.

"I don't know, man. I'm not a clock puncher. I never had a real job before, and I'm afraid I'd let you down."

He turned and looked right at me. "Sam, I know you better than you think. Trust me, the last thing you'd be to me is a disappointment. "

Then it hit me. He wasn't watching the road. At all. The car was driving by itself, straight down the highway. It took a lot to keep from reacting. I smiled, shook my head. "No thanks, man. I appreciate it, but I'll be all right."

He sighed, his eyes finally finding the road again. "Some days, I just can't win. Okay, pal, where to?"

"The Welcome Pagoda in Chinatown."

"I don't mind dropping you off at the door."

"Oh, I know," I lied, "I just want to walk home. Stretch my legs, get acquainted with the streets again."

He nodded, and I could tell he didn't believe me. But he answered cheerfully, "You got it."

We drove in silence until he screeched to a stop in front of the familiar landmark. Only the natives were up this early. I got out of the car quickly, knowing he'd want to shake hands. "Well, Caddy, thanks for everything. Really, I appreciate the chance to turn things around."

He nodded. "Glad I could help." He handed me a business card. "Listen, you change your mind about the job, you give me a call. I'll be here before you can hang up the phone."

I looked at it. A name and a phone number, nothing else. "I don't doubt it."

"See you around, Sam." I didn't like the way that sounded at all.

"Drive safe," I replied. I turned on my heel and walked quickly away, not looking back. Passing under the Pagoda's shadow was a transforming thing. I felt comfortable again. At home. It was time to get back to my life.

The early morning streets were choked with delivery trucks and pedestrians on their way to work. Old women carried bags of fresh food home. Commuters boarded buses. Everybody went about their business thoughtlessly. I spied a person or two that I knew and nodded to them. They did double takes at me in my suit.

When I spied my building, I almost broke into a run. The door banged open like it always did, and Benny popped out of the wall to greet me. "Sam! You back. I been so worried!"

"Hey, Benny." I put the bulk of my winnings on the counter. "Sorry this is late, man."

Benny blinked at me, then almost hugged me. I had to step back fast to avoid getting numbed. "Oh Sam, you dumb idiot! I no care about the money! You think everyone in this building is caught up on rent? Don't wander off like that again, you may get killed next time."

I self-consciously looked at the floor. "Yeah, but I still feel bad. I don't want to be a deadbeat."

"Hey! Where you get the nice suit?" he accused.

"Oh, this thing. It was a loan from a really weird guy."

"Hmm. It's not you."

"No," I agreed, "you're right, it's not. I'm gonna go up-stairs and change."

"Okay," he smiled and waved. "Oh, wait! I forgot. Your mail." He handed me a stack of letters. On top was an envelope from the Armitage Foundation. I opened it and found a sizable check, along with a letter of apology from the department. My stipend, plus a little extra, thanks to the sale of some recent occult items at a private auction.

Benny leaned in. "Good news?"

"Yeah, Benny, real good news. Food, rent, clothes, and supplies."

He walked back through the wall. "I knew your luck would change."

"Benny, you don't know the half of it." I walked upstairs to get out of the suit and into my rickety, comfortable bed.

The Dragon in Repose

WORSHIP

Chu Sheng Kai opened the door to his bedroom and stepped into the darkened hallway. Su Yun, the houseboy, stood to the left of the door, bleary-eyed but awake. He bowed and produced a waist-length jacket. Chu put it on, walked down the long hall to the back door, and let himself out.

At five in the morning, the temperature was a brisk sixty degrees. Chu walked through the garden, taking in the smell of the orchids and turned earth, and stopped briefly at a small wooden gate with a pillared arch over it. He drew three symbols in the air and pushed them with his mind into invisible locks. The gate swung open silently, and he passed through it.

He followed the trail that wound serpentine through the property on Nod Hill. The path curved up and around the hillside, forcing him to exert himself. No dogs barked and no one disturbed him at this early hour. The exercise felt good, and he concentrated on keeping his mind clear.

He paused briefly when the Buddhist temple loomed into

view. The building was only ten years old, but it had the look and feel of a traditional temple from the Mainland. There were little differences, such as the larger scale and size, and the use of modern building materials. To the communities surrounding it, the Buddhist Temple was a well-groomed monument to cultural diversity and one of the grand sites of the city. For thousands of people in Chinatown, it was also a place of worship. It was Chu's secret project, and he was very proud of it.

The gates were already open, and he could see orange-robed monks going about their business. Chu walked down the path and into the public grounds. He bowed to the temple, then lit incense and said a quick prayer for his family. That done, he stepped back and moved into the temple itself.

Fu Yan faced the door, sitting with his legs under him. When Chu entered, he stood and bowed. His usual attire, the much-repaired shirt and jacket, adorned with pouches and gourds, was gone. He wore a matching set of loose, black pants and shirt. Here, Fu Yan didn't look like a beggar or a drunkard. The eyes that shone out of his gnarled brows were calm and clear.

Chu shed his coat with a shrug. He was dressed in a similar fashion to Fu, but his pants were gray. They bowed to one another and assumed identical stances. Legs bent, arms outstretched. Fu started moving and Chu followed him, always a fraction behind. As Chu moved through the Tai Chi positions, he concentrated on his breathing and emptied his mind. Soon, the trance-like state spoke to him and he listened intently.

They spent an hour moving in harmony. Finally, Chu straightened, eyes open, and bowed deeply. Fu Yan did the same. Chu then sat down in a lotus position and watched Fu go through the kata of the Eight Drunken Fairies. After waltz-

ing about like a woman, he ended the kata by flipping up-
side-down and collapsing into a lotus position in front of Chu.

"As always, your technique is flawless," Chu said.

"You know, I could teach it to you," Fu nodded, "It's not
as if you don't have the time."

"No thank you, old friend. I have other means at my
disposal. You are lucky to get me to practice Tai Chi."

Fu scoffed. "You love Tai Chi. I think you are scared
you will have to get into a fight."

"You forget: the wise man avoids a fight."

"Or has younger men fight it for him," Fu taunted.

"Would you have me killed?" he asked in feigned shock.

Fu thumped his chest. "If your enemies killed you, I would
avenge your death." They both laughed at the childhood
promise they once made to each other. Fu stood and stretched.
"Let's collect my fee."

They strolled out of the temple and into the commons,
where two of the monks were selling sweet rice pudding,
mangos, and various buns. Fu selected a bun, a mango, and
a cup of pudding, and Chu paid for it. As they ambled back
to the path, Chu said, "You should charge me more for Tai
Chi lessons."

Fu shrugged. "You shouldn't pay my tab at Doyle's."

"I do it because we are friends, and I don't get to spend as
much time with you as I would like."

Fu nodded. "And I appreciate every kindness. But our
old fighting debts are long over with. We are old now." He
thumped Chu on the chest. "Even if some of us don't look
it."

Chu sighed. "We have talked about this before…" He
glanced behind him at the temple one last time before it vanished between the trees.

"And my answer is still the same. No thank you." He

finished off his rice pudding and pocketed the cup.

"Does it bother you that I..."

"No, it doesn't." Fu put half of the bun in his mouth and talked around it, "but I think it bothers you. That's part of why you are so nice to me."

Chu frowned. "That is not so! You are my oldest friend."

Fu nodded again. "I know. But still...Anyway, I thought you should know that your newest son was at the bar last night..."

Chu's lips tightened. "I don't want to hear about his revels."

"...but he drank club soda all night and sat in a corner."

"He did?"

"Yes. I think he is close."

"Let us hope." Chu sighed. "Anything else of late?"

"No, but that doesn't mean that things are quiet in the neighborhood." Fu tore the skin off his mango with practiced ease. "My offer still stands. If you need me, have that jackass son of yours, Jiang Shui, call me so I can beat him to your house." He motioned towards the back of Chu's estate ahead of them.

Chu smiled at the rivalry. "I know. Thank you." They patted each other on the back as Chu stepped inside his gate. "Take care. Perhaps you could join me for dinner tomorrow?"

Fu scratched his chin under his beard. "It's my night off. Okay, sure."

"Good. I'll see you then."

Fu waved and continued walking around the side to the street out front. Chu made his way back through the garden, where Su Yun had tea and breakfast laid out for him on the veranda.

BUSINESS

Jiang Shui wore a gray, European-cut jacket over a black turtleneck sweater. His legs casually crossed, he did his best to relax in the antique red velvet chair in Chu's office as he sipped his tea. Chu regarded his second-oldest son with interest.

"And what of the impending war?" he asked.

Jiang uncrossed his legs and sat up. "Do you want to hear this now? Or wait until our guests leave?"

"Tell me now."

Jiang pulled up an expensive leather case from beside the chair and flipped it open, withdrew several sheets of paper, and slid them across the massive desk. Chu picked them up and read them while Jiang spoke.

"This is our organization, converted into military units. That column on the left represents what we can afford to lose."

Chu frowned. "What do you think are our minimal losses?"

"I don't think there are any minimal losses. "

Chu put the papers down. "You don't think this is necessary, do you?"

Jiang took a sip of his tea. "I didn't say that."

"We take action only when there is no alternative."

"Yes, and being masterful is not always appropriate. Don't give me the Tao, Father, I can match you verse for verse."

"Don't forget your place." Chu reached for the intercom, ordered some tea for himself and sat back. "We will go to war. We have no choice. Wan Fei Ying has seen to that. Besides," he said with a smile, "you are forgetting the di Lessa family."

"I didn't forget, I just chose not to count on them." Jiang Shui stood up and straightened his clothing. "I think you are taking too many chances."

"The Dragon in repose has more choices than the Tiger at war."

Jiang frowned. "Who said that?"

Chu leaned closer. "Your grandfather."

The Liu family stood in his office, tightly clustered together, heads down. They wore their Sunday best, smartly ironed and pressed. The elder Liu's suit was at least ten years old and was the appropriate cut and color so that it could be worn to a wedding or a funeral. Mrs. Liu's dress was crisp and new and looked homemade but well made. The son was taller than both of them, which put him at no more than 5'6". He wore a blue blazer with matching shirt and starched blue jeans. Chu coughed. "Please, sit down." They did so, shuffling to the couch as a single entity.

"Mr. Liu, I understand your son is a senior in high school now." He looked at the boy, a gangly-limbed youth with glasses.

Mr. Liu nodded. "He has been accepted at Berkeley. He is to be an architect."

Chu looked at the boy. "What is your name?"

"Shou, Sir." He also wouldn't look Chu in the face.

"Why do you want to be an architect?"

Without hesitation, he said, "So I can redesign my father's grocery store. I hate the way it looks."

"Look at me." The boy did so. Chu focused on his eyes and asked, "Is that the only thing you want to do?"

"No, I want to start a new wave of architectural style that fuses the beauty of our culture with the baroque decadence of the early twentieth century art nouveau and change the world," he said quickly, then looked down again.

"Excellent!" Chu beamed. "A true artist."

"Our son is already very gifted..." his mother began.

"Remember your place!" Mr. Liu barked in Cantonese.

"No, it's all right." Chu walked around in front of his desk and folded his arms. "You were saying?"

She looked up, grateful. "He is very gifted as an artist. He received a scholarship. His tuition is paid for."

"I must confess, I am now confused. What is it that you want of me?"

Mr. Liu hesitated before he spoke. "We have saved every penny for our son. That money will go to pay his room and board. But he needs one thing in order to find his wife and find true happiness and be a leader."

Chu waited until it was apparent that no further statements were forthcoming. "And that thing is?"

Liu waved to his son. "Show Mr. Chu." The woman buried her face in her hands. The boy looked up and smiled widely.

Chu took a step back. "I see." He walked back around behind the desk and sat down. "How much will it cost?"

"I have an estimate..." Mr. Liu dug around in his pocket and produced a pink slip of paper. "He is a friend of the family."

Chu looked at the paper. The dentist was Chinese, and his office was in Chinatown. He read dollar amount at the bottom of the page and sat back in his chair. "And you know what the price for this would be?"

They nodded.

"Very well." He opened the desk drawer and dug around inside, brought out a sheet of paper. "I want you to read this over carefully. Look at the number at the bottom. That is how many years I am asking in exchange." He handed them the sheet. They crowded around it, peering anxiously. Mr. Liu looked up, surprised.

"Only two?"

"Yes, what did you expect?"

He shrugged and replied, "Well, you hear the stories..." His wife nudged him. "We accept."

"One year from each of you. Not the boy."

They nodded again. Chu reached for the intercom. "Send Jiang Shui in, please."

FAMILY

Michael Chu picked at his food. The elder Chu ate with gusto and pretended not to notice. It was an old game they played, and he always won. Michael pushed his plate away and stared out at the garden from their vantage point on the veranda. Su came out and cleared the table and left sweet buns and fried bananas, Michael's favorite dessert. Michael ignored them. Finally he stood up to address his father.

"I am concerned about Wan Fei Ying."

Chu looked at his watch and noted the time with a small smile. A new record for his son. He sighed. "What now, youngest one?"

Michael bristled at the name but pressed on. "He has attempted to assassinate you three times in the past year and you do nothing against him. He kidnapped your granddaughter. He sent outsiders against you. He has driven wedges between you and members of this family..."

"Adopted members, Michael. Never forget that. Real

family, never."

"He saved your life!" Michael hissed.

"And then brought more outsiders to my home. Are they more important than our family?" Chu took out a long thin pipe and began packing it with tobacco and herbs from a red and green pouch.

"Of course not." Michael composed himself, but just barely.

"Is that what is really bothering you, Michael? Ya Shen?"

"No, not Sam. It's David Wan. Jiang says you are planning to go to war. I just want to make sure that the family will be protected."

"You mean your family." Chu lit the pipe and puffed slowly.

"I don't want my little girl hurt again. Or my wife."

"Michael," Chu said between clouds of sweet-smelling smoke, "did it ever occur to you that we are already in the middle of a war?"

The startled expression on his youngest son's face was priceless. "I don't understand."

"You must become the blind man eating a won ton. You can't see, but you know what has gone down."

Michael rolled his eyes. "You know, I hate that Confucianist crap, Dad."

"And you know I hate being called 'Dad,' son." Chu sighed. "There are two kinds of wars. The kind fought with men and money, and the kind fought with will." He gestured to the empty chair in front of him. Michael looked at the chair, his father, then sat down grudgingly. "I hate it when you stand over me, too. I am glad you married a short woman."

"You didn't give me any real choice in the matter, now did you?" Chu pressed his lips together. Michel rolled his eyes again. "Sorry. Cheap shot. Okay, so, what am I missing that you haven't told me?"

Chu began repacking his pipe. "The problem is, Wan Fei Ying fights a different war than I. He is currently expending men and money. I am resisting him with my will and my will alone. Not once has he seen a sign of weakness from me. Nor will he."

Michael sat back. "That seems unwise."

"Yes, it does. But it is not. I know Wan Fei Ying. I grew up with him, remember? He fights for the honor of your dead mother, whom he feels I took from him."

Michael was stunned. "I-I did not know that."

"No one knows that." Chu lit the pipe again. "So he throws all he has to throw at me. And it's a lot. And he feels that he is crippling me, because there is panic around me. What he does not know is that I have been gathering my strength while he is expending his." He drew on his pipe and blew out the smoke. "So, you don't need to worry about me."

Michael looked at his father, aghast. "I'm still processing the fact that David Wan is doing this because of Mom."

Chu regarded his son for a moment. He cocked his head in thought and then pointed at Michael with the stem of his pipe. "Perhaps it is time to involve my sons fully in my history once and for all. There is more that you do not know. Much more. What I have to say will anger you. "

"Father," Michael began, "If it's about how she died, I think we already know."

"You may suspect, but you don't know everything. Leave it, for now, Michael. We will finish this later." Michael got up to leave. Chu asked, "Can you come to dinner tomorrow night?"

"Me, or all of us?" Michael asked, moving toward the

door.

"Everyone, of course. I want to see my granddaughter. We'll have a nice, family dinner, like we used to. Then we will all have a nice, long talk."

Michael shrugged and said, "Okay, sure. Usual time?"

"Always."

"Right. Always." Michael left the terrace to his father and his smoke.

PERSONAL

The mail arrived on a small ivory tray, delivered by Su Yun. Chu sipped tea and looked at Su Yun as he fumbled with something in his coat pocket. "Master, this also came for you." He produced a small parcel wrapped in brown paper.

"Did it come in the mail?" Chu asked.

"No, it was delivered by hand." He laid it down on the table and stood there expectantly with his hands behind him, a noticeable change from the daily routine.

Chu stared. "What are you doing?"

"I was told to wait and see if you have a reply."

Chu looked at the package warily. "Do you recognize the delivery boy?"

"Yes, Master."

"Well, who is it?"

"It's Ya Shen, Master."

"Send him away. There is no reply." Su left quickly. Chu sighed and picked up the package. His name was written across the front of the hand-made rice paper wrapping. He thumbed open the flap and slid the object out. It was a silver hip flask, such as would hold bourbon. It was scuffed and dented. He uncrewed the top and noted that it was clean, no trace of alcohol smell. Taped to the back of the flask was a note. He read it once, twice. Then he called Su back to his office.

When Su appeared, Chu was writing a note. "Take this to Ya Shen's home. Ask him to join us for a family dinner tomorrow night." Su bowed and left.

Chu picked up the phone and dialed a number. "Ya Shen has passed the test. I am holding his apology in my hand," he said to Jiang Shui.

"Do you think he had help?"

"I am certain of it," Chu said, "but this time, he kept it in the family. That is good."

"Well, he didn't come to me," Jiang said huffily.

"Have you spoken to Mi Hei about it?"

"It wasn't Mi Hei, father," Jiang said with confidence. "She hates him."

"Be wary of what a hateful mask may hide."

"What do you mean?" asked Jiang, suddenly suspicious.

"Nothing, nothing. You know your daughter, yes? There is nothing to worry about."

"Yes, well..." In a different tone of voice, Jiang said, "Now, about Bowen."

"Please, son, let's leave this until tomorrow. It will keep. We are all having dinner tomorrow night, and we will work all of this out. I promise."

"All right." Jiang hung up, his pride wounded.

Chu smiled. Everything was falling into place.

They came late at night, after the servants had gone to

bed. Chu was in his bedroom, reading from scrolls older than anything in his house, when the cricket in the brass cage stopped singing. Without thinking, he dropped to the floor, scroll in hand, and rolled under the bed.

They slid between the closed window, paper-thin, but when they touched the floor, they were solid and real. Each demon carried something different in its malformed hand. The leader clutched a lantern. Behind him, the drooling one held a scroll. The last one carried sharpened chopsticks. The soul-gatherers. Minor demons from the third level of Hell. Their services could be bought by mortals, and the price was steep.

He could hear them jabbering at one another in their demonic dialect, asking questions concerning his whereabouts. Chu waited until they had crossed the length of the room and were between him and the full-length mirror that was angled away from the bed, then crawled out and stood up. "What is the meaning of this?" he said in a clear, strong voice.

They turned and started forward.

"We seek a soul..." Lantern-Bearer said.

"...to take back to our master..." added Scroll-Reader.

"...for his amusement..." finished Chopstick-Waver.

Chu planted his feet in the traditional attack stance of the demon hunter and recited the prayer of righteousness. "Do you know who I am?" he said, his voice an octave lower. "I am Chu Sheng Kai, son of Chu Long Yan, sorcerer and demon hunter. His skills are my skills, and it is a shame to have to use them on lesser beings such as yourselves!"

"Strip the soul from his body, so that we might sup on his bones," said Lantern-Bearer. Chopstick-Waver vaulted forward, and Chu met him with an Iron Palm that sent him straight back into his brothers. They clattered to the floor like bowling pins, and Chu pressed the advantage. He withdrew the Eight Trigram Prism from his pocket and angled it so that the light bounced off the larger mirror and onto them, giving the room an unearthly glow.

"Do you know what this is?" he asked the tangle of demons on his floor. They shrank back but didn't answer. "It's the I-Ching Mirror of my father, Chu Long Lan, the prism he tamed one hundred demons with."

"No!" said Lantern-Bearer.

"Not the Mirror!" said Scroll-Reader.

"Be merciful!" said Chopstick-Waver.

"I will show you exactly the same mercy you would have shown me." Chu raised his hand and inscribed a Force of Will sigil in front of him and hung the prism in place. In the light of the prism, they could not move, and they communicated this fact to Chu in foul language, cursing him with leprosy, cancer, and a dozen other maladies while he stood over them, laughing.

Chu soon grew tired of their coarse language. He walked through the door to his study and opened up the cabinet, selected a carefully labeled clay pot, and returned to his unwelcome guests. He uncorked the clay pot and poured the thin, foul-smelling liquid over the demons, who howled in protest. Chu then took the lantern, scroll, and chopsticks from their limp appendages and set them aside. He intoned a prayer to his ancestors, then took out the matches he'd been lighting his pipe with all day. "When you go back to Sung Ti, remind him that what he fights for will not balance any scales. My father subjugated him, and I will do the same if he comes to my home again."

He struck the match and dropped it on the demons. Bright red fire shot up, waist high and heatless. The demons screamed as the flames quickly ate through them. They would reform in Hell, without their trappings of office, and have to tell their tale to their superiors. The outcome would not bode well for Wan Fei Ying.

The fire was gone, and so were all traces of the scuffle. Someone softly knocked on the door. "Come in."

The door opened. It was Su, looking very tired. "Master, I heard something..."

"It was nothing. While you are up, would you bring me some tea and buns? And take these things and put them in the vault." He gestured at the objects on the bed. Su walked in and gathered them up in his arms and wordlessly set about his tasks. Chu sat on the edge of the bed and went back to reading his scroll.

DINNER

The table was surreptitiously cleared, and Michael Chu's wife, Kim, and child, Elizabeth, discreetly excused themselves. Steaming rice wine was poured and tobacco offered. The dining room was suddenly transformed into a war council. Chu looked out at the people gathered around him. On the left side of the table sat Michael and Sam Bowen, his adopted son. On the right side of the table was Jiang Shui and his daughter, Mi Hei. Directly opposite him was Fu Yan. They wore a mixture of expressions on their faces: discomfort, humility, curiosity, anxiety. He smiled at them in turn.

"Thank you for dining with me tonight," he said. "Your presence here lends me strength...for my confession." He stood up and began to pace, concentrating on his story. "All of you know some facets of my personal history. Some of you grew up hearing stories, while others of you have embarked on a campaign of self-study." He glanced briefly at Sam, who cut his eyes. "In order to tell you why you are all here, I must tell you the whole story. Please, indulge me."

"I was born here, in San Cibola, in 1850. My family had founded the Xian Hong Yue triad to protect the people here from civil injustice. Other triads formed and served to lead the community, but we were the first. Due to the nature of San Cibola, I exhibited a remarkable aptitude for sorcery at an early age. My family sent me back to China for training from magicians and priests. My only contact with my family was through letters. For thirty-five years I trained to become the most powerful sorcerer in China. In 1890, my master was killed, but not before passing on to me the secrets of immortality. I walked the path of the Hac Tao and learned many terrible, destructive things."

"Hac Tao?" asked Sam.

"It means, literally, 'the black way'." whispered Jiang Shui.

"I was sent back to my family, where I became the sorcerer for the Xian Hong Yue. The Eternal Red Moon. By then, our family was engaged in criminal activity. Opium. Prostitution. Gambling. As were all of the triads. We warred with one another. I fought sorcerer's duels, battled demons, and killed many people for the honor of the family. I was eventually promoted to Advisor to Chin Lin. Together, we made the Xian Hong Yue the most feared name on the West Coast. That lasted until 1938."

Chu paused, took a sip of rice wine, and continued. "Chin was murdered in his bed by a demon. His wife was undisturbed. She woke up to find him in pieces. The murder was my fault. I was supposed to protect him with magic spells.

242

We knew that an attack would come, and I did nothing to stop it. "

"Why not?" asked Sam, which brought scowls from Jiang Shui and Mi Hei.

"I was too drunk to perform the spells," said Chu.

Sam clamped his mouth shut and sank back in his chair. Chu continued. "For my shame, I left the family to atone for what I had done. I went back to China and immersed myself in study. I climbed mountains, fought monsters...anything I could do to punish myself."

"When I returned to America, it was 1951. I was ready to rejoin the family. They gave me a position on the council. No war duties. I was to observe and learn the business of our family. It was at this time I met three people who would alter my destiny. Fu Yan," he gestured at his friend at the end of the table, "who was training to be a martial artist. We drank and caroused together. It was the two of us who met Lo Lu Mao, your mother, one night at a public dance. She was there at the dance with Wan Fei Ying. He was older than your mother, older than I looked, and already a lieutenant in the Xue Yin Triad. She was being courted by him. Unsuccessfully, it would seem."

Chu refreshed his glass and sat down. "We dated privately while I clashed with Wan Fei Ying publicly. I was forbidden by the council to use my abilities, which frankly suited me just fine. We were still at war with the Xue Yin and any breach of etiquette would be disastrous. In spite of the difficulties, Lu Mao were married after four years. The Xue Yin tried to stop the wedding, but we prevailed. That year, your oldest brother, Nan Tieh, was born."

Everyone glanced at one another. "Nan, it seemed, had my gift. Sorcerous aptitude. He was sent away by my uncle to receive the training I did. It broke our hearts. So a few years later, Jiang Shui came into the world. Thankfully, he didn't have my gift."

"Nor much of anything else," quipped Fu Yan. Jiang gave Fu a go to hell look.

"Finally, we felt like we could be a family. Except for Wan Fei Ying. He would not leave your mother alone. We had to threaten the Xue Yin with retribution to get him to leave us alone. He left soon thereafter for China. We should have cared, but we did not. That was another mistake I made."

Chu looked at the table for a minute before going on. "In 1965, Tu Chuang came to us."

"Who?" asked Sam.

"Me," said Michael, unhappily.

"Yes, that is his real name," said Chu. " It means, 'strong skull,' and I think you can see it is an apt name for him. Now we had three sons. We were as complete as we could be. We had forgotten about Wan Fei Ying."

Fu Yan made fists and stared at nothing.

"Three years later, your mother was killed. Someone, we didn't know who at the time, sent an infernal, a magic-eater, to the house. It was meant for me. I was not there. It should have left. But, you see, earlier that day, we had made love. It grabbed onto the energy from our union and drained Lu Mao of her life force."

Sam frowned. "I don't understand."

Fu Yan said quietly, "Tantrism. Exchanges energy with your partner."

Chu nodded. "She was infused with my spirit, and I with hers." He paused. "I still have her spirit with me to this day." He drank some wine and continued in a clearer voice. "Three days later, she was buried. I saw Wan Fei Ying at the funeral. No one knew he was back. We fought at the gravesite, and as the people pulled us apart, he said to me,

'It's not as if you won't have the time to find another bride.' He had discovered my secret of longevity. The trip to China was to do research on me and maybe to receive some training as well. Now he swims in negative Chi. He is entangled in evil."

"With David Wan, as he was calling himself now, back in town, things became difficult for the family. I was tired of fighting with the Xue Yin, the Hundred Hammers, and all the rest of them. I wanted out of the criminal activity. In 1976, I became second-in-command to my cousin, Lim Pao, the last relative of my uncles. I began to slowly influence him to pull out of drugs and prostitution and put our money into legitimate businesses. At this time, Wan Fei Ying assumed control of the Xue Yin and began taking over the areas we vacated. No one thought this was a good idea. Lim Pao hung onto the gambling venues for another ten years, until he was cursed with Reptile Flesh and was killed. By then, Xue Yin and the others had all of the criminal activities in Chinatown. We had real businesses that made honest money."

"I took control of the Xian Hong Yue and founded Red Moon Enterprises. I disbanded all of the tongs. I told the people that our family would become community leaders instead of community problems. And yet, the attacks still continued. Wan Fei Ying. Angry because I wasn't home the day he tried to kill me. I endured it for years, even grew to like it. It made it feel like your mother was still alive and I was competing for her affections again. But, this last year, Wan Fei Ying has become desperate. My life is now at stake, as is the life of my family. And that is my story." He sat back and began filling his pipe.

For a long minute, no one spoke. It was Michael who broke the silence. "So, Father, when do we go to war?"

Chu looked at his youngest son and found him wearing a face he did not often see. "And do you all feel this way?"

Everyone nodded.

"Well, my family, we must wait for the last player in this drama." Chu lit his pipe. "Your eldest brother's training is complete. Soon, he will be coming home." Smiles bloomed around the table. Chu filled everyone's glasses again and said, "Now, let's discuss what will happen when he gets here."

Night of the Stomp

The invitation arrived in a plain white envelope. Inside was a printed card in my name. On the back, it said:

You and a guest are cordially invited to
an old-fashioned Halloween Stomp,
San Cibola-style.
Costumes are required, and you must
present this invitation to get in.
Time: October 31st, 8 PM until Whenever
Place: 926 Tigris Avenue, Eden Park
RSVP to Ian Rosewood, 899-7734

The last Halloween party I went to was my freshman year of college. After I hit the road, I quickly saw more than my fair share of ghosts and monsters on the regular days, so I tended to lay low on the one day they were supposed to be out. Even then, I occasionally ran into trouble. I resolved to talk to Ian and scope this little shindig out before I committed to it. I dialed the number listed.

"Pocket Shop, this is Ian."

"Ian. Sam Bowen."

"Hey, Sam. Did you get your invitation?" he asked excitedly.

"I'm looking at it right now."

"Good, good. So, you coming?"

"Well, I don't know. What's a Halloween Stomp, any-way?"

"Oh ho ho. I could tell you, but that would spoil all the fun. You'll just have to show up to find out."

"Do I have to wear a costume?" I asked.

"Hell, yes! Look, are you coming or not? I'd really like to see you there. As a favor to me."

"But why?"

Ian paused. "I can't tell you yet. But when you get there, you will understand. I promise you'll have a good time, okay? Okay?"

"Yeah, okay, I'll be there."

"Great! You bringing a date?" he asked.

"No, I'm coming stag." I hung up before he could try to convince me otherwise.

The party was two weeks away. I went to Serendipity to look through Thad's old books, but there was nothing that talked of any Halloween Stomp. Ivy, Thad's protégé, was just as clueless. She spent most of her time trying to learn Thad's Byzantine filing system. We did compare stories and discovered that we were both invited and that Ian strong-armed her into showing up as well. This would either be a classic party or a colossal waste of time.

"Hey, Silas?"

"Yeah, Sam?"

"Ever hear of a Halloween Stomp?"

Silas burst out laughing. "What am I, the fount of knowl-edge all of a sudden? Okay, for all the rest of you who got an invite to Rosewood's to-do, I'm only gonna tell the story one more time and that's it, so listen up." Several of the after-noon patrons at Doyle's gathered around the bar to hear Silas' story.

"Back in the '50s and '60s, there were several cliques in the Neighborhood. Not like now, where everyone does their own thing. Ian, for example, was a part of the Tigris Avenue Regulars, an informal group of hell-raisers and monster hunters. Ian's mentor, Kelsey O'Roarke, was one of the last of the bare-handed demon fighters, if you know what I mean. The group was headed up by Howard Reese, who was a pretty powerful sorcerer. He and his group were the favorites in town for a long time. They partied, tore this place up more than once, and occasionally did some community service that got them some ink in the *San Cibola Stranger*, before it went belly up.

"Okay, you know what kind of place the Founder's Cemetery is on Halloween, right? Well, one All-Hallow's Eve back in, oh, probably '57, someone got the bright idea of taking a trip out to the Founder's Cemetery to check out the scene. Back then, only the walls were protected, and it was hell keeping the gate barred. James Allison even put armed guards on the property. Anyway, Reese put all the guards to sleep, and they conjured the gate open. Now, at this point, it's almost midnight, and the gang is pole-axed drunk, trying to stump each other at Tombstone Trivia. Sure enough, one of the dead spirits starts to come out of the ground, scaring the shit out of Howard Reese, who automatically just stomped on his head. That disrupted the spirit, and it sank back into its resting place.

"Everyone broke up laughing, and Reese put charms on everyone's feet, and soon the whole cream of the Neighborhood crop was running around the graveyard, staggering drunk, stomping on the heads of the emerging dead spirits, like some demented Whack-a-Mole game. So, next year rolls around, and Reese trucks out these special boots he's made, leather with an iron sole, and protective symbols etched into it. Everyone gets 'em, and it became something of a tradition until the late sixties, when Peter Midnight put a dampening field over the whole cemetery." Silas wiped the bar with his ubiquitous rag to indicate the story was finished.

Someone in the back asked, "What happened when the drunken sots missed a spirit? Did they let it walk around?"

"Uh, no," Silas answered. "One guy was designated the sober sorcerer, and he would banish any spirits that made it through the boots."

That answered my basic question, but I didn't know how or where Ian intended to throw a Stomp. All of the graveyards were magically locked down on Halloween so nothing would get up and walk around. Oh well, not my problem, I said to myself. I finished my beer and left.

"Hey, Mi Hei, you got any plans this weekend?"

She looked at me like I'd just thrown up on her. "Why?"

We were in the study of Chu Sheng Kai's mansion, translating texts, and as usual, she was mad at me because of the haphazard way I do research. A month ago, I found a number of collected memoirs from the 19th century, and she was having real trouble deciphering the handwriting.

"Oh, well, I got invited to a costume party on Halloween, and I thought you might like to go."

She closed the book she was working on, marking her place with her paper. "Are you asking me out on a date?"

"Not by definition, no."

She crossed her arms. "Okay, what do you call a date?"

"A date is where a man asks a woman out for the purposes of furthering a romance. He buys dinner, there's a kiss at the end of it, that kind of thing."

"Mm hmm. So, what is this, then?"

"It's a go-with. As in, 'do you want to go with me.' Platonic."

"Related," she said.

"Adopted," I corrected.

"Foreigner, what makes you think I have any interest in doing any extra-curricular activities with you at all?"

"We work together a lot. We've been in fights together. Hell, you've even saved my life. Whether you want to admit it or not, we're partners."

"This is my job, Round-Eye."

I leaned closer to her. "Not for me. For me, it's a way of life. And I've made great efforts to fit in with your family and to understand your way of life. Are you so narrow-minded that you don't want the chance to see things from my point of view?"

She looked at the table, doing battle with herself. When she looked up again, it was with the resignation that comes when you know you have to go to the dentist. "Okay, what should I wear?"

"I am doing a simple, easy costume. I suggest you not go overboard."

"What time?" she asked.

"It starts at eight o'clock. We can meet here and head out. Sound good?"

"Sure. But look, no funny business, all right? I mean it."

"Right, like I'd pull anything," I said. "Let's knock off for the rest of the day."

"Fine," she said, standing up, "I have to go make my costume anyway." I watched her walk out, smiling. I now had a ride to the party.

Halloween is a big deal in San Cibola. For the whole month of October, everyone has a little spring in their step. The Neighborhood, in particular, is jumpy and excitable.

Some of the Neighbors are more energized, as this is the one of the few times a year that they can walk about in public and get away with it. Others in the community are more on edge, as they have much work to do. In fact, the build up of energy routinely threatens to overrun the city every year, and much time and effort is expended in keeping everything under control. Guards are posted at every graveyard to keep people from getting in or out, several of the local sorcerers are employed to watch for any unauthorized summonings, and sales on protective magic go through the roof. In Chinatown, the Jen Long keep an all night vigil, armed with weapons from Chu's private occult arsenal. Arcadia always goes overboard with a parade and two-day festival that would rival anything in New Orleans. The Gaslight and the Campus districts become overrun with drunken college kids in groups of twelve or more, toga parties, dances, and revels. Last year, I hadn't been in town for too long, but I knew enough to stay indoors all night, not that I got any sleep. This year would be different, I said to myself. I was part of the community now.

I spent fifty dollars at the UNC Spirit Shop; I bought a pullover sweatshirt, some purple and white face paint, a beer stein, and a big foam finger. The Seafarers were playing for shit that year, which would make the costume a little funnier. As I studied the cartoon fisherman on the plastic stein, I remembered a story I ran across about how the mascot used to be the Whalers, but some young activists in the sixties got offended and started a student protest. The college voted to change the mascot to something more eco-friendly. Near as I could tell, all they did was take the harpoon out of his hands.

I brought everything over to Chu's house and spent half an hour painting each side of my face a different color. I put the sweatshirt on over my T-shirt, which was tucked into my blue jeans. White canvas Converse sneakers completed the look.

As I sat in the den and waited for Mi Hei, I debated whether or not to take my duffel bag. It was a party, sure, but it was also a Neighborhood party. There could be trouble, even if no one wanted any. I spent the rest of my time transferring useful items to my pockets. The bag would stay in the car.

Mi Hei finally showed up, entering the front door loudly. She ran through the house, calling my name. I let her. She got to me eventually, out of breath. "Didn't you hear me?" she asked.

"I heard you, I just didn't want to add to your noise..." I trailed off.

She was wearing a black unitard with black gloves that went to the elbow and thigh high black boots. Across her hips was a silver belt. Two cat's ears were affixed to her poofed-up hair. It was Catwoman. She looked amazing.

"That's your costume?" she said.

"Go Seafarers!" I laughed. "Seriously, you look great."

"You look like a dork."

"I'm a college student."

"No, you're a dork."

"Oh my goodness, look at the two of you." It was Chu Sheng Kai, in his evening smoking jacket. Before we could do anything, there was a flash and a pop. "Your father will be so pleased."

She looked down at her outfit. "If you say so, Grandfather."

I bowed. "Chu-San. We are about to leave for the party."

"Before you go, I have something for you." He ducked around the corner and came back with two Hershey bars. "Treats, no tricks, right, Ya Shen?"

I bowed again. "Yes, sir. Thank you."

Mi Hei shot me a look and whispered, "Brown noser."

"Have a good time at the party, you two," Chu beamed at us.

"Okay, we have to go now," said Mi Hei as she grabbed me by my shirt and hustled me to the door. "Good night, grandfather!" she yelled behind us, and pushed me out the door.

We pulled up to the house at the end of the street. It was a huge, towering three-story house that overlooked Nod Hill. Happy, yellow light spilled out of most of the windows, but it wasn't enough to make the house look anything other than what it was: a rambling, creepy old mansion.

"Looks like something from Scooby Doo," Mi Hei said, parking her car along the street.

"So, would you be Daphne or Thelma?"

She pretended to think about it. "Hmm, probably the one that would hate you more."

"Nice," I said, walking up the steep, curving sidewalk. "Now, look, I know some of these people, but not all of them. If you get nervous, just stick close to me."

"Terrific."

Up on the porch, I could hear people and music. I suddenly felt very self-conscious, as if I didn't belong here. Especially dressed like a football fan. I rang the bell and saw, through the stained glass, someone coming in response. It was Ian. He opened the door, smiling. He was clean-shaven and dressed as a priest.

"Sam!" His eyes darted from me to Mi Hei, then back again. Through his smile, he asked, "Is she a Good Neighbor?"

"Ian, this is Mi Hei, my assistant and translator. Mi Hei, this is Ian Rosewood, my supplier for all of my weird, heathen barbarian magic."

"Hello," she said, extending a hand and smiling.

"Call me Ian," he said, shaking her hand.

"Mi Hei is the granddaughter of Chu Sheng Kai. She's with Jen Long Security." I said pointedly, in answer to his earlier question.

Ian nodded, still smiling. "Well, don't just stand there, come on in!" He pulled us both through into an entrance hall decorated with orange and black crepe paper. There was a double set of doors in front of us, leading to a den full of people, and a dining room beyond that. To the left and right were the sitting and living room, also filled with people. Ian slapped my shoulder. "Hey, the food and drinks are straight ahead. Just make yourself at home, okay?"

"Cool, thanks." I guided us through the people to the dining room, mostly to get a beer, but also to take stock of our surroundings.

The house was in the process of being restored. The wooden floors were newly refinished, and I could still smell fresh paint and construction. The walls were mostly bare save for a few old paintings, original to the house, I imagined. Except for standing items like the china cabinet, all of the furniture was covered with sheets. Brass fixtures, expensive lamps, and statuary. This was an opulent house at one time. I wondered how Ian acquired it.

We grabbed beers and hugged the food table self-consciously, not yet ready to mingle. Everyone that was here seemed to know each other and talked loudly. It was an older crowd, maybe Ian's age or older. Most of them were dressed in simple evening gowns and tuxedos with the sole addition of domino masks or the fancy kind on sticks. I did see another priest in the bunch, though. Several wore no costume at all.

"I feel ridiculous in this outfit. You're just an embarrassment," Mi Hei said.

"Why? Everyone is dressed up," I said.

"No, there's a bunch of people in here who look perfectly normal..." she trailed off and then nodded slowly. "Oh, right."

"Come on, let's take a quick stroll," I said. She put her free hand on my shoulder, and we eased through the crowd to check out the other two rooms.

The living room was more of the same. A smaller group, in more interesting costumes, was chatting about nothing in particular. Several partygoers were lined up along the fireplace mantle, not talking. I recognized a couple of people from Ian's shop and Doyle's. We ducked out and checked the sitting room.

This room was almost too crowed to get in. There was a big clamor, but we couldn't see what was going on. Someone was telling some story, and we came in on the punchline. I turned to Catwoman. "Well, where to?"

"Back to the food table." As we inched back to the dining room, she asked me, "Why are so many people dressed like Drew Carey?"

"What?" I asked.

"Over there." She pointed to a guy in horn-rimmed glasses, a pillow under his jacket, and slicked-down hair, talking to Deedle, Ian's helper at the Pocket Shop, and his wife. I sincerely hoped his wife's ass was part of her costume.

"They're all dressed as Mike Bretz."

"Who?"

"Local guy. Very powerful wizard."

She looked again. "Does he really look like that?"

"Actually, that's a very romantic likeness."

"Excuse me," said an older woman dressed in a mountain of black satin lace, "but I have *got* to get something to drink before I *die*." We moved to the side as she flung herself at the food table, snatched a wine glass full of Merlot, and drained it. "Gods, but I have *got* to get more tanked than this if we are going to survive the night." She looked at us. "*Wonderful* costume, darling, you *have* to tell me where you bought that *belt*."

Mi Hei looked down at her waist. "I...um..."

"*You*, on the other hand, do that 'blend in with the mundanes' bit a little *too* well," she said, looking me up and down. "I *refuse* to use 'Norman' when there is *nothing* wrong with the word 'mundane' in the first place. I cannot *stand* vulgar contractions. Hello, Dee Anne *Powell*." She extended her hand. She was doing a good job of keeping herself together, in spite of some hard living that was visible around her eyes. Everything else on her was carefully crafted to accentuate her assets and play down her defects.

"Sam Bowen," I said, shaking her hand. "This is Mi Hei."

"Wipe that makeup off, and you two would make a *cute* couple."

"Oh, we're not together," Mi Hei said quickly.

"So, who do *you* know here?" she asked, ignoring that last comment.

"Ian. I pick up things from him from time to time."

"*Sweetie*, there's no need to be coy," she said, tossing back another glass of Merlot with a flourish. "What do you practice? Tantric? Sorcery? Witchcraft?"

I glanced at Mi Hei, who was listening with interest. "Um, nothing specific. A little of this and that, really."

"Oh, a *dilettante*," she said with a wave of her hand.

"No, not a dilettante," I said, getting angry. "I've got a wide background in—"

"*Dearest*, don't take offense. Some of my *best* friends are dilettantes. Or, they *were*, anyway. Most of them are dead."

To change the subject, I said, "So, you know Ian?"

"*Darling*," Dee Anne leaned in for emphasis, displaying impressive and ample cleavage. "I know the whole *room*."

Mi Hei whispered into my ear, "I'm going to mingle," and then she was gone.

Cursing her, I turned my attention back to Dee Anne, who was smiling like she had the goods on me. "So, you were one of the original Tigris Avenue Regulars?" I asked.

She blinked. "Oh *my*, has my reputation *preceded* me?" she batted her eyelashes.

"Truthfully, no." Her face fell. "I mean, I just heard about the group recently. I was guessing."

"Well, it was a *good* guess. Yes, I used to run with *Ian* and *Howard* and *Kelsey* and all the rest of them. Me and *Maddy*, don't you know."

"No, I don't."

"*Fontaine*. Madylene Fontaine. The *artist*?" She raised her eyebrows.

"Oh, her!" I gushed, still not knowing who the hell she was talking about.

Dee Anne snatched up a third glass of Merlot and grabbed my arm with her free hand. "Come on, I'll *give* you the nickel tour of Reese Manor." She pulled me away with considerable force before I could protest.

We walked through the crowds, parting the knots of people easily. She took me from room to room, telling me what used to be there, and describing any room in detail when we ran into locked doors. There was a stretch of rope across the upstairs, so we couldn't wander around the second floor. Dee Anne proved to be a knowledgeable guide. She told me about the house, pointing out the features of the various rooms and recounting amusing stories from the apparently infinite number of parties thrown here back in her day. She told me what objects and furniture were missing from each room. Mostly, though, she dished the dirt on the party-goers.

Dee Anne did indeed seem to know everyone and spoke to them all. I noticed the expressions on people's faces when they first saw her. There was a mixture of affection, envy, fear, hatred, scorn, and confusion. But all of them said hello back. All of them. I eventually figured out why. Dee Anne was one of the Powells. Yeah, those Powells. She was filthy rich. That fact alone accounted for some of the looks she got. I got some interesting looks from the people we encountered. Some must have thought I was her new boy-toy. Who knows what the other people thought.

"That guy," she said, pointing to a middle-aged Hispanic man dressed as the Pope, "

is *Father* Rodrigo Munoz. Roddy and I had a *fling* before he went to seminary. I think I *drove* him to it. Anyway, now he works here, on loan from the *Vatican*. One of the branches of the priesthood that is thought *not* to exist anymore, if you know what I mean."

I nodded.

"The two men he's talking to, the one on the *left*, is Bonesy Blake. He's a *musician*. One of the hangers-on, like me. The other guy is Calvin Rumsey. *Used* to be pretty nice, until he got *elected* to the Neighborhood *council*. Now he's a real *asshole*."

"Did you have a thing with him?" I asked.

"Thank *God*, no. I thought *Bonsey* was cute, but that was it. Cal, *never*. He was too nerdy."

"And those two at the table? The big guy trying to eat *all* the finger sandwiches is Tony "The Rock" Roccoro. He was our resident big dumb guy. Every group has one. *Owns* his own moving company now. That *schmuck* he's talking to is

Roger Sheenan. Roger is Howard Reese's *cousin*. He's a *stage* magician. No one ever liked him. I have *no* idea why Ian invited him."

She pointed out several others to me, with anecdotal remarks for each of them; the nature of each made it very clear as to who was on Dee Anne's A-List and who was not. The party was livening up as more people came in and joined the eddy and swirl. I started looking for Mi Hei as we meandered, so I was completely unprepared for the man in the tuxedo and turban who barreled into me and threatened to take us both to the ground.

"Please excuse me," said a familiar voice.

"*Robert*!" Dee Anne shouted gleefully. She pulled the man out of my arms and gave him a tremendous hug. "Sam, this is Rob Stonehill, one of my *favorite* people in the whole world." He was wearing a formal tuxedo and a stylish purple turban with a fake red gem set into the front.

"Stonehill."

"Bowen."

"Oops," Dee Anne said, covering her mouth, "looks like *you* two have a little history."

"Just a skosh," I said. "So, are you the guy Nostradamus warned us about?"

"No, Nostradamus was an asshole. Look, Bowen, as much as I'd like to stand here and joust for the lovely Ms. Powell's affections, it would be in our mutual interests if you would walk the kitchen with me right now." He was glancing over his shoulder as he talked quickly and quietly. I saw what he was looking at. Standing in the entrance hall was Rosemary, formerly of Doyle's, and Morrigan, formerly of a job we both worked on. I tried to kill her, she tried to kill me, and Stonehill almost killed her. It wasn't pretty. She swore vengeance on him for shooting her, but I was pretty sure she wouldn't hesitate to crush my skull in an instant.

"Ah. Good point. Dee Anne, please excuse us."

"Oh, no, hotshot, I'm coming *with*. I *must* hear this story."

"What are you, a reporter?" I asked as the three of us tore through the crowd to the dining room.

"No, I'm *rich*."

In the relative safety of the kitchen, we bumped into Ian, who warmly greeted all of us, and he in turn introduced us to an older, pleasant-looking woman named Camille Hanschen. While Dee Anne, Ian, and Camille caught up on old times, Stonehill and I talked about our options.

"You think she's still pissed?" I asked.

"I'd bank on it," he said easily.

"Can you get us out of here?" I asked.

"I can get out of here just fine, but you should know I don't— "

"Oh, never mind. I know what you are going to say already."

He smiled at me and turned to Dee Anne. "How are your nephews?" he asked.

"How should *I* know? My sister *hates* me and despises me in *turn*, so I never get the full report on *anything*. They are doing a lot better, if that's what you mean. Mum has the *whole* family in therapy now, and they're making progress."

"Good to hear. Send them my best. Is this the back door, Ian?"

"No, that's the pantry."

"Good enough. See you around, Bowen." He stepped into it.

"Okay, what's with *you* two?" Dee Anne asked.

"Well..." was as far as I got.

"Sam!" I looked and saw Rosemary Tetherwall, ex-waitress at Doyle's and new founder of the current San Cibola

Pentacle. The Pentacle was a five-man (or, in this case, woman) peace-keeping organization, privately funded, that handled Neighborhood disputes. Rosemary was dressed as Emma Peel, and attractively so. She was smiling. Morrigan, wearing a simple green dress, looked at me with open-mouthed wonder. She started forward, favoring one leg slightly. I took a step back. Rosemary saw all of this and got in between us.

"Morrigan, whatever happened between you two is ancient history."

"That fucker tried to take my head off!"

"You were gonna kill Stonehill! And me!" I said.

"All right, that's enough of that!" Ian barked. "The same rules that go for Doyle's apply here, okay? No bullshit, from either of you."

The kitchen was silent for a couple of beats, then Morrigan broke the standoff with, "Rosemary, I'm going for a drink. You want anything?"

"No, I'm fine, thanks," she said quietly.

Morrigan nodded, then pointed at me. "Stay out of my way, Bowen." She stalked to the dining room.

"Don't worry," I muttered. Then louder, I said, "Thanks, Rosemary. Ian."

Dee Anne patted me on the back and resumed her conversation with Ian and Camille. Rosemary stepped closer. "You're welcome."

"Great costume," I said.

"You like?" She stood on tiptoe, smiling. "You know, if you want to thank me properly for saving your life, you could always buy me dinner."

"Well, I..."

"Bowen!" We all turned around. Mi Hei, her hands on her hips, wearing a scowl. "Have you been in here the whole time? Hiding from me?"

"What? No! I had to duck in here..."

Rosemary looked at me, her eyes suddenly cold. "I'll see you around." She turned on her heel and walked out, pausing only add to Mi Hei, "I should have let her take a swing at him."

"Yes, you should have," she replied.

I turned to the crowd. "Dee Anne, Ian, Camille, thanks for everything. I'm going to get drunk now." I walked out to cheers from the oldsters. Mi Hei followed me, still bitching.

"You aren't really going to get drunk, are you? What about your promise to grandfather?"

"No, but this night is a prime example of why people are so fond of alcohol." Out in the dining room, the place was packed. Everyone from the front of the house had now migrated to the back. "I'm going to go this way," I motioned with my head back to the front. "You coming?"

She shrugged and fell in step. I went back to the living room, where several people in my age bracket were congregated. James Allison was holding court, literally, in his judge's robe and powdered wig, talking to several of the regulars from Doyle's, while Ivy stood shyly in the corner. Leaning against the fireplace, one hand on her ear, was the Maori woman, Susan Kururangi. She was active in keeping the Neighborhood trouble in Oceanview to a discrete minimum. She wore her work clothes. I walked over to her.

"Susan, right?" I said.

She nodded, distracted. "What do you want, Bowen?"

"Just wondering where your costume is?" I said.

"Can't afford to wear a costume tonight," she said. I looked closer and saw she had a small radio in her hand, pressed to her ear. "I have to work."

"So, why did you come?"

"Ian made me. Excuse me." She slipped the radio into her leather jacket and left the room quickly.

"Tough girl," Mi Hei said. I looked across the hall and saw people pouring out of the sitting room.

"Come on," I said. "Let's go see what's so cool about this room."

The sliding door had closed, so I pushed it open again. The room was fully furnished, from restored antique chairs to old wooden trophy cases and a score of pictures in antique frames. The trophy case was packed. It looked like a museum exhibit. Standing close to one of the pictures was a big, wide, and tall man. He had long red hair that hung past his shoulders, and he was wearing a white poet's shirt and leather pants tucked into black boots. A pirate, I guessed. He was walking slowly from photo to photo, studying each in detail.

I looked at the nearest group of photos. Party pictures, most of them. Guys and gals dancing. People laughing and smoking. A very young-looking Ian Rosewood with a lampshade on his head. Several photos of a dapper-looking man with a cigarette holder in his mouth. Underneath a few of the pictures were typed captions. One picture of him and a gorgeous woman in his arms, in full evening wear, had a caption underneath it: Howard and Jeanette Reese, 1959. They were smiling at each other and looked very much in love.

The man was very close to me now, so I said, "Some party, huh?"

He snorted, without looking at me. "Back in the day, the cops would've been here twice already," he said in a thick Irish brogue.

"Oh really?" I said. "You think we ought to turn things up a notch?"

264

"Ah, it's nae good anyhow. Everyone's gone now. Scattered to the four feckin' winds."

"Ian's still around, and Dee Anne, and several others whose names escape me right now."

He looked at me for the first time, tears in his eyes. "Ya doon't understand. Everyone's gone. It was lightnin' in a feckin' bottle, lad. Ye've got the look about you. Doon't go the way we went, boyo."

"What are you talking about?" I asked him.

"Ya silly wee bastard. Ya got shite in your ears? Study what happened to us. Doon't do what we did, ya got it?"

A cold chill crept down my back and settled in my stomach. "What's your name?" I asked.

"Kelsey O'Roarke," he said, "Pleased to make your acquaintance, Sam."

He looked completely solid, but there was still no way I was touching him. "Do you live here, Kelsey?"

"No," he sniffed, "I wish I did. No, I'm in Hell, Sam. And I'm bloody miserable." The way he said it, it wasn't a metaphor. He leaned in closer to me. "He talks about you…"

Someone walked through the door. I turned to see Ian, standing there, grave-faced. "Ian!" I said, relieved.

"I'm glad you're here now, Sam. I wanted you to see this," he said.

"What? You mean—?" I turned around to face Kelsey, but he was gone.

"Yeah, this room is the legacy of the Tigris Avenue Regulars." He walked over to the display case and looked inside it. "Here are some of the things I found as I was cleaning up the place."

"Ian, you had a partner named Kelsey, right?" He nodded. "What happened to him?"

"How'd he die, you mean?" I nodded. "He was getting

older and not taking it well. He insisted on going back out into the field, even when it was obvious to everyone that he was drinking too much, not taking care of himself, that kind of thing. He didn't want to admit to anyone that he was not invincible. We had a fight about that very thing, and he stormed out of Doyle's.

"Later that night, he was asked to sit-in on an exorcism with Roddy Munoz. Actually, we both were asked, but he told them he could do it alone just fine. Well, he goes to the exorcism, and everything was going just fine, until the demon came out. It was big, bigger than they thought it would be, and Kelsey fell to fighting it...and he lost. It took his head and galloped away."

"Jesus," I said.

"Roddy didn't know what to do at the time. He was still in training. We had a system, checks and balances, you know? Had I been there, I know I could have saved him. We were both pretty stubborn."

"Ian, there's a lot of ghosts in this house," I told him.

"Yeah, I know," he said, staring at a studio portrait of Jeanette. "That's partially why I wanted all of you over."

"And the rest of the reason?" I said.

"There will be an announcement. Stick around," he said and walked out of the room. I decided to follow him out and bumped into Mi Hei as I exited.

"Look," she said, "Do you want me to hang around or not?"

"What are you talking about?"

"Before I could walk into the room, you shut the door and locked me out!"

"But I didn't— "

"Look, tell you what. I'm going to go back to the food table and get drunk. Come get me when you are ready to go." She marched off.

What a night this was turning out to be. I walked back to the living room and chatted with Ivy for a bit. We were joined by an older man named Jeremy Wilkinson, formerly of the *San Cibola Stranger*, the late Neighborhood newspaper. He and Thad were writing partners, and he was helping Ivy with Thad's filing system. We talked about books and Thad for a while. Eventually, the pulse of the party flowed back into that room, and we were forced to evacuate or be crushed in the swirl of bodies. I ended up on the front porch with a bunch of people who were smoking and chatting in quieter tones. I spotted the Moko, the Fae, and the Tong (I didn't know their names, but they commanded a measure of respect from the crowd at Doyle's, where I saw them occasionally), talking to Ian in earnest tones. He nodded sympathetically. I really wanted to overhear what they were talking about and tried to lean in, but I was blocked by a man joining me at the porch railing, mimicking my stance.

"I'll bet you don't recognize me, Hoss."

I turned my head and looked up at Cadillac Arlington Nicholson. "Hello, Caddy," I said, my heart racing.

"Aw, shucks, I didn't think you'd remember me." This time he was wearing a black suit with a red rose.

"What are you doing here?" I asked.

"Hell, this wasn't even my idea. Some of the boys heard about old Ian fixing up the house and wanted to see it. They dragged me here, you know?"

"They dragged you," I said, as a bunch of things fell together all at once.

"Well, I drove." He smiled. "Can I get you a drink?"

"No, I don't think so. In fact, I don't think you and I have anything to discuss anymore."

He put a hand on his hip. "That a fact?" he said. "Well,

I ain't the type to hold a grudge, myself, Sam. You still got my card, you know how to get in touch with me. I'll set you up, just like I promised."

"You'll pardon me if I don't take your promise for a whole lot."

He nodded. "Yeah, well, sooner or later, Hoss, you and me are going to have us a little sit-down."

"Let's make it later," I said.

He shrugged and finished his drink. "Suit yourself."

From inside the house came the rapid clang of a dinner bell. "Excuse me, Old Son," I said and turned my back on him, muttering a quick prayer of protection as I went back inside.

Everyone was crowded into the dining room. Those who couldn't fit inside leaned in from adjoining rooms. Ian was talking. "...everyone for showing up tonight. I realize some of you are going to be busy later on." Laughter from the crowd. "But I wanted to make this announcement before any more of us got hurt. "Ian moved through the room slowly, directing his voice to the ceiling so all could hear. "There are a lot of old friends in the room tonight. Some of you are almost famous." More laughter. "Some of you haven't changed a bit." This brought jeers for someone called Laslo, who was an infamous drinker, according to Dee Anne. "I have changed, though. When Howard...died...he left me this house and all its contents. Well, I don't want the damn thing. So I'm giving it to you."

Murmurs from the crowd, mostly confused. "I've decided to set this house up as a refuge, a sanctuary, for the Neighborhood. I'll be fixing the place up, restoring it, and that front room is my first project. A little shrine to my good friends, many of whom aren't with us anymore. The rest of the house will be a hostel. We'll be a connecting point for other groups. You can hold meetings here, receive medical treatment, lay low, etc. Just like Howard used to do for us." Someone started clapping, and everyone else joined in.

"You ain't trying to horn in on my business, are ya?" James Allison bellowed jokingly from the crowd. Everyone chuckled.

"No, way, Jim. It's BYOB here," said Ian, smiling. "I'm not doing this alone. You all know Cammie Hanschen," he drew her in under his arm. "She's going to live on the premises and run her clinic out of one of the rooms. You all know Prentice Two Moons? Where are you, Prentice?" She raised her hand. "She'll be working and living here as well. This can be a safe haven for Neighbors who are down on their luck. And it'll be sort of a clubhouse, too, for you young'uns to kick back. We'll be living off of donations, so..." he looked down, then looked back up at the crowd. "And it seems we've got our first one right here." He held up a check in his hand. "Ten thousand dollars from Dee Anne Powell!" More clapping and cheering.

Dee Anne stuck her head up over the crowd. "Maddy is *here* now, and we have agreed to help with the restoration of the house!" I looked for Maddy and found an almost identically dressed woman, unmistakably an artist, standing beside Dee Anne, smiling at the room.

Ian resumed his speech. "Back in the day, we were a family. This was our home. I can't rebuild my family, but I can start a new one. Maybe you youngsters can learn a thing or two from us old farts." He looked right at me. I nodded and smiled. "Well, that's about it. Everyone can go back to drinking now!" Everyone clapped some more.

Someone tapped my shoulder. It was Mi Hei. "You ready to go yet? I'm getting drunk, and I'm getting bored."

"Actually, I kinda want to stay," I said to her. "Do you

mind?"

"I guess not. It's just, well, rude, is all. I mean, I'm with you and I want to leave…"

"Hey, you've been telling everyone all night that we aren't together, okay? So, don't get all coy and clingy on me now. Don't worry about me, I'll get a ride."

She colored visibly. "Oh, fuck you." With that, she vanished into the crowd.

The old Bowen charm gets 'em every time, I thought. I tried to be mad at her and ended up being mad at myself instead. With nothing better to do, I made for Ian in the crowd. "Listen, Ian, there's something I have to tell you about this house…"

Ian leaned in real close to my ear. "I know. Meet us in the trophy room in half an hour. We'll talk more then."

I needed some food, so I strolled back to the remains of the party trays and found Rino, one of the bouncers at Doyle's, talking to a guy dressed as an accountant. "Hey, it's Kentucky Bowen," said Rino.

"How you guys doing?" I asked.

"Not bad, not bad. Bowen, this is my good friend Drew. Drew, this is Kentucky Bowen." I shook his hand. He tried to be manly.

"Hey, Drew, does he give everyone those wise-guy nicknames, or just me."

"Well, I don't have a nickname…" Drew said.

"Oh, yeah you do, Pally," said Rino, clapping Drew on the back. "We call you all kinds of things when you ain't around."

"Gee, thanks," said Drew.

"So, what brings you two here?" I asked.

"I got an invite at Doyle's, and decided to show Drew some of the Neighborhood colors."

"Really, Rino, I get enough color every day," said Drew. I nimbly snatched the last of the pigs in blankets from Rino, who was having trouble talking and grabbing at the same time.

"Drew, you work in the office. What color can you possibly get that compares to this?" Rino settled for the celery stuffed with peanut butter, which he crunched loudly.

"Well, y'all be good over here. Nice meeting you," I said and made for the living room, where I could sit down.

I ate in relative solitude and spent a nice ten minutes talking to one of the old-timers, Chelsea, and her Norman husband. He was tickled pink at all the eccentrics his wife used to know. We kept the conversation light for his sake. Finally, I heard Ian making noises in the trophy room, so I excused myself and went to see what he was on about.

There were a dozen of us: Rosemary, Father Rodrigo, Dee Anne, Cal Rumsey, The Moko, the Fae, the Tong, James Allison, Deedle, Stonehill, myself, and Ian. Ian had dragged a large, wooden box into the center of the room and was resting one foot on it as he talked.

"Okay, I invited you to a Stomp, and I mean to have one. I don't want to get too gossipy, but Howard left a lot of unfinished business around here. And, no doubt, some of you have seen one or two uninvited guests here as well." He bent down and pulled the lid off of the box. Inside were a bunch of metal shoe soles with leather straps. "I had these made up special for the party. I would consider it an honor if you all would help me christen the house by stomping the shit out of it."

"Ian, *darling*, what about the *floor*?" said Dee Anne, looking at the shoes in horror.

"Don't worry about that, Ma'am," said Deedle, taking a metal sole from Ian and fastening it to his shoe, "I'll just buff it all out again."

"Here, put these on, just strap them over your shoe like a sandal," said Ian, handing me a sole. I looked at the bottom. They were iron, reasonably thin, with seven different symbols carved into the length of the sole. Reinforced leather straps and metal buckles ran across the top of the arch and behind the toes. A leather cuff kept the heel in place. I sighed and strapped it to my right foot.

"Ian, do these keep score like the old ones?" asked Dee Anne.

"Nah, they don't change color or any of that shit. This will be fun, but it ain't no game, if you get my meaning."

We were all shod. Ian looked at each of us in turn. "Well, the party is still going on, and that grandfather clock in the hallway is about to strike midnight. All of you kids take the downstairs. Me and the old-timers will handle the upstairs." They all tromped out, Dee Anne cringing every time the metal hit the wood floor.

We looked at one another for a moment. The Moko, the Fae, and the Tong left as a single unit. I looked at Rosemary and Stonehill.

"I thought you left?" I said to Stonehill.

"Where's your girlfriend?" asked Rosemary.

"I didn't go anywhere," said Stonehill.

"She's not my girlfriend," I said.

"Come on, Rob, let's go." He took her arm, smiled at me, and walked out of the room.

Well, shit, I thought.

The clock struck the first bell of midnight. The room got colder almost instantly. Upstairs, I could hear loud thumping and clanking. The rest of the party-goers cheered and joined in on the fun, if only symbolically.

In the middle of the room, surrounded by pictures of dead heroes and beautiful women, I began to stomp.

Endgame

No one would have given him a second glance. He drove into town from Las Vegas, Nevada, in a rented Honda Civic, wearing a god-awful Hawaiian shirt and baggy shorts. His white socks were hiked almost up to the knees; his feet were encased in black tennis shoes. With the camera in his hand, and his genial smile, he looked just like one of the millions of Asian tourists you see every year in San Cibola.

A powerful sorcerer? Hardly. He looked too young, for starters. Realistically, he had twenty years on me, but you would never know it to look at him. No doubt, the family secret for longevity was alive and well. Plus, even though he fairly glowed with energy, he lacked that purposeful look that was characteristic of the rest of his family. As soon as he walked into the room, though, all of my bits of junk I used to detect magic went nuts. So, there was a lot more going on behind that wide-eyed innocent smile.

It was just after two o'clock in the morning when we heard the bell ring, and not a minute later, the excited houseboy ushered him into the study where we were all gathered. Chu stood up and bowed, then embraced him warmly. Jiang Shui (Chu's second-oldest son and leader of the Jen Long security force), followed suit. Michael Chu (the youngest son and director of the Chinatown Cultural Exchange Center), was greeted next. I hung back with Fu Yan (Chu's childhood friend and bouncer at Doyle's), and Mi Hei (Jiang Shui's daughter and my assistant). They were playing Mah jongg, and I was still trying to pick it up. After a minute or two of talking in low tones, Chu brought him over to us. We stood as he introduced us in turn. When he got to me, Chu said, "And this is your adopted brother, Ya Shen, Sam Bowen."

He looked confused for a moment, glancing between his father and me. Then he shrugged and gave me a huge hug. "No differences exist between me and my American family!" he gushed.

"Nice to meet you, too," I said.

He was Nan Tieh, or 'man of iron.' He was Chu Sheng Kai's oldest son and his greatest weapon in the war with David Wan.

The next day, Nan was at breakfast with all of us, much more composed. He still couldn't resist the occasional grin as Chu filled him in on the situation at hand. Nan listened intently, but as soon as his eyes strayed to the garden or us, he would look down and smile. I couldn't help thinking that had any of us been as gawky while Chu was talking, the old man would have handed us our heads.

Chu did notice, however. He laid a hand on Nan's shoulder. "My son, I know it is difficult for you. It is difficult for all of us. You have been so patient. Now that you are here, we have one more task yet to do. Then we can all relax. Do you understand?"

Nan nodded. "Yes, Father."

I listened to all of this without looking at them, concentrating instead on my Chinese breakfast. Chu provided me with a translator spell, much better than the one I used before to spy on him. I got everything spoken and written with no static or buzz in my head, plus the spell would occasionally translate pictures and symbols for me. My being able to understand what everyone was saying solved a lot of logistic problems for everyone. Also, it kept me very busy in the past two weeks.

My tutoring duties at UNC were suspended during all of this, and Benny Wan (my landlord), was forwarding all of my correspondence to Chu's estate. I slept in the main guestroom (my room, as it was called, owing to the frequency with which I found myself convalescing there). The others stayed at the estate intermittently. Only I was requested to remain on hand at all times until it was all over.

Mi Hei and I were on guard duty, along with Jiang Shui, Michael Chu, and Fu Yan. We were the inner circle, offering protection to Chu Sheng Kai, while the Jen Long and a few private agents took care of the legwork. I was initially pissed, until Chu explained that he needed his best men close to him for now, and while I'm waiting, why don't I go get a book to read? So, for the past two weeks, I tore through Chu's library, finally able to work in the manner to which I was accustomed, while Fu Yan kicked Mi Hei's ass in Mah jongg, chess, and a bunch of other games that I had never seen before. Thanks to Chu's translator spell and Mi Hei growing up in an all-male household, I was also learning the finer points of Chinese swearing.

Chu turned to all of us. "As you know, the Blood Shadow triad is no more, thanks to the efforts of the di Lessa crime family. This is a major blow, but it will only aggravate Wan Fei Ying. We need to gain a measure of things on the streets." He turned to Jiang Shui. "I want your daughter and Ya Shen to reconnoiter." Jiang Shui nodded, then nodded to Mi Hei. She stood up.

"Come on, Foreigner." she said.

Chu held his hand up. "I will not tolerate your abuse of Ya Shen, Granddaughter."

She immediately turned to me. "I'm sorry," she said with

everything but her eyes. "Let's go, Bowen."

As we walked out of the room, I heard one of the men whisper, "Strongest will I've ever seen,"

They didn't know the half of it.

We drove through Chinatown leisurely, making a lot of stops. At Benny's, I ran into my apartment to pick up some stuff. We went to Zhu's Noodle Hut for food and stood on the street corner, playfully hurling insults at the demon while he howled with rage. At the Asian Market, Mi Hei ran in to grab random groceries while I stayed in the car. All of this was supposed to look like normal errands, which they were. But our carefully plotted route took us through most of Chinatown, crisscrossing through several of the hotspots. We kept smiles on our face and cranked the radio. To the casual observer, we could have even been on a date. Good thing they couldn't hear us inside the car.

Mi Hei had been acting pissy and irritable ever since her dressing down at the breakfast table. I gave up on trying to calm her down after the first ten minutes and settled into my usual pastime: aggravating her to the point that she got too mad to speak. It didn't always work, but it beat sitting there passively and just taking her abuse.

"Bowen, just shut up."

"Answer the question first."

"I don't even know what you're talking about."

"Oh, come on, you've watched television before, I've seen you." I was thrown into the passenger door as she made a hard left.

"Maybe so, but I never watched those stupid shows."

"That's bullshit. We all watched those shows, whether it was the first time, like me, or in reruns, like you. Don't try to wriggle out of this one, Mi."

276

"If I answer the question, will you shut up?"

"Absolutely. I promise."

She sighed. "Okay, I think that Starsky and Hutch's car —"

"The Striped Tomato."

"Whatever. I think the Striped Tomato is faster than the General Lee."

"Are you nuts?" I shouted. "That was a street car. The General Lee was built for racing, for Christ's sake! What's your reasoning behind that lame-ass idea?"

She fumed. "You said you would shut up about it if I answered your goddamn question. Well, I answered it, so you have to shut up."

"Fine, I'm shutting up about that. Now I'm starting a totally separate discussion about how you could think that the General Lee is somehow inferior to the Striped Tomato."

"Fuck you." She turned the radio up louder.

We were deep in the heart of Chinatown now, and the plan was to do a quick zigzag through the neighborhoods, then get back to Crane Street, post-haste.

"You're just mad because you know you're wrong."

"Bowen, I don't care! It's a stupid television show that I don't even like, about stupid crackers that remind me too much of you, and none of this really matters anyway because it's all make-believe!"

"Then what are we supposed to talk about?" I asked. "You don't think I'm funny, you have no interest in my past —"

"That's not true," she interrupted, holding up her finger warningly. "You won't let me read your journals, so what am I supposed to do?"

"Ask me, I'll tell you anything."

She smiled sweetly. "Haven't you figured out by now

that I hate the sound of your voice?"

"You're a real piece of work." I looked out the window to plan my next volley. On the narrow street, we were forced to slow down due to the parked cars and foot traffic. I could see small knots of gang members that I didn't recognize. It was tough to get a picture of what they looked like without staring, but it was obvious that they were up to no good.

"Mi Hei," I said.

"I see them," she said, turning to smile at me.

"Who are they?" I asked.

"They are the Winter Storms tong." She said their name in Chinese, but I got the translation.

"Yeah, well, what are they up to?"

"I don't know, but they're connected with David Wan's organization. If they are out on the streets, then they are his new muscle."

"The second stringers, you mean."

She looked at me. "Hey, anyone can shoot a gun."

"Let's get out of here," I suggested.

"Way ahead of you." She made a right, then a left, then a right, and then we were back in the commercial zone. Her sudden change from bitchy to agreeable always made me nervous.

"Hey, let's stop for a drink. I'm dying of thirst."

"Coke, right? Not beer."

I rolled my eyes. "No, not beer. Just pull over somewhere, will you? I'll buy you a Diet Pepsi."

There was a corner grocery store up ahead. She pulled along side the curb to let me out. "You want anything else?" I asked.

"Not from this place."

"Snob."

"Commoner."

I slammed the car door without meaning to and walked inside. This was one of the thousands of family businesses that operated in Chinatown. I could smell food cooking and hear children being scolded by a woman with a shrill voice. A short man with thinning hair sat behind the counter and watched a game show I couldn't identify.

The store stock was a mixture of things I see every day and food I would never eat on a dare. I walked back to the cooler and grabbed sodas for us both. As I turned around to walk back up the aisle with shrimp-flavored cookies, the lights turned gray. Up at the front counter, the man was a shadow, and the television invisible. I looked outside to see if there was an eclipse when I caught a glimpse of him, moving sideways through my peripheral vision. The Chinese sorcerer working with David Wan. Then it hit me: I was in the Dream-State. He pulled me into it with no effort and without my knowledge.

The last time I saw this guy, he was pinned to a warehouse door with my Bowie knife sticking out of his neck. My bad for not making sure he was dead. As he materialized in front of me, I could see the hate on his face clearly. No matter what else, he meant to kill me. Gone were the flowing robes of his last Dream-Form. Now he wore tight-fitting, modern-looking black garments. He was ready for combat, not ceremony.

"The barbarian hedge-wizard returns to interfere with my master's plans," he said in his peculiar sing-song fashion.

"No, I'm just getting a drink," I said.

Surprise flickered across his face for an instant. "A translation spell. How quaint. You don't even bother to learn, only taking shortcuts. And speaking of short cuts, I think I owe you for this." He opened up his shirt at the collar, exposing a horrible bloodless wound. "In the waking-world, I can't even speak. You have scarred me beyond repair."

"Boo-fuckin'-hoo. You were going to sacrifice a little girl to a demon."

"Insolent." He slapped me hard and fast. I never saw it coming. The force of the blow knocked me to the ground. He was on top of me before I could move. "Remember this?" He withdrew my Bowie knife from behind him and showed it to me. Dim, threatening runes had been etched into the blade. "You left this behind last time, so I thought I'd return it."

He brought the knife straight down to my throat. I caught it on one arm, and it opened up a red gash. His strength was unbelievable. This is ridiculous, I thought, I'm not even asleep. Suddenly, he looked up over his shoulder and was gone in an instant. I sat up, and just as suddenly I was out of the Dream-State and I was looking at Mi Hei as she lunged between me and the grocery store owner. I was on the floor, and food was everywhere. The owner had a gun and was screaming for Mi Hei to take her crazy friend and get out, and also to pay for everything I busted up. I stood up and felt something warm on my arm. Blood flowed from the slash in my jacket sleeve.

I put my hands up, just as Mi Hei managed to get the grocery store guy to put his gun down. "I don't want trouble. We'll go." Mi Hei handed the man a wad of cash, and we hurried out to the car.

"What the hell happened?" she asked once we were driving.

"We have to get back right now." I showed her my wound. "I was attacked astrally by that creepy wizard who tried to kidnap Elizabeth earlier this year. They are so on to us. And he's really got it in for me."

She shook her head. "So, in other words, it's all your

fault again?"

Back at Chu's estate, one of the servants patched me up while Mi Hei filled her father and grandfather in on what we'd observed. After she was done, I told them what happened to me. Jiang Shui looked worried, but Chu kept his cool.

"Father, if this is true, then we must bump the timetable up."

"Not necessarily," said Chu, "we will simply do what has served us well all along."

"Nothing," said Jiang Shui, his voice tight. He wore his blazer with the Jen Long emblem.

"I know you are nervous. All of you. But you must trust me." Chu turned and left the room.

I looked at Jiang Shui. "Do you trust him?"

"He is my father, Ya Shen." Jiang followed Chu out the door.

I looked at Mi Hei for an explanation. "That was Chinese for 'don't be stupid,'" she said.

"No, really?"

"You and your translator spell," she scoffed. "You get the words, but not the true meaning."

"Oh, I get plenty of true meaning around here," I said easily.

"What is that supposed to mean?" she asked, but I was already halfway to the study to catch up on my reading.

That night, fierce winds tore at the estate, forcing the Jen Long guards into their shack. The house creaked and groaned against the unrelenting push of wind. It seemed to be coming from all sides at once.

Chu looked up at his ceiling and said to me, "He is looking for you."

I came and sat down beside him. "Who is he?"

Chu took his reading glasses off and rubbed his eyes. "Do you really want to know?" My look answered his question. "His name is Bai Xin. Wan Fei Ying found him adrift in the Sea of Black Blood and nurtured him back to health. He has served Wan ever since. His power is great, but narrowly focused. He can only do certain things, but he has total mastery of the Astral Plane."

"The Dream-State," I murmured.

"There he is most powerful. The flesh is his weakness."

"That much I know."

A particularly fierce gust of wind dislodged a piece of the roof. We followed the sound of tiles cascading and hitting the ground outside.

"Sir, what if that wind gets in here?"

"Then it will carry you out by the same way it got in."

"Great."

Chu put up a hand. "Don't worry. The house will hold together."

I walked back to the table with my books and research and went back to transcribing from a very interesting book I found.

No one slept well that night. We met at the breakfast table, each carrying various degrees of irritation. I think I was the worst. Half my night was spent keeping impossibly-long silver snakes from injecting poison into my dream-self. Bai Xin wasn't going to let up, now that he had found me.

We were quietly eating sweet buns and rice when Michael Chu came barreling into the room. "Father, you need to see this," he said, and continued into the den. We got up to follow him.

Michael was standing in front of the television. "I saw this and came right over." He turned it on.

An anchorman was talking, but the first thing we saw was the graphic floating over his shoulder: MURDER IN CHINATOWN. We listened to the newscast.

"...have not ruled Mister Chu out as a suspect yet. The names of the victims are not being disclosed at this time. This tragedy comes right on the heels of the Blood Shadow triad massacre not two weeks ago and casts much doubt on the effectiveness of the Chinatown precinct to protect and serve. Once again, a family of seven was found dead in their homes not an hour ago, mutilated and murdered. Written in the victim's blood on the wall was the name, 'Chu Sheng Kai.' Mr. Chu is a prominent local businessman and community leader..."

Michael turned the television off. "What are we going to do, Father?" he asked for all of us.

Chu Sheng Kai folded his hands in front of his chin and said nothing.

The doorbell rang.

Chu said, "I am sure we will all have to talk to the police. We will use my office. Everyone remember your cover stories. I am going to get dressed. Jiang, get our lawyer on the phone. The rest of you, go finish your breakfast." He strode from the room.

When it was my turn to talk to the detectives, I put on my good-old-boy routine and yessir'd and nosir'd them to death. I was a friend of the family, you see, here to visit m'pal Chewsan and his niece, Mi Hei. We just hung out, y'know, talking and what-not. See, I'm fascinated with Oriental culture and so forth, and lots of times we'll all talk for hours and hours about Chinese culture and kung fu and all that kinda stuff. Anyway, it got to be late, so instead of takin' the bus back to my apartment, they let me crash in their guest room. Yessir, I work at the college, tutoring and stuff. Nosir, we was all here the whole time.

I was really glad when they were done with me. While detectives Frick and Frack threw me twenty questions, four uniformed cops stood in the living room and tried to look scary. We talked to them in shifts and learned some interesting things. It seems that the victims were hacked completely to bits with several large knives, maybe even machetes or swords. Many of the organs were missing from the bodies. Chu's name was written on the ceiling, in Chinese, looking down on the artfully arranged family below. The real and only lead any of them had was a knife found at the scene of the crime, a knife that had gone missing at the Chinatown Cultural Exchange Center about a month ago. It had been used to make some cuts, but the cops didn't think it was the primary murder weapon. It was designed to point the cops at Chu Sheng Kai, nothing more. There were no fingerprints, no signs of forced entry, and no signs of a struggle. It's the kind of thing that freaks Norman out. It doesn't make any sense.

Four hours after their arrival, everyone finally left except for the leading investigator and Chu's lawyer. They spoke in Chu's office for an hour and came out of it with a plan. Two cops in plainclothes would guard the gate that night instead of Jen Long. Two more policemen would patrol the grounds. This was to prevent any concerned citizens from trying to get in, and it would also serve to keep tabs on the family.

I spent the day reading and writing, partly to keep busy and partly to keep away from the palpable tension between Chu and his sons. Everyone except Nan Tieh, that is. He and Fu Yan were playing Mah jongg, and for once, Fu was getting his ass handed to him.

I fell asleep in the middle of the book.

I am chasing a man through the streets of Chinatown.

Every window I pass is a restaurant, with the carcasses of geese hanging in the window. The guy keeps trying to lose me, but I keep pace. We round the corner to enter the cul-de-sac to my apartment. I make with a flying tackle, and he goes down. As I turn him around, I can see his face. It's me. Then he pulls his face off, only instead of another face below, all I can see is an empty, black void that sucks me in as I scream—

Mi Hei shook me awake. "Hey, Bowen. It's dinner time."

"Thank you," I told her sincerely.

She shook her head and walked to the dining room.

I excused myself early and went to my room. It took some effort to rearrange things so I had enough space on the floor to draw a medicine wheel. I pulled out my totems and arranged them according to prominence. The larger protective animals went to my back. The clever, problem-solving animals went up front. I used up the last of my tanis leaves to put myself under. I plunged into the Dream-State quickly, dodging a screen of silent, whirling blades. I looked back at the astral traps that lay hovering over the house. That son of a bitch Bai Xin really had it out for me.

I flew quickly, covering hundreds of miles, occasionally looking back over my shoulder to see if my hunter was behind me. When I was sure he wasn't, I stopped and waited at the edge of a magnificent cliff. The wind coursed through my dream-self, tugging at my heart, begging me to fly. In the twilight, I could see tiny points of light off in the distance that might have been campfires. I lifted my head back and called out to Brother Raven. Then I sat down to wait.

It didn't take long. Brother Raven, looking much smaller now that he wasn't in San Cibola's sphere of influence, fluttered at the cliff's edge for a few seconds, then landed in my lap like it was his own personal nest.

"Many Feathers," said Raven. My Indian name. I've got a lot of names. Some of them aren't so nice.

"Brother Raven. It is good to see you again," I sang.

"You are in trouble again, aren't you?"

"I am being hunted by a negative spirit."

Raven tilted his head up. "And you want me to help you?"

"Just deliver a message for me."

Raven sighed and looked away. "Very well. Who shall I give the message to?"

"Coyote."

Raven took to the air, beating his wings and sending a spray of feathers into my face. "No! I won't do it!"

"Raven, it is the only way. I cannot beat my hunter. He is hunting me in the Dream-State."

"That is not my fault. If anything, it is yours. You should have kept in practice."

"Would you rather he kill me?" I asked.

"Many Feathers, you are playing one evil against another. No good can come of this."

I looked at the bird. "What if I let you council me on this matter?"

Raven landed. "I will not do it alone. I will bring Brother Hawk as well."

I nodded. "Do that. It will be good to see him again."

"That's what you think. He's still pissed at you." Raven turned into an updraft of wind and soared away.

When I descended back into my physical form, it was morning. I was surprised to find Mi Hei asleep in my bed. I yawned and stretched and gave her a gentle nudge. "Hey, you," I said.

She sat up quickly. "Bowen! What- uh…"

"What are you doing in my bed?" I asked.

She looked at me, awake now, and then looked at the

circle on the floor. "I, um, came in here to check up on you and found you sitting in your, um..."

"Medicine Wheel."

"Right. So, I decided to stick around in case you freaked out or something like that. Guess I fell asleep."

I was really touched but didn't know how to tell her that. Instead I asked, "Did I freak out?"

"No. You made some dumb noises, but you seemed okay."

The door opened. It was Jiang Shui. I jumped back quickly, and Mi Hei sat upright. "Father!"

Jiang Shui didn't say anything. He turned and walked back down the hall. Mi Hei muttered, "Oh shit," and followed him out the door.

The television was on when I walked into the den. Three families murdered in the night, sixteen people in all, cut to unrecognizable bits. Also present was Chu Sheng Kai's name, this time carved into the stomach of one of the children.

Jiang looked out the front window. "There are people at the gate. The police are having trouble keeping them out."

Michael turned off the television. "Well, at least the authorities know it wasn't Dad."

Chu said nothing. He kept his hands folded in front of his mouth, the gesture of prayer. I don't think I ever saw him that worried before. We were all looking at him for guidance, orders, something. He stood up and said, "Let's have breakfast," and walked out of the room. Jiang scowled and followed him out.

We ate in silence. Even Nan Tieh was somber. He was finally getting it. I ate ravenously. Dream-walking always took a lot out of me.

When Chu finally broke his silence, it was to speak to me. "Ya Shen, was your journey of any use last night?"

All eyes were suddenly on me. "Yes, I think so. That is, I hope so."

"Good. Do you need any help from us?" he asked.

"Um, I don't think so," I said, a little awed by such deference, "but if I do, I will let you know."

"Good. And are you well-rested?"

"Sure," I answered. "Still hungry, but that's normal."

Chu turned to Jiang Shui. "Set up the meeting. This afternoon, at five o'clock."

Jiang smiled. Chu turned back to address the table. "Today, we go on the offensive."

This was the set-up: Chu and his entourage would meet with David Wan and his entourage. I was not to be there, and if my absence was noticed, the reason would be that just because I am adopted doesn't mean I had a place in the proceedings. The real reason was because I would be driving our secret weapon into David Wan's territory for the sole purpose of wiping them out. If Nan Tieh got into trouble, I was to help bail him out.

I spent the day in preparation. Chu sent runners out for supplies through the police barricade. He let me use his workroom, and for about four hours I was in alchemical Nirvana. In spite of these new keys to the kingdom, I felt a familiar tightening in my stomach that I didn't like. Magical combat always freaked me out. Self-defense was different; you didn't have time to think, only react. Dueling meant you had to go to the trouble of figuring out what could do the most damage to someone and prepare that.

Five minutes shy of five o'clock found Nan Tieh and me in Michael Chu's car, cruising down Redwood Street towards the Winter Storms main hangout. Nan wasn't smiling anymore. He all of a sudden looked a lot like his father.

The cell phone beside me rang and I picked it up quickly.

"Talk to me," I said, looking for a parking spot.

It was Mi Hei. "Wan just showed up."

"Is Bai Xin there?" I asked.

"I don't see him."

"Shit."

"Sam? You okay?"

"Yeah, sure. Call me if he shows up. Let it ring once, then hang up."

"Okay."

I parallel parked by the mouth of an alley and looked at Nan. "You ready?"

"Yes, pale but exciting cracker brother."

Damn Mi Hei... "Just make it Sam, okay?"

"Okey-dokey." We got out of the car and started walking. At the corner of Redwood and Tang Street, we made a left and stopped. The sidewalk was knotted with Winter Storms, going in and out of businesses, looting and robbing and pillaging. Pedestrians on the street, mostly residents, had to walk a gauntlet of hostile gang members and jerking cars. Glass broke, women screamed, and music blared. I looked at Nan, who whispered, "Berserkers."

"Right. Okay, you ready?"

"Yes. Are you?"

I nodded.

"I need to see their gang symbol very clearly."

"Right." I stepped into the fray, fists cocked. A young woman was running towards me with an even younger gang member in hot pursuit. Her jacket was torn and half-off her shoulder. She was terrified. The kid had a knife. I grabbed her hand and pulled her quickly forward, off her feet, stepped between them, and clotheslined the kid. He hit the ground with a clap, all five points at full extension. I dropped my knee into his stomach and knocked the wind out of him.

There was genuine panic in his eyes as he tried to draw a breath and found that he couldn't. I dragged him to the street corner as the woman tried to thank me and hug me over and over. Nan tactfully got her out of my way. The kid finally got air in his lungs, so I broke a rib with my boot heel. Now every breath would bring a sharp stab of pain. I rolled him over, onto his ribs, and put my foot in the base of his spine. His gang symbol was very clearly visible on the back of his jacket.

I leaned in on him hard and said, "Scream and I'll snap your spine." He bleated and quietly sobbed. "Nan, this gonna work for you?" I asked.

Nan stepped in quickly. "Yes, that will do fine. Hold him still, please."

"Whatever you're doing, hurry," I said, looking around. We were starting to get some attention from a couple of gang members. "I'm about to be busy."

"One minute," he said, scribbling furiously on the palm of his open hand.

A pack of kids broke away, headed towards us. I could clearly see a knife and a baseball bat in the hands of two of them. "Nan, they're coming."

"Steady…"

The guy under my boot started to scream for help. I bore down on his spine, but he just screamed louder. They broke into a run.

"Shit, Nan, hurry up!"

"Okay!" He stood up and grabbed my hand, forcing the fingers open. He carefully drew a glowing, red symbol with a peculiar little calligraphy pen. The Winter Storms were ten yards away and closing.

"Okay, now what?" I said.

"Slap them. Open hand, like this," he made a striking

motion. "Skin to skin, you see?"

"What will that do?" I asked as the leader cocked his bat back for a running swing. We went in separate directions to split up the pack.

"Put the mark on all of them!" he shouted. "That's only step one of the plan!"

Goddamn ceremonial magic, I thought as two of the gang members tried to circle around me. I grabbed the bat as it came at me and sent explosive physical energy through it. The bat erupted in the man's hands and he screamed and backed away with huge shards of wood protruding through his skin. While his younger companion stared, I slapped him full in the face, leaving a light red mark that was the mirror of the one in my hand. He howled and swung blindly at me in anger, but I danced beyond his reach and smacked the kid with the bat on the back of his free hand. I immediately turned to help Nan, who was grappling with his last Winter Storm.

I grabbed Nan's attacker by the collar and yanked him off. Without missing a beat, Nan reversed his own momentum, pivoting on one foot, spinning, and slapping the kid on his forehead. I threw him to the ground and made to kick him, but Nan held me off.

"Wait." He pulled me back, and sure enough, the five of them were standing slack in the street, mouths slightly open.

I put my hands on my knees and wheezed, "Good trick, now what?"

Nan drew the same symbol on their hands. Looking at my own hand, I saw what looked like the Winter Storms symbol crossed with another symbol I couldn't identify.

"Phase two," Nan said to me, smiling. Then he said to the transfixed gang members, "Brothers in symbol. Gather yourselves up."

Without a word, the five Winter Storms turned and went

back into the melee. I crossed my arms and watched as little by little, the fighting came to a stop. Grateful citizens scurried through the listless bodies and ducked into shops and locked doors behind them.

"Impressive, Nan," I said, and I meant it.

"Thank you. Now, phase three."

He wiped off the symbol on our hands. That done, he threw a handful of amber dust in the air and drew a complex pattern, lightning fast, in the cloud. He turned his back to the street and shouted, his voice strong and clear, "You are all dogs, fighting over the same little bone."

I watched them kill each other for a few minutes as he directed the spell, eyes closed in concentration. When their ranks were thinned by half, he held up his hand. "Perhaps one of your masters has your bone." They broke apart, falling into clusters, and headed in four different directions. One group walked right by us without so much as a twitch.

I looked at Nan Tieh. "Will that get them all?"

"Most of them." he said. "And terrify the rest who might stumble across them."

"Complicated spell," I commented, "poetic, but complicated."

"But it hides the truth from the authorities. No mysterious deaths. All knives and bullets. That they understand."

I took one last look at the carnage in the street. "Come on, let's get back home."

We beat Chu's group to the house. Fu Yan was waiting for us, though, and we told him everything we had done. He listened without comment until we were finished. "We had best prepare for a home defense tonight."

"You think?" I asked.

"I know. Wan Fei Ying will have nowhere to go. Even if

they kill his tong members before they can lay a hand on him, which is very likely, then he will have nothing left but offense. I hope your father knows what he is doing.

Just then, the doors flew open and Jiang Shui was carrying Mi Hei, blood dripping behind them. Chu and Michael followed, with Michael barking orders into a cell phone and Chu shouting for every servant in the house. "What happened?" I asked over everyone's screaming.

"Ambush," Jiang said tightly. "She took the bullet intended for Father..." he broke off, and then I couldn't follow them down the hall to my room for all of the people suddenly in my way.

I waited outside the door, trying to listen to what was going on. It was some time before everyone filed out quietly. I looked at Jiang Shui and Chu Sheng Kai, the last to leave. "She's going to be all right," Chu said.

"Is it bad?"

"It's not good," Jiang Shui said, "but we have some strong magic inside her right now."

"Can I see her?"

"She's resting," Chu said.

"Sam," said Jiang, helping me to my feet. "Will you stay with her tonight? And watch over her?"

I glanced at Chu, who nodded slightly. "Okay."

Jiang nodded thanks, and we moved into the living room to talk.

The reports came in later that night. They were confused and conflicted, but one thing was certain: the Winter Storms were no more. They razed two safe houses to the ground and did considerable damage to David Wan's estate before they were all shot and killed.

"They will come tonight," Chu said as we ate dinner. "Even Wan Fei Ying."

"Endgame," said Fu Yan.

"If this is true," I said to Chu, "then I am going to be busy tonight."

"It will be all right," he said to me. "We will stay up and wait for them. Your nemesis cannot find you in his dreams if you are not dreaming. He will have to lay eyes on you to bring you to the astral."

I nodded. "So, what is the plan?"

Chu turned to Jiang. "Call in all of the Jen Long. Stake out the grounds, but not the house."

"But father, we need men inside to…" Jiang started.

"No, we don't. The four of you will defend me. I don't think we will have anything to worry about, once Ya Shen takes care of the Bai Xin, the White-Hearted Man."

Jiang shook his head. "I wish I could believe you." He picked up the phone and spoke into it. "It is done," he said, hanging up. "Excuse me, I have to go get ready to be killed." He left the table.

Nan leaned in and whispered to me, "So, does that mean he is a chicken shit?"

"No, it means you've been watching too much television."

I was stationed in the exercise room, which had a set of double glass doors that opened up onto the back terrace. Nan took the front. Fu Yan staked out the kitchen and servant's quarters. Jiang Shui patrolled the guest wing. Chu sat in his study.

This is so fucked up, I thought.

•

Bai Xin floated over the Chu estate, chortling in his rage. Down below, the attack on the Chu estate had started. The battle was physical, messy. He had no taste for it. But none

294

of that mattered so much as the job he was given, the job he would have begged for, anyway: kill the white man that was helping Master Wan's enemy.

Bai Xin could see the flashes from the gunfire on the ground and knew that the rest of Master Wan's thugs were meeting their fates even now. He closed his eyes and sent himself out into the Grayscape, feeling for the blond devil. He wasn't there. Bai Xin would have to pull him in before he could kill him. He ran through his catalog of sorceries, trying to decide which one would last the longest. Oh well, he thought as he descended to ground level, he was sure something would come to him.

The shields around the house were embarrassingly easy to get through. The lock on the back door was joke; he turned paper-thin and slid between the seams. As he willed himself back to three dimensions, he took stock of his surroundings.

He was standing in a long hallway with straw mats on a hardwood floor. To his left was an open door. Bai Xin could see the darkened shapes of exercise equipment around the perimeter and a large opening in the center of the room. A modern dojo. Light from outside spilled across the floor, and he could clearly see a human shadow. He stepped inside, and his heart leapt with joy. It was his prey. He was standing in front of the double doors, facing the room, arms folded in front of him.

Bai Xin reached out, taking in a deep breath, and drew them both into the grayscape easily, comfortably. "You were waiting for someone, I see? Maybe me?"

Sam Bowen said nothing.

"Have you nothing to say now? No insolent quips?"

Silence.

Bai Xin started walking towards him. He willed the bowie knife into his right hand and held it loosely. "Don't mock me with your silence!"

He lunged at Bowen and grabbed him by the collar with his left hand. He didn't resist. Bai Xin drew his arm back and plunged it into Bowen's heart. Instead of flesh, the knife broke through a hard, charcoal-like crust, into a hollow center. Bai Xin looked down at the hole, then looked into Bowen's face.

It wasn't Bowen.

He was holding onto the scruff of a dark gray pelt. Blue eyes were yellow. Face was snout. Hands were claws. It was a man-sized dog or wolf. The mouth flashed, and he felt warmth and wetness on his throat. He tried to scream but found that he couldn't. In the monster's jaws was a hunk of bloody meat.

Bai Xin did the only thing that came to him. He pushed off and fell back into the waking world.

•

The look on that bastard's face was priceless. He opened his eyes, staggering back and holding his throat.

"How?" It came out of his mouth as a horrible whisper.

"That was Brother Coyote," I told him, "and if you slip back into the astral, he'll finish the job."

Bai Xin visibly composed himself and slipped into his now familiar fighting stance. "Then I shall break every bone in your body myself," he croaked.

I smiled and walked a wide circle around him and stood in the middle of the dojo. From behind my back I withdrew two slender metal objects. His eyes widened.

"Remember these?" I popped the fans open.

"You had them all this time?" he mouthed.

"Yeah, and boy, are they fascinating. I've had a long time to figure out what they are and what they do. That little

296

trick you did, where you separated my soul from my body? That's just the tip of the iceberg. Did you know they can also paralyze?"

I crisscrossed the air in front of me, outlining the form of the second sigil of lamentation. Glowing green threads erupted out of thin air and encased his limbs like a spider enveloping its prey. The more he struggled against them, the quicker they appeared. In seconds, he was completely immobile. That didn't stop him, though. He started some spell, singing in that horrible rattling whisper. I held the fans at specific angles, said the command words, and shoved the fans into his neck. They went all the way through without cutting flesh and stopped his incantation in mid-sentence. His eyes widened in horror.

"I've been doing my homework. I know these fans can also transfer your energy to me and leave you a ghost. The trouble is, you could still cause trouble for us in that form."

He shook his head, trying to speak, but nothing would come out.

"On the other hand, I did make a promise to someone, a promise that I would hate to break, as it would cause me all kinds of problems."

Fear was giving way to anger, now that he thought I wouldn't kill him. I could also see the paralysis starting to wear off.

"Actually, I think this would be an ideal time to try out a new spell with these. What do you think?"

I made the specific angles with the fans again, this time, with a new command word. Across Bai Xin's heart, I carved a certain Navajo symbol, so he would be easier to track in the astral. He screamed soundlessly, and I turned the fan up and ran it through his brain.

"Give my regards to Brother Coyote," I said. He collapsed on the floor and twitched for a few moments. His body was intact, but the silver tether that held his spirit to his body was gone. I stared at him and thought about what I had done. Only the sound of gunfire broke my reverie.

I ran into the study to find the place crawling with Jen Long, leftover thugs from David Wan's empire, and Jiang Shui and Nan Tieh. Jiang had been shot in the arm, and Nan was still crackling with energy. Three of the Jen Long guarded a small knot of seven or eight gang members. A few more Jen Long sat on the floor, wounded. Fu Yan appeared with a guy in a headlock. We all started talking at once, but fell silent as Chu entered the room.

"Where is Wan Fei Ying?" he asked.

"He's not here, the coward," Jiang said, wincing. "We've searched all of them, and he is nowhere to be seen."

"My son, you have done well, but you are in error. He is here. I can feel him. The stink of his magic is all over these men." He walked over to the knot of captured gang members. "Is this everyone?"

"Everyone who is still alive," said Jiang.

Chu closed his eyes and began to hum, taking deep breaths. Everyone watched in silence. He stood up and slowly walked up to one of the gang members in the front of the group. "All Jen Long clear the room. Take everyone but him with you. You," he indicated us, "stay here."

When we were all alone with the gang member, Chu said, "I think it's safe to drop the disguise now. You are found out."

"Pig." The gang member's form shifted and wavered, and then there was a crooked-looking old man in his place. "You won't kill me, Chu. You don't spill blood anymore, unless it's to further your miserable existence."

"One could argue that your death will go a long way towards furthering my existence. All the pain you've caused me, my family, this community. Your greed and your jealousy. Now they have unmade you."

"You unmade me!" he screamed. "You took my bride from me, my role in the community, you took my life!"

Chu shook his head sadly. "No, you made your own way, as we all did. You followed the path of empty vengeance to its conclusion. You wanted an ending. Now I shall give you one."

He stepped back and sat down, lotus-style in the middle of the room. "You are quite right. I will not spill blood. Someone else wants to do that."

Chu's head lolled back, and a strange sound came from him. Yellow energy danced around him and lifted him off the ground. He started chanting, but I couldn't make out any of the words. The glow coalesced into a face, a woman's face. She was young and beautiful. Her hair danced in a wind that none of us felt, and she looked upon the room with an air of peace.

Chu gasped and collapsed, "I...believe...you already know...my wife, Lu Mao."

Jiang Shui breathed, "Mother."

Wan Fei Ying's face twisted in disbelief and fear. Suddenly, the beautiful woman's face was a mask of rage. She flew at him, shrieking. He threw up his hands, but the light encompassed him completely. The room glowed with the brightness of the sun. I could hear screams but couldn't tell whose they were. I couldn't see anyone or anything.

All at once, it was dark again. The revenant and Wan Fei Ying were gone. Chu lay crumpled on the floor.

"Help me!" cried Fu Yan, running to Chu. Everyone surged forward and carried him to his bed. Fu rang for the servants and turned to address us. "Jiang, you stay. Nan, you too. Bowen, call Michael and get him over here now. We have a lot of work to do."

I did as I was told and wondered if Chu was going to be all right.

As it was, Chu came a lot closer to death than anyone was willing to admit. I went to see him the next day.

"Well, this is a switch," I said, standing over the bed.

"Not really," Chu said, smiling weakly. "I was sick when you and I first met."

"Are you okay?" I asked.

"I will be," he said. His eyes were sad. "I stopped missing her because she was always close to me. Now she is gone."

"I don't think she could ever really leave you, sir."

He smiled. "She liked you, you know. She is the reason you are a part of this family."

I didn't know what to say. "I'll let you get some sleep. We'll talk more later."

Chu rolled over and closed his eyes. I went from his bedroom to mine. Mi Hei was sitting up in my bed.

"Foreigner."

"Prude. How you feeling?" I sat down at the foot of the bed.

"I hurt all over. I got shot. How would you feel?" She crossed her arms and scowled at me.

"Oh, I've been shot, I know how it feels."

"Really?" she looked skeptical.

"Yep." To change the subject, I asked, "Are you glad this is all over?"

"Sort of."

"They told me what you did. That was very brave."

She shrugged. "It's what I was trained for. I didn't think

I'd ever have the chance to use it."

"You think I hold you back, don't you?"

She looked sideways at me. "How do you mean?"

"Well, you said it yourself, you don't like translating books for me when you could be out kung-fooing bad guys."

Mi Hei picked at the bedspread. "It was a shit assignment at first, but you can't really say the last year has been boring."

"No, I guess it hasn't. Well, I'll let you go." I stood up to leave.

"Hey, Bowen."

I paused at the door. "Yeah?"

"Thanks for helping us out."

I grinned at her. "Hey, you're family."

Printed in the United States
3636

9 780970 484154